When The Soldiers Came

Kesli Gleason

Published by Kesli Gleason, 2024.

This is a work of fiction. Similarities to real people, places, or events are entirely coincidental.

WHEN THE SOLDIERS CAME

First edition. January 1, 2024.

Copyright © 2024 Kesli Gleason.

ISBN: 979-8223365341

Written by Kesli Gleason.

Table of Contents

Chapter 1 1
Chapter 2 9
Chapter 3 19
Chapter 4 31
Chapter 5 43
Chapter 6 57
Chapter 7 67
Chapter 8 85
Chapter 9 99
Chapter 10 117
Chapter 11 129
Chapter 12 139
Chapter 13 151
Chapter 14 163
Chapter 15 175
Chapter 16 185
Chapter 17 193
Chapter 18 203
Chapter 19 211
Chapter 20 223
Chapter 21 229
Chapter 22 237
Chapter 23 245
Epilogue 257

To all those that give their lives for the right cause. Those that belive freedom for others is more important than their lives. Thank you for all you did and continue to do.

Chapter 1

Thirteen year old Leanne Martin started every day with a song as she skipped lightly down the stairs. She and her eighteen year old brother, Jameson, lived with Jameson's best friend, Marius Decrocles, in a small clock shop in Reims, France.

She hopped through the kitchen door, tied an apron around her waist so as not to spoil the dark blue dress she wore, and got prepared to make breakfast. She pushed a black headband into her shoulder length brown hair, keeping it out of the way.

The home was small. In the front was the small clock shop that Marius and Jameson ran. Through the side door in the shop ran a little corridor to get to the living room, it was quaint, with one door to the kitchen, one to the shop, and one to the stairs. In the living room was a small three-person sofa and a squishy armchair. An oak cabinet held a clock and some other small nick nacks. A rug covered the floor. The small kitchen was an addition to the original property so it popped into the alley. There was just enough room for the stove, the table, and the door to the alley. It was a tight fit, but Leanne liked it. It was easy to keep warm in the winter. When it got hot in the summer, they only had to open the door to let fresh air run through. There were only three rooms upstairs: One for Leanne, one for Jameson, and one for Marius.

Leanne started humming as the pot boiled. A step on the stairs made her smile and hum a little louder. She ran a hand down her navy blue dress with buttons in the back from the neck to her waist. She dropped in the packet of cider and stirred it quickly with a spoon just as Jameson entered. Jameson had brown hair, like her, and soft green eyes. He loved nature and enjoyed teaching Leanne all about it when he could. He picked a new tune to whistle every week, and did it whenever he wasn't talking or eating. He hung his huge coat on the pegs by the door and seated himself at the table. "*Bonjour*, Little Bird." he said cheerfully. "How are you?"

Leanne smiled as she placed the cider in the center of the small table. "*Bonjour*. I'm great. Where's Marius?" Her honey-brown eyes sparkled and smiled at the corners as she heard steps on the stairs and Marius entered.

He was a broad shouldered young man with an easy grin. His bright face and easy manner drew people to him. He had dark hair and bushy eyebrows but that only added to his appearance. Laugh lines crinkled around his mouth and sky blue eyes. To Leanne, he was part of the family not just a friend.

He grinned at her. "You look beautiful." He seated himself and gratefully accepted the cup she placed in front of him.

"*Merci*." She lifted the small loaf of bread out of the oven and placed it beside the cider. "That's all for breakfast. But there should be more for lunch." she said gaily.

Marius smiled. "It's perfect. Do we have jam?"

Leanne nodded and hurried to fetch it out of the small cupboard above the stove. Jameson cut the bread and served a slice to each one of them. "What's happening today?" he asked as he took the jam from her outstretched hand.

She settled down. "Nothing new. I'm going to go to the market, but I do that everyday. Oh," She paused with her cup on the way to her mouth. "Mademoiselle Azéma stopped me in the market yesterday. She said she had a clock that was an hour behind and was wondering if you could do anything about it?"

Marius nodded. "Of course we can. Jameson, you want to go?"

"Sure." A comfortable silence settled over them as they ate.

Leanne looked at her watch. The simple black band was tight around her wrist and the white face told her it was time for the bible. She walked into the living room and returned with the faded black book. She retook her seat and handed the book to Jameson.

"*Merci*." He opened the book and spent the next ten minutes reading aloud. Without fail, this happened every morning.

After ten minutes, Leanne looked at her watch again. "I've got to go. And you've got to open the shop. See you soon. *Adieu*." She slipped her light jacket on, grabbed the basket beside the door, and disappeared into the alley. It was September 1, 1939. The weather was nice and a sweet breeze blew down through her hair. She hurried down the street, waving to everyone she passed, and greeting those she knew by name. Waiting on the corner was a girl that matched her age and height. She wore a pink colored dress and a light gray jacket that went to the bottom of her dress. A basket hung on her arm.

"*Bonjour*, Rose!" Leanne hurried to catch up to her best friend.

KESLI GLEASON

Rose Bonnot was the daughter of Bella and Gaston Bonnot, two of the best tailors in Reims. She was a pretty girl with bright blonde hair and diamond blue eyes. She had a small face, delicate nose, and a small dimple on her cheek that appeared when she smiled. She came from a large family with two older sisters, Angelica and Josephine, two older brothers, Marcel and Théo, and one younger brother, Charle. Her sisters had moved out, one to Paris and the other to Lyon. Marcel had moved to America when he was eighteen. That was five years ago. Rose and her brothers, Théo and Charle, were frequent visitors to the shop. Rose smiled. "*Bonjour*, Leanne. How are you? How are Jameson and Marius doing this beautiful morning?"

"I'm amazing. And they're doing fine, thanks for asking."

The girls walked down the street, chatting and laughing. They got to the market and started gathering what they needed. Leanne made sure to get cider, jam, flour, sugar, yeast, oats, and some milk. Rose's basket was similar. Rose wandered around as Leanne took her change. "*Merci*." Leanne smiled at the salesman and turned around. "Rose?" She looked for her friend. "Rose!"

"Leanne, over here!" Rose's voice sounded oddly happy.

Leanne hurried to her. "What is it?"

"Oranges!" Rose cried happily. "They have oranges!"

The girls ran toward the cart. The sweet, tangy smell of oranges filled the air as they neared the cart. The man laughed at their happy expressions. "They cost a fortune girls. I almost couldn't get them myself."

Rose reached into her pocket. "How much?" Her eyes were round and filled with joy.

"Five *francs*." he replied heavily.

WHEN THE SOLDIERS CAME

"Oh." Rose frowned. "I don't have enough."

Leanne shook her head. "Me neither. Thanks anyway."

Rose sniffled as they started to walk away. "Wait!" she said suddenly. "How much do you have? Maybe we'll have enough if we go in on it together."

Leanne brightened. "I have two and a half."

"I have three. That's more than enough. We'll each pay two and a half."

The girls hurried back, both pulling the coins from their pockets.

"We'll take one." Leanne announced placing the money on the counter.

The salesman smiled at them. "Glad to hear it. Here you go. Enjoy." He waved as the girls walked away.

Rose held the orange to her nose and closed her eyes as she inhaled deeply. "We should open it now; it smells divine."

Leanne caught her arm and pulled her out of someone's way. "Excuse us, sorry." she called back to the man that had skirted out of their way. "Rose, open your eyes. And we can't eat it now. We have to share it with Jameson, Marius, and Théo."

Rose sighed. "Yeah, you're right. Okay, let's go. Come on. Let's get there faster." The girls raced down the street until they stopped in front of the clock shop.

Jameson was behind the counter fixing a watch. Marius was standing by, matching the time of a different watch to a clock hanging on the wall. Théo, acting like their apprentice, was sweeping the floor. Leanne and Rose waited until the customers had gone before hurrying inside.

"We got a surprise for lunch." Rose cried happily.

Leanne kindly plucked the orange out of Rose's hands and hurried into the kitchen. Jameson looked up from the counter as Leanne disappeared.

"What kind of surprise? Is it sugar?"

Rose laughed a high, girly laugh. "You'll have to wait and see," she smiled. "Leanne will bring it out." She fluttered her eyelashes at him, blushing when he smiled at her.

Marius smiled. "This sounds interesting. Théo, will you close the store?"

Théo, a tall, muscular eighteen year old, dropped the broom. "Sure." He had blond hair like his sister, but his eyes were a cloudy gray. He smiled at his sister as he walked by. "Are you ready for the test Monday?"

Rose nodded. "*Oui*, I've been looking forward to it."

Jameson exchanged a look with Marius. They didn't have enough money for schooling. Both boys had aged out of school and all the money they earned went to food so they never had enough to send Leanne to school. It was a sore subject with them, Leanne was a little sister to both of them, and they both wanted to take care of her. When someone brought up school, they felt as if they'd failed somehow. Jameson taught her to read and write every chance he got, and she was fluent in German and Italian, but he still wished he could send her to school. There was something happy about the thought of her having many friends her own age that made him wish that school was a part of her life.

Leanne chose that moment to walk out, carrying a plate with bread, jam, a small bit of meat, and the orange slices. Jameson gasped in amazement. "Leanne, where did you get that?"

Marius echoed his shock. "How much did it cost?"

WHEN THE SOLDIERS CAME

Leanne smiled. "If I tell you the cost it will ruin the taste. Come on, dig in!" The next half hour was pleasant, spent in laughter and joy. Little did they know that it was going to change.

Chapter 2

Leanne sat down that night and pulled the bible from its place in the cabinet. She opened to a place and started reading silently, mouthing the words as she went. Marius was counting the small amount of money they'd earned that day and Jameson was assembling a pocket watch. Leanne looked up. "Jameson, what's S-A-L-V-A-T-I-O-N?"

"Salvation. It means to be saved." He responded, taking a break in his work.

"*Merci.*" She smiled, then turned back to the bible.

Marius looked up. "I think it's time for the wireless." He dropped the money in a small box and handed it to Leanne. She placed the bible in the cabinet and put the box behind it. Jameson wrapped up the pieces of the watch and raced to place them in the shop. As he returned, Marius switched on the wireless. A man's voice echoed through the room. Two sentences bounced off the walls. All of France was in shock.

"This is the eight O'clock news. The Germans have invaded Poland."

Leanne gasped as she stared at the wireless with wide eyes,

"The Germans invaded?" She aimed her question at Jameson.

Jameson hurried to shut it off. His usual kind and calm face was angry and dark. Leanne shuddered. She didn't like seeing him like this.

"I think it's time for bed." He retorted, not even acknowledging her question.

She winced at his sharp words, but got to her feet and hugged him. "Good night, Jameson," she whispered, placing a soft kiss on his cheek.

Some of his anger seemed to melt. He hugged her back. "Good night, Little Bird."

She grinned a little at the nickname and went and hugged Marius. "Night."

She kissed his cheek and hurried up the stairs. As her footsteps faded, Jameson and Marius exchanged looks, knowing their happy life was about to change.

The days passed quickly. War was declared and soldiers started moving out. Leanne knew something was off. Marius never smiled anymore and Jameson never sang or whistled. It was quiet in the house. Days turned to weeks, and weeks to months. Soon it was March 1, 1940. Leanne's birthday had passed, and she was excited to be fourteen. She couldn't forget Jameson's birthday only a week earlier. There had been a shadow hanging over it, for he seemed to regret the fact that he was now nineteen. Leanne heard talk in the streets. The Germans were advancing, fighting their way into France. The fear of the Germans haunted Leanne's dreams. Some nights, when the dreams were too real and horrible to face alone, she would crawl into Jameson's bed and curl up in his arms. He always had something comforting to say, and she would fall asleep quickly, knowing there was nothing to fear.

The morning was gray. Storm clouds rolled over Reims. Thunder clapped and rain began to pour. Leanne started the cider as she did every morning. Yesterday she'd gotten a little extra food from the market so she didn't have to go today. She tapped her fingers, waiting for the water to boil. Marius tramped down the stairs with heavy steps. Leanne looked at him.

"What's wrong?"

He shook his head. "Nothing." Slowly he took his seat. "Leanne, did any mail come yesterday?" He asked softly, picking at the white tablecloth she had made a few months ago. His strong, careful fingers traced the pattern on the fabric.

Leanne blinked in surprise. *They hardly ever got mail, why would he expect something now?* She dropped the cider in the water.

"No. Why? Are you expecting something?"

"I don't know. Something may come. Will you check?"

She nodded as she bent over to check the bread, "If you want me to. Where's Jameson?"

"He's coming." A voice said on the stairs, "See, here he is." Jameson stepped through the door, spreading his hands wide. A fake smile plastered his face.

Leanne smiled, "It's time to eat." She pulled the bread out of the oven and placed it on the table followed by the cider along with their three white cups and plates. They ate quickly, Jameson mentioned something that he had to do, but before he got up, Leanne stopped him, "Jameson, what about reading?"

She loved books, almost more than anything else in her world. The bible was her favorite, and she enjoyed starting each day with it.

Jameson shrugged and nodded, "Oops, forgot."

Leanne watched him as he got the book, *'He never forgot the bible.'* She thought to herself, *'He enjoys reading it as much as I enjoy hearing it.'* As he sat down she noticed how wide his eyes were. His lips said the words, but she could tell his mind was somewhere else. She heard a soft thumping and looked at Marius whose fingers were drumming on the side of his chair. Sweat formed on his lip, and his leg was bouncing up and down shaking the small table. She wondered what was wrong. After only a few verses, Jameson placed the book down and she noticed his hands were trembling, "Leanne—" He started, but he only got that far. A quick, sharp knock sounded on the alley door.

Leanne got to her feet and opened it. Standing in the doorway was a tall man. A brown beard covered his chin, cheeks, and mouth. Black eyes stared sadly at the two young men seated at the table. She met the man's stricken gaze with a smile, "*Bonjour*, Officer Rouzet." She danced to the side, swinging the door wider, "Won't you come in?"

She gave him another quick smile, but it faded as the police officer stepped inside. As she closed the door, she shot a quick look at her brother. Jameson was sitting ramrod straight, his face red and his eyes nervous. Marius was slouched, his hands were still. She frowned. She couldn't remember the last time Marius's hands were still. Something was off, she could tell. The very air felt heavy. She shifted her stance. In the quick silence, it was uncomfortably hot now. She shook off the feeling of gloom and thought, *'What could be so bad anyway? The Germans were far from Reims, barely on the border of France.'* Leanne smiled as she latched the door, "It's hot in here. Should I open a window?" She asked Jameson.

He went to answer but Officer Rouzet cut him off, "*Non*." His voice was heavy, like Marius's steps that morning, she recalled.

Something was off, *'Why was Officer Rouzet here? Why was Jameson nervous? And why was Marius still?'* She wanted all the answers but decided not to ask. It would be safer that way. She trusted that Jameson would tell her what she needed to know. She pulled out another cup from the small cupboard and set to getting the officer some of the warm cider.

Officer Rouzet smiled at her, "*Merci*." He took a quick sip, "It's very good. Almost as good as my wife's, but don't tell her that." He winked at her.

She smiled for politeness' sake, but her mind was whirring. *'What was he doing here?'* She went to sit on the small chair beside Jameson but stopped as Officer Rouzet held out a hand,

"Excuse me, Leanne, could I speak to your brother and Marius alone for a moment?"

She froze but added a quick smile on her face and nodded. "Sure. I'll be outside."

She grabbed her blue raincoat from its peg and hurried outside. Every piece of her body wanted to lean against the keyhole and listen to what was being said, but she didn't think Jameson would like it. Slowly she paced in the front of the shop. No one was looking at the clocks and watches in the wide window, so she walked over to study them. She loved the clocks. Each hour of her day was filled with their ticking. It had been annoying at first, but now she reveled in it. Each one was set to the same time, and the time was said to be the most correct time in all of Reims. She glanced at her favorite clock. Small...about the size of her fist. It was made of a golden colored metal. The tiny hands were black, but it was the numbers that she loved. Each one was a different colored bird. A black bird for one, a blue for two, a red for three, and so on. Jameson was sure someone was going to buy it, but she prayed that that wasn't the case. She waited, wondering if she should go check the mail then shook the thought away. Jameson wouldn't know where she was and he'd worry if she was gone. Footsteps sounded in the alley and she ran around the small house. Officer Rouzet whispered a kind farewell as he walked beside her. She hurried inside before Jameson closed the door. Something was off, but it wasn't the same nervous, tenseness from before. It was different...but she wanted it to go away nonetheless. She hung her coat up and turned to the table. Marius had his arms crossed on the table with his head resting on them. His shoulders were drooped and his feet were sitting loosely beneath his chair. Jameson was leaning back against the wall. His eyes were closed, but she knew he was awake. His left arm was laying in his lap and his right hand was resting on the table. She paused. In the center of the table were three letters. One had Jameson's name. One had Marius's. And one had hers! She hurried to the table and reached to grab her letter. No one had ever written to her. She didn't have any friends out of the city. What could it say? As her fingers brushed the soft paper, Jameson's hand fell on hers. She raised her eyes. Jameson's soft green ones rested on her face. "Not now, Little Bird. Later."

WHEN THE SOLDIERS CAME

She frowned. "What is it, Jameson?" She hardly even recognized the nickname now.

Marius sat up quickly. "Not now!" he shouted. "Just go!" He pointed up the stairs.

Leanne gasped. Feeling tears in her eyes, she fled. Her light steps made no sound on the creaky stairs. She hurried across the tight landing and fell into her room. It was a small room, like the rest of the house. There was a small wardrobe, holding her dresses and boots. Her bed was in the farthest corner, with a white rug beside it. Other than that, the room was bare. She threw herself across the bed and buried her face in the pillow. Marius had never yelled at her before! She sobbed softly. *'I'm older.'* she thought. *'but that doesn't mean I can't cry like I used to.'* It wasn't a long time of crying, but she stayed in her room for most of the day. Her feelings were hurt and she felt sad. She didn't know what was wrong, but there had to be something.

Leanne wished she could talk to Rose, but Rose was in school. It would still be awhile before she got out. She sat up and pulled the pillow on her lap. Her fingers ran across it. It was soft and comforting, like Jameson's arms, she thought sadly. A tentative knock on the door made her jump slightly. "Who is it?"

Marius called through the thin wood. "It's Marius, can I come in?"

Leanne didn't hesitate. "*Oui.*" She placed the pillow back in its place.

Marius opened the door slowly. "Leanne, I'm sorry I shouted. I'm nervous and scared, and I took it out on you. Can you forgive me?"

She smiled and got up and hugged him. "*Oui*," she whispered into his shirt.

Marius smiled, too. "Leanne, Jameson and I have something to tell you." He started back downstairs. She hurried after him. Her quiet steps were drowned out by his loud, heavy ones. She noticed the same feeling as she stepped into the living room. Jameson was seated on the sofa, Leanne's letter and his were sitting loosely in his hand. Marius's letter was on the arm of the armchair. It looked as if he'd left it there when he'd come up to apologize. Leanne skipped to Jameson's side and sat beside him. "What's going on?" she asked softly. "What did Officer Rouzet want?"

"Leanne—" Jameson muttered. How he wished he could spare her from this. "—Leanne, our government has decided to send troops to help the people in Poland, Denmark, Norway, Austria, and Czechoslovakia." He was speaking in a tone that reminded Leanne of mothers when they talked to their children.

"So," she asked. "What's wrong with that? I think we should help them. It's not fair that we have everything while they have nothing."

Jameson winced. "I know, Little Bird, I know." He had to remind himself that Leanne was grown. She wasn't the same, frightened ten year old that he'd had to care for.

"Leanne, Marius and I are being sent to Denmark to be soldiers."

"*Non!*" Leanne cried. "Jameson—" She searched her mind for words to say, but couldn't find any.

Madame and Monsieur Granet had a son that became a soldier. He had only been a soldier for a few weeks before he'd been killed. What if Marius and Jameson die, too?' She gasped at the horror of her thoughts. She spun to Marius, wishing him to start laughing and yelling that this was a joke, but his face remained pained and sad. She blinked back the hot tears that filled her eyes. "When do you leave?"

The words that Jameson whispered shattered Leanne's sheltered world.

"We leave at the end of the week."

Chapter 3

The next morning was filled with sunshine, but Leanne didn't notice. She felt as if all the happiness had drained from her. *'Jameson was going to war. He was going to be a soldier. He'd probably die.'* The thoughts raced through her head as she stared at the dark ceiling. Her watch told her it was time to make breakfast, but she didn't want to move. If she did, she'd have to face Jameson and Marius, and she couldn't bring herself to face them. Then she remembered Rose. Rose would be waiting for her at the corner so they could go to the market together. Rose's family wasn't poor, but they weren't rich anymore. They could only afford two days out of the week for Rose and Théo to go to school since the declaration of war.

'Father give me thy strength. I need it terribly,' she thought as she rolled out of bed and hurried down the stairs. The small pot was filled with water in no time, and the cider was made. When no one came down the stairs, Leanne began to get worried. She pulled a loaf of bread from the oven and placed it on the table; the cider soon joined it. She waited tensely at the kitchen door. This was the latest that Jameson and Marius had ever come down. The morning had a strict routine that they all followed without thinking. Leanne would wake at 6:50 and start breakfast. Marius and Jameson would come down stairs

at exactly 6:58. They'd wait two minutes until food was on the table, and then eat. Breakfast was done in ten minutes. Then they'd talk about what they were doing that day for another ten, and then there was the bible for a third ten. At 7:30 Jameson and Marius would open the shop and Leanne would head to the market.

Leanne looked at her watch. It was 7:10 and they still hadn't shown up. She tapped her foot as she waited. She'd never had to wake them before and she was worried about doing it now. Maybe they were sick. If that was the case, she'd have to open the shop herself and get the doctor at lunch, skipping the market until later. She waited another two minutes before hurrying upstairs.

"Jameson?" She called, knocking on the door. "Breakfast is ready!"

No answer. Leanne's breath quickened.

"Jameson?" She knocked louder. The door gave under her fist and swung open. Jameson's room looked identical to hers, except the rug was blue not white. The bed was perfectly made. The room stood empty.

Leanne allowed the door to swing closed as she turned to Marius's room. "Marius!" She didn't ask if he was there. She was worried and she was going to yell. "Marius!" She didn't wait for the door to open but quickly turned the handle. Again, the room was empty. There were clothes scattered around his room and on the green rug but no Marius.

She turned and ran down the stairs. Her breath was quickening. *'Did they leave early? Did they leave me here alone?'* She pushed the thoughts away and forced herself to calm down. They must have had a perfectly good reason for leaving. They'd be back as soon as possible. But at the moment, breakfast was ready. She had to go to the market. She quickly drank her cider, placed the half full pot back on the stove, and pulled the bible onto her lap. Once she finished tripping through the hard words, she replaced the book, cut a slice of bread, and hurried outside with her basket. She ate the bread as she walked down the street. People smiled and waved, but she could tell they were tense. Eyes held unspoken fear. Hands trembled as they returned after waving. Shoulders were tight. Leanne hurried down the street, feeling a small bit of relief as she saw the familiar figure waiting for her, but it was soon lost as she saw tears on Rose's face.

"Rose!"

She ran and held her friend an arm's length away. "What has happened? What's wrong?"

Rose pressed her hands to her face. Tears trickled slowly between her fingers, coming in ones and twos. Her shoulders bounced as she sobbed.

"Rose!" Leanne shook her gently.

Rose took a gasping breath and moved her hands.

"Théo is being sent away!" she cried and held Leanne's gaze for a second before replacing her hands.

Leanne blinked back her tears,

"Jameson and Marius, too. I wonder if anyone will be left."

"That's not all," Rose gasped, her voice breaking. "Mama and Papa have decided that we're moving in with my sister, Angelica. We're moving to Paris! We leave when the soldiers do!" Tears poured down her face. She threw her head down, sobs ripping relentlessly from her mouth.

KESLI GLEASON

Leanne gasped and felt the tears slip down her face. She took shuddering breaths trying not to cry. Numbness crept up her body. Her knees sagged, and she sank to the ground, unable to stand. The rough stone bit through her dress and cut into her knees, but she didn't care. The only pain she felt was in her heart. Both girls cried, not knowing what else they could do. After a while, Leanne looked at her watch. It was nearly 12:00. Surely Jameson and Marius *must* be back by now. A part of her brain, the part that wasn't completely numb, told her she should get home; but she couldn't leave her friend. She sobbed without tears until she could quiet them. Slowly, numbly, she got to her feet. Leftover tears dried on her face. Pain shot through her legs and blood rushed to her toes. She staggered for a moment until she regained her balance. Once steady, she caught Rose's arm and pulled her up.

"Come, Rose," she whispered softly. "Let's get you home."

Together the girls stumbled down the street. Their baskets hung, forgotten, on their arms. The money they were supposed to have spent at the market still lay in their pockets unused. Leanne made sure that Rose was safely home before heading back to the shop. Her steps were heavy.

'Father,' she thought miserably, *'why is this happening? Thou art taking my brother and my friends! What did I do wrong?'*

She felt no peace from her small prayer. In fact, she felt worse. Her heart felt as if it had dropped to her boots. She felt dizzy and sick but was too weak to do anything other than keep putting one foot in front of the other. The shop loomed in front of her, but she couldn't face Marius and Jameson right now. She hurried past. Her green dress swirled around her ankles. Her boots made heavy sounds on the walkway. She ducked her head and brushed more tears off her cheeks. Her eyes were burning. The tinkling of a bell not too far away warned her that someone had come out of the shop. She didn't know who it was. Honestly, she didn't want to.

"Leanne?" Jameson's voice was concerned, watching his sister walk by the shop surprised him. "Leanne!" he shouted again, noticing the way her head was bowed.

Leanne heard him calling her but shook his voice from her head. She wrapped her arms around her chest and sped up, trying to get away from this part of town. Heavy boots followed her.

"Leanne!" Jameson tried again.

Leanne felt tears burn her eyes and knew she couldn't go any further. She dropped to her knees, hung her head, and sobbed. She rocked back and forth, wishing that the nightmare would end. Jameson caught up to her and placed a loving hand on her shoulder.

"Leanne, what happened?" His eyebrows drew together and his lips pursed.

She wiped her nose with her wrist and tried to answer, but any noise from her throat was a sob. Knowing now it was useless to try and speak, she gave up and turned away from her brother. Jameson sat beside her and pulled her into his lap like he'd done when she was little. His hands rubbed down her arms and back. People walking by pointed and gawked, their eyes filled with confusion. No one said a word. After all, if it wasn't hurting them, then why draw attention to it? They hurried by, getting back to their business. Soon Leanne's sobs turned to sniffles and she was able to speak. Jameson held her close and asked once more. "Leanne, what happened?" He was soft, but firm.

Leanne took a careful breath before starting.

"The Bonnots are moving to Paris." she said slowly, feeling more tears swim in her eyes. "I'm never going to see Rose again." She buried her face into Jameson's shirt, but she didn't cry. She'd finally run out of tears. "The Germans aren't even here. They're not even close. So why are people so afraid?" She jerked her face up to look at Jameson, her eyes demanding an answer.

He frowned, unsure if he wanted to tell her. Leanne caught his hesitation. Fear made her skin go cold. Her heartbeat picked up rapidly.

"Jameson, what's going on? What aren't you telling me?"

She looked into her brother's face, seeking the reassurance and comfort that she could always find there, but she was disappointed. His usual calm eyes were worried and filled with fear. His lips were tight.

"Jameson?" She leaned away from him, her eyes raking his face. "What is it?"

He took a deep breath. Tears swam in his eyes, making Leanne hang onto and dread every word that came from his mouth.

"The Nazis are fighting their way to Reims as we speak." He made sure to emphasize that it was the Nazis, not the Germans. "Soon we'll have air raid drills and fire drills, evacuating practices, and even hand to hand combat training. Hopefully it never comes down to that." he added as an afterthought.

Unease settled on her, followed by another wave of fear. Leanne frowned.

WHEN THE SOLDIERS CAME

"But what am I supposed to do? When you, Marius, and Rose leave, I'll have no one. Not a single friend." Her stomach rolled with dread at the prospect of being left alone, even in the town where she'd grown up.

Jameson thought for a moment. "A kind couple has agreed to take you in. They live on the other side of town. They seem sensible. They honor our flag." His voice was slow and cautious.

Leanne hated it, but she knew that honoring the flag was important to Jameson. Some of their neighbors had sided with the Germans, even though they didn't know what the Germans were doing. All they knew was that there was a war. And the Germans seemed unstoppable. She shivered a little, despite the warm breeze.

"How do you know them?" she asked.

For Jameson's sake she made it sound like she was curious, not dreading it.

Jameson smiled, but it went as fast as it came.

"The letter," he responded. "Officer Rouzet had written to them. Apparently he's an old friend of the Monsieur Lucroy that owns the house. He and his wife have agreed to take in many children that have no home. Most are around your age and they are happy to care for another. I have arranged," he said slowly, picking his words carefully, "for you to go and live with them when Marius and I leave. I was planning on sending you to Uncle Pinchon out in Riom—" He shuddered and his voice trailed off. "You'll have to get to the Lucroy's home by yourself, but you're fourteen. I know I don't need to worry. When we leave, you can spend one more night in the shop, but then, please, go to the Lucroy's. They'll keep you safe until the war is over and I can come and fetch you. Leanne," he grinned at her, "can you do that for me?"

Leanne smiled through her grief. For Jameson? Anything.

"Of course, Jameson. You act as if I'm still a little girl."

She made herself grin wider.

Her response brought a smile to Jameson's lips.

"I don't know why I doubted you."

He ruffled her hair as he pulled himself and her from the ground.

"Let's get back, I think Marius is waiting for lunch."

The air raid siren just kept wailing. It went on and on and on. A high pitched screaming sound. Leanne wished it would stop. It hurt her head. She felt jumpy. She hated this dark, dusty, crowded shelter she was in and her stomach pinched uncomfortably.

'When was the last time she'd eaten? Lunch yesterday,' she recalled. The air ride drill had happened an hour before dinner.

To distract herself from her muttering stomach, she looked around the room for the umpteenth time. Jameson was sitting beside her with his head leaning against the wall. He looked as if he was asleep. His clothes were rumbled and disheveled but there was a faint smile on his lips, and it brought one to Leanne's. Marius had found some friends and was having a lovely time catching up with them. Their laughs and jokes echoed in the silent room. People around her cowered in fear. Children clung to mothers as they huddled beside their husbands. As she looked around, her smile faded. Her eyes were drawn to the Bonnets. Even in the dark she could see Rose. Théo was holding one of her hands. Leanne could see his lips moving, though she was too far away to hear what he was saying. She could see the tears running down Rose's cheeks as easily as she could see stars on a clear night. She turned away. She could easily guess what Théo was talking about. It was all everyone ever talked about now. The soldiers were leaving tomorrow.

The thought that some would never see France again was excruciating. Curiosity and despair drew her eyes back to her friend and her family. Monsieur and Madame Bonnet were sitting side by side. Their eyes drawn from the dark wall opposite them to the small discussion between their son and daughter. The little brother, Charle, was wrapped in his mother's arms. His small blonde head was turned in the direction of his brother and sister. A confused glint in his blue-gray eyes.

Leanne turned away and stole another look at Jameson. His face remained calm and unreadable. She wished she were as calm as him. To try to calm herself, she leaned her head against his arm as another siren wailed off into the distance. She sat wondering when they'd be able to go back home. Her stomach voiced annoyance. Suddenly a huge boom sounded, the lights flickered and dust fell from the ceiling. A few people screamed. Leanne rolled her eyes. *Oui*, she was nervous and jumpy, but she also knew it was fake. There wasn't a real air raid or anything like that going on, just drills and more drills like the ones that had been going on for the past three days. Jameson looked at her. A smile crinkled his face, but he didn't say anything. Another hour crawled by. Followed by another. Then finally the "All clear!" rang out, telling everyone that they could go home.

KESLI GLEASON

Leanne sighed gratefully and glanced at her watch as she waited until it was her turn to climb the ladder out of the shelter.

It was 6:00 in the morning. Her stomach complained again, but she couldn't help but smile as her head came into the clean morning air. The smile faded quickly though, as she pulled herself out of the shelter. Reims was quiet. Even more so for the fear that was running through the rest of its people. Jameson caught her hand and together they waited anxiously for Marius. Soon his bushy head popped from the hole and the three started home. Marius tried to get them to talk. Jameson would answer, but his answers were always one word and stiff. Soon, Maruis gave up, and they collapsed into silence.

Marius pulled the key to the shop from his pocket and unlocked the door. Leanne hurried to the kitchen as the boys went upstairs to change. Her eyes were drawn again and again to the empty pegs by the door and the barely visible bags in the living room. Her throat tightened and every movement felt forced. She felt a tear slip down her cheek but quickly brushed it away. Now was not the time. Even then, she allowed another quick glance at the bags, wishing that somehow they'd disappear. Wishing that she'd wake up and find that it was all a dream. Just to be sure, she pinched her arm hard. It hurt a lot. Again the feeling of despair wrapped a cold and unrelenting hand around her heart. She knew it would take a while for this feeling to go away.

A special breakfast was on the table today. She'd made muffins, scones, cider, and even had apples and cheese to put on the bread. As she called Jameson and Marius to the table, she felt the tears start again. They ate in silence. The ticking of the clocks seemed magnified in the gloomy silence. Leanne wanted to speak; wanted to say anything that would end the awful silence that hung over the table, but she couldn't. What was there to talk about?

A knock at the front door made them all jump. Jameson hurried and opened it. Leanne could hear his cheery voice welcoming someone inside.

"Leanne," he called to her. "Will you set another place at the table?"

She didn't answer, but she knew he didn't need her to. She got up swiftly and grabbed a cup and plate, wondering who would be coming over this early, especially after a typically long air-raid drill. Their guest was someone Leanne had never seen before. A tall man with gray hair, a gray beard, and black eyes. He wore a blue uniform with three gold bars on his sleeve. He smiled at her,

"*Bonjour*, I'm Captain Hauet." He took her hand and kissed it softly.

She smiled. "*Bonjour*. Am I safe in assuming that you are Jameson and Marius's Captain?"

Though she forced cheerfulness and welcoming to her voice, she didn't suppress the anger that heated her body, she even had to bite her lip before she said something rude and hurtful.

He laughed. "*Oui*. I am their Captain. I was coming over to tell them to report to the station at nine. Jameson has invited me to stay for breakfast and the smell of those muffins was too promising for me to turn them down."

He meant it kindly, Leanne was sure, but it came across differently. He was here to *force* Jameson and Marius to the train.

KESLI GLEASON

'Father, wilt thou spare them? I need them!' she cried in her head, moving her gaze to Maruis and Jameson. Her lip quivered and tears threatened to spill down her cheeks, but she knew that Jameson wouldn't want a scene with company over. Especially their captain. So she bit her lip, blinked back the tears, and smiled. Looking back at the Captain she knew he was obviously waiting for an answer. She widened the smile.

"*Merci*, Jameson taught me the recipe."

Her heart burned painfully. The tears burned in her eyes, but she didn't let them fall. She couldn't.

The captain nodded to her then turned back to the boys.

"I brought your uniforms. They're in my bag."

Leanne spent the next hour forcing herself to laugh and smile with the men. Each time Jameson smiled, it sent a stabbing pain to her heart. *He seems glad to go!* She forced herself not to cry. She ignored the gnawing at her heart and mind, and made herself enjoy the company of the captain. After making another pot of cider, it seemed apparent that Captain Hauet was staying as long as he could, so Leanne made her exit swiftly and quietly into the shop and out the front door.

Chapter 4

Leanne stood straight with her head held high, her eyes stoney. Tears swam in them, making her sight blurry. She felt empty. Too much pain was building in her chest and it was easier to just shut down and stand still, not saying anything, not looking at anything. Marius and Jameson stood beside her. Both wore their uniforms: Horizon blue overcoats, trousers, and caps, a white undershirt, black boots, and finally, a gun over one shoulder. They were handsome, with calm faces and bright eyes. They'd already accepted the fact that they were going to board the train. That they were going to war and nothing they did would stop that.

The train platform was crowded. Soldiers stood out like stars in a dark night. Splashes of blue on a black canvas. From her position she could see the Bonnots. They weren't far, but Leanne felt as if they were miles away. Rose clutched a small bag and a train ticket. Her arms were tight around her brother. Théo was dressed the same as Jameson and Marius, but instead of calm, his face was written in sadness and terror. Leanne caught a few snatches of their conversation. His Mama telling him to write, his Papa telling him to be brave, Rose begging him not to leave, and Charle crying and crying, but not understanding what was happening.

A train pulled into the station. Its brakes squealed and threw sparks as they ground to a stop. The scarlet engine on the train was beautiful. The many windows sparkled in the morning light. Gray smoke and white steam launched out of the smokestack, flying into the blue March sky. Leanne tore her eyes away from the train.

'Please, Father, keep them safe, keep them all safe.' she pleaded, looking back to Rose and her family.

Théo was looking a little uncomfortable. When his gray eyes met hers, he made a motion toward her and gave a questioning glance at his Papa, followed by an indiscernible question. His Papa nodded and Théo quickly walked over to where she, Jameson, and Marius stood.

He smiled. "Sorry to impose."

Jameson took his hand happily and shook it, his face lifting in a smile.

"No worries. Leanne is so choked up with tears she's not very talkative."

It was meant as a joke, but it was so sad it cut to Leanne's core. She bit her lip, fought the tears in her eyes and the pain in her heart, and quickly turned away. She moved swiftly across the wood platform, Jameson's pleading apology sounded behind her. She didn't stop until she threw her arms around Rose. They hugged for a moment, their tears mingling down their faces.

Rose pulled back. "Will you write to me?" Her face was sad, but a small hopeful smile curved the corners of her lips. "I'll write to you first, then you'll have my address, and you can write to me."

The pleading in her voice wasn't lost on Leanne.

WHEN THE SOLDIERS CAME

"Of course I'll write to you. You're my best friend." Leanne pulled her back into a hug. "Just because we're living in different places doesn't mean we can't be friends." She forced her voice to remain level and calm. Although, under the surface, she was nothing of the sort. She felt a hand on her arm and turned. Jameson was standing there. His face was no longer calm. A scared sadness had taken over.

Leanne didn't need him to say anything. The train was here. He was here to say goodbye. He led her away from the other people then he dropped to his knee as he held her shoulders.

"Leanne, I'm sorry. I didn't mean it. I wasn't trying to hurt your feelings, I just wanted to lift the mood a little."

The tears in his eyes made Leanne feel guilty.

She threw her arms around his neck, "I'm not mad, Jameson. I'm just scared. Oh, what am I going to do without you?" she sobbed.

Jameson hugged her tightly. "You'll do just fine. Madame and Monsieur Lucroy will look after you. Officer Rouzet said he'd take you to them if you wanted."

"*Non*." she whispered, tears rolling down her face, "I'd rather go alone."

Jameson managed a half smile. "I know, I told him that."

She felt her small defense crumble and didn't try to stop the tears from flowing. "Just come back!" she squeezed him tightly, "Please! Jameson, come back to me!"

Jameson blinked back his own tears.

"I will, Leanne. I promise. I'll be back. I love you, my sister."

He buried his face in her hair.

Leanne sobbed, her tears making hot trails down her cheeks.

"I love you, too, my brother."

The train's whistle blew loudly, its scream made Leanne's head pound painfully. She leaned back, placing her hands on Jameson's cheeks. She raked his face with her eyes, trying to commit every single detail to memory. The whistle screamed again. Jameson placed his hands on hers and slid them off his cheeks. He quickly got to his feet.

"I'll come back." he whispered huskily. Leanne had never heard him sound like that and it scared her worse.

He dropped her hands and moved backward toward the train, trying to keep her in sight. All around them women, girls, and children were crying as sons, husbands, brothers, and uncles made their way to the train's doors.

"I'll be back!" Jameson shouted above the din.

"I'll be waiting!" she cried, dancing on tiptoes to see him. "I'll be waiting! *Au revoir!* May God keep you! Tell Marius farewell!"

Jameson's face became blurred in the mass of people pressing forward.

"*Adieu!* I'll miss you!" he cried, despair filling his eyes and voice.

He disappeared for a moment as he was shoved onto the train. The train lurched as its engine lept against the steel that held it back. More steam and smoke, and the train started moving. Leanne shoved through people.

"Jameson! I love you!" she called, her eyes frantically searching for him.

WHEN THE SOLDIERS CAME

She saw his face in a window, his hand was reaching for her. She struggled, her dress catching her legs.

"I love you!" she screamed above the train. She forced herself faster and touched his hand with her fingers.

"*AU REVOIR!*"

The train picked up speed and her hand slipped out of his.

"*ADIEU!*" The train sped away carrying Leanne's heart with it.

"I love you, Jameson." she whispered brokenly. She stood gasping, hot tears streaming down her face.

'Father, bring him back to me. Please! I can't live without him.' She felt her heart break as she turned back.

'One painful good-bye.' she thought miserably. *'One more to go.'*

Oh, if only the Bonnets could stay one more night! A night spent with friends would lessen the pain of the double good-bye, but she knew that was impossible. Nothing would change their minds.

She pushed back through the crowd until she got back to Rose, Charle, and Monsieur and Madame Bonnot. Nobody spoke. Even when the scarlet train was out of view, the five of them remained silent. Another train rolled from the direction the soldiers had gone. This one was less magnificent. The dull gray engine was covered with rust. The cars weren't much better. The windows were covered in a layer of oil and grime. Suddenly it seemed like there were a million things to say. Each unspoken word pounded in Leanne's head and mouth, choking her. Tears swam in her eyes as Monsieur Bonnot smiled. "Come, Rose. Charle. We've got to get going. Good-bye Leanne, God keep you." He gave her a hug then stepped back.

Madame Bonnet walked up to her and threw her arms around Leanne. "I feel awful about leaving you here alone. I should have talked with Gaston. We should stay with you." Tears blurred her beautiful eyes and threatened to ruin her flawless makeup.

Leanne again forced a smile through her tears. "I'll be alright."

Madame Bonnet squeezed her tightly. "I know that."

Madame Bonnet struggled to keep her tears and sobs in check. "I just feel as if I'm leaving one of my children behind." She stepped back. Her lips pursed as she swallowed each sob as it rose. She took a pure white handkerchief from her purse and dabbed at her eyes. "Oh, I love you, Leanne. I've always loved you."

Leanne nodded. Then dropped to her knees throwing her arms around Charle. "I love you, *Copain*."

His thick toddler arms went around her.

"Bye-bye." he whispered.

Leanne rose. Madame and Monsieur took Charle by the hands, walked to the train, and handed the conductor their tickets. Leanne watched them, tears blurring her eyes. Charle waved to her, but it was apparent by the smile on his face that he didn't know how painful this goodbye was. He'd never get to see this friend again.

It took a few seconds, but Leanne finally returned her eyes to Rose. Rose's eyes were red and puffy, her face shiny and blotchy.

"I don't want to go. I don't want to leave you here alone."

She looked over her shoulder at the city or Reims. It had been their home for forever. Leaving it seemed wrong.

WHEN THE SOLDIERS CAME

Leanne couldn't even force a smile, everything was too real. It was all too fast,

"I'll be fine, Rose." she said through tears. "I have a home to go to. Don't worry about me. I won't be alone. And, I'll write to you until the war is over, and then you can move back and I'll be able to go to school with you."

Even as she said that, she knew that would never happen. Even if the war ended, she and Rose would never see each other again. The pain of that thought ripped through her heart. She and her friend would never get to see each other, ever again. Tears rolled rapidly down her cheeks, creating dark spots on the cold concrete ground.

Rose nodded sadly, her throat too thick for words, Monsieur Bonnet called her from the train steps. "Rose! Come on, Darling!"

"Oh," Rose hugged Leanne again, tears leaking down her face. "I'll miss you so very much, Leanne. May God keep you." she cried.

She slowly walked toward her Papa, wiping the tears from her cheeks. Her shoulders hunched, her chest caved. She looked defeated. In a way, she was.

'Keep her safe, Father. Keep her safe.' Leanne murmured under her breath, she wondered if Rose would look back, but she didn't. Leanne waited until Rose was on the train before brushing the new tears off her face. Dancing on tiptoe again, she waved enthusiastically as the train started moving. Each turn of the wheels sent a stabbing pain through Leanne. Each movement of her hand made her want to fall to the ground sobbing.

Rose opened the grimy window she sat beside and waved back. The train picked up speed. Again, Leanne set out running after it.

"Don't forget me, Rose! Don't forget me! Please!"

She stopped running. Her dress spun around her shins. She threw her arm in the air and waved. The empty feeling in her heart doubled, but she refused to cry again. "Don't forget me!" The words started loud, but faded as the train roared over them. Rose leaned out the window as far as she dared and waved. A sad smile twisting her lip. Tears running down her face and off her cheeks. Her mouth opened and she looked like she said something, but the train was too loud and too far away for Leanne to hear what she'd said.

Leanne watched painfully as her friend's face became a small smudge of white against the train, and all too soon she and the train were gone, leaving the faint wisp of smoke behind them. People started leaving and Leanne couldn't help but feel jealous and hurt all at the same time. They all had families or friends to go home with or to, she had no one. Not a single friend to give her a hug and tell her it would all work out.

No, that wasn't true. God was still here. He would help her. She reminded herself.

She walked back to the center of the station platform. Her heart felt as if it had been torn in two and each piece taken in a separate direction. Her head whipped first to the east, then to the west, as if she was trying to decide which train she'd see first. *'Father keep them all safe, please.'* She felt horrible. She wondered if she'd seen Jameson smile, or heard him whistle as he came into the kitchen for the last time. If she'd ever see Maruis laughing as he reassembled a watch, keeping up a steady, engaging conversation with the owner. If Rose would ever smile at her again and hug her. She wondered if she'd ever feel happy and alive again.

She stood there watching, until a hand fell on her shoulder. "Go on, Darling."

The station guard smiled at her. "Get on home." He had a kind face and a sympathetic smile.

Leanne was too scared to say she didn't want to go back to the now empty house and decided to leave without a word. The streets of Reims seemed darker than usual. The occasional person she saw hurried by without a word, but she didn't care. She didn't want to talk to anyone. She'd rather be left alone. Each step was hard. It felt like her boots had been turned to lead. Before she knew where she was, she found herself at the alley door to the shop. She sighed. She'd have to go in sooner or later. Slowly she slipped the key from her pocket and opened the door. The house was dark, and she didn't want to turn on the light. She hurried up the stairs in the dark and fell into bed, fresh tears streaming down her face. She buried her face in the pillow and bedclothes and sobbed. A new nightmare had begun.

When she woke, she didn't feel any better. Her head hurt from crying and still the empty feeling clung to her like a unrelenting fog. She swung her legs over the side of the bed and walked heavily to the wardrobe. She'd packed all her dresses yesterday, minus one. She pulled the soft, brown fabric over her head and set to buttoning the three buttons on her chest.

She took a small brush and blue hair ribbon from the bag on the floor and quickly tied her hair from her face. She slipped her shoes on, grabbed her bag, and hurried down the stairs.

The living room felt empty. She walked to the cabinet and pulled the worn bible from its place along with the small money box Marius had hidden there. She slipped the box into the bag, but seated herself on the sofa with the bible. Routine has a way of happening even if the world has been changed. Leanne didn't feel comfortable starting the day without the Word of God. She spent ten minutes studying the comforting words before adding the book to the bag. As she stepped in the kitchen, she noticed the letter from a while ago. It was laying with its flap open on the table. She stepped to it and picked it up as if it was made of ash. She gently pulled the paper and read quickly. It was the letter from Monsieur and Madame Lucroy. It had their address. That was good. When she'd told Jameson she wanted to go by herself, she didn't remember she didn't know where it was or how to get there. At least now she had a starting point. She tucked the letter into her pocket and opened the alley door. She was tempted to eat something but shook off the feeling. She wasn't hungry. She only wanted to prolong parting from the house.

Everyone already knew that the clock shop would be closed until further notice, so there was no reason to open the window. She cast one last, lingering look into the house then, heavily, she closed the door behind her and locked it. She pressed her hand to the smooth wood and laid her forehead beside it.

"I'll miss you." she murmured. Quickly, before the tears could run again, she turned and walked out of the alley.

WHEN THE SOLDIERS CAME

She heard money jingling in her pocket and thought of the bikes that could be rented, but decided against it. She'd rather walk. The day was warm and pleasant. The smell of rain was in the air, and it brought a smile to her lips. She loved the rain. She decided there was no reason to feel glum and gloomy. There was nothing she could do about her position except smile and hope for the best.

Chapter 5

It was a large house. Tall, gray brick walls led to a great iron gate. Perfect spheres sat atop the stone pillars. Looking between the bars, Leanne could see a gravel path lined with hedges leading to the house. A stone fountain stood in front of the porch. The house was white with pillars holding an impressive looking balcony above the front porch. Almost twenty windows were visible on the front of the mansion. Tall trees grew on the large yards to the sides of the hedges and path. Leanne checked the address again. This was the right place. But how was one to get the owners to know that someone was here? She spun around, looking for a knocker or a bell rope. She didn't see anything. *'Please let this be the right house.'*

A quick movement in the yard brought her eyes back to the gate. A young woman was hurrying down the path, the gravel crunching beneath her shoes. She was wearing a black and white maid's dress. She had stunning auburn hair and shining green eyes. She stepped to the bars. "Name, Mademoiselle?" She smiled. It was king and inviting.

Leanne figured the maid couldn't be more than a few years above her own age. "Leanne Martin." she stated softly, "And who are you?"

The woman smiled. "Claudia Courtial. It's a pleasure to meet you, Mademoiselle Martin." Her face was small, framed by her red hair. She had a tiny nose, and thin eyebrows. But it was a kind and gentle face filled with friendship.

Leanne grinned. "Please...call me Leanne. Mademoiselle Martin doesn't sound right." Already she knew that she'd like Claudia.

Claudia opened the gate and beckoned Leanne in. Leanne smiled as she complied. *'Merci, Father.'*

Claudia started back down the gravel path, her steps light and swift. Leanne stared at the house as she neared it, each step making her eyes widen. Claudia opened the wide front door with a golden knocker and motioned for Leanne to go inside. Leanne entered and expected Claudia to follow, but she didn't. She only smiled that sweet smile of hers.

"Edgar is in the room to your left. Don't be frightened. He's a kind man."

She closed the door without another word.

Leanne stood in front of the door, her jaw slightly agape. She was looking at a large entrance hall. Two large staircases were on either side of her. A large, expensive Spanish rug covered most of the floor at her feet. Oak furniture stood against the walls, their surfaces gleaming. Glancing up, she was shocked to see a huge, diamond chandelier dazzling the center of the ceiling. The stairs, walls, and ceiling were of polished marble. The floor was of dark oak and polished until she could see her reflection in it. Lace curtains blocked the light from the identical windows on either side of the dark oak front door. She took a few tentative steps and spun around, looking at everything. The Bonnets had been considered rich before the war, but even then Leanne had never seen anything remotely close to this kind of rich. She stopped and looked at the room to the right. She couldn't see much. A glowing fireplace lit the room, a mahogany desk barely visible in the doorway. Papers were scattered across the gleaming surface. A bookcase was on the opposite wall filled with the reds, blues, greens, and blacks of covers. Another Spanish rug decorated the floor. She loved books, and on impulse, took a step toward the room. Someone cleared their throat from behind her and she jumped, a small squeal of fright escaping her lips.

"Sorry, sorry, Mademoiselle."

The voice was rich and kind. She spun to face the speaker. He was an elderly man, with snow white hair and gentle hazel eyes. He wore a black suit and tie, the outfit of a butler. A gold watch shone on his wrist.

"*Non*, that was my fault." Leanne offered. "I should have been paying more attention."

She felt strange standing in the majestic house, she rubbed the front of her skirt. The simple brown dress seemed out of place in the house where silk and satin were probably worn for all occasions, not wool and cotton. Footsteps made her look up. She caught a glimpse of dark brown hair and shining brown eyes in one of the rooms before the door closed. She cocked her head, wondering who it was.

Edgar smiled at her. "I should have noticed you weren't paying attention and waited for you to turn around. Come, Mademoiselle Martin. I'm to see you to your room, and, once you're settled, take you to meet Monsieur and Madame Lucroy."

He swept his arm out, motioning to the stairs.

It took Leanne a moment before she moved. It was a breathtaking home, but she wasn't used to being treated as some important person. She was just Leanne, no one special. Her steps echoed as she climbed the stairs. Edgar followed her. The upstairs was just as magnificent as the down. The landing wrapped around and connected to the other staircase. A dozen doors followed the curve of the wall. Each one was of the same dark oak as the front door. Their knobs were of brass and each one had a lion head knocker in the center. Just like downstairs, everything was made of marble. The floor of dark oak. She looked across the curved balustrade and found herself level with the chandelier. She gasped. It was even more beautiful up close than from afar. Small rainbows danced across the ceiling as the light caught the diamonds at the right angle. Edgar opened one of the doors in the center and cleared his throat. Leanne started and turned around, an embarrassed flush creeping across her cheeks. Edgar smiled softly.

"Welcome to your room. Once you get settled, Mademoiselle, come downstairs and I'll take you to the living room."

He waited for her to walk into the room before closing the door behind her.

Leanne lost her breath again. The room was gigantic. It was small when she entered, but once she got away from the door it widened out. Again the walls and ceiling were marble. The floor was less polished, but the same dark color. In the farthest left corner was a bed so big she would have gotten lost in it. There were no windows, but that didn't come as a surprise, she must have been in the center of the house. A mahogany wardrobe was against the right wall, its face shining. It was ten times bigger than the one at home. A small, carved bench was at the foot of the bed. Another door led off into a small bathroom. Even the bathroom was pretty. A mirror was on the wall above the sink. A porcelain bathtub was tucked into a corner. She turned and walked cautiously back into the room. She placed her small bag on the bench uncertainly and carefully touched the bed cover. It was satin, and the pillows looked like silk, the kind that came from China. Another rug covered the floor, but this time it was a solid sky blue color, the same as the bedspread, pillows, and sheets. As she looked at everything, she realized something was missing. Not in the room itself, but in the whole house. Something was off. She shrugged, figuring that she'd guess what it was later. She took her bag again, opened the wardrobe, and gasped in shock as she saw it was already full of dresses, coats, jackets, and shoes. The dresses were magnificent, in shimmering pinks and purples, deep blues and reds, bright greens and yellows. The coats were lined with fur and made in a beautiful fashion, the kind that buttoned on the side of the chest, not the center. The shoes were all polished until she could see her reflection in them. All were her size and ranged from a slip-on summer pair, to a thick, fur lined winter boot. She took her dresses from the bag, smoothed them out, and hung them up in the small part of the empty rack, sighing as her hands rubbed against the now coarse wool and cotton. The slippery silk brushed against her hand. She shook her head and turned away. She folded the bag and set it on the floor or the wardrobe. She closed the wardrobe and walked to the door.

'Merci for giving me a place to stay, Father.'

As she dismounted the steps, she realized what was missing, the house didn't have a home feeling to it. The doors had been opened for her, but it seemed as if love was something these floors had never known. Laughter had never rang from the walls.

She dismounted the steps and smiled at Edgar.

"The room is amazing. I've never seen sleeping quarters so large."

Edgar returned her smile. "Well, Mademoiselle, now you have. Come, this way."

He led her down the hall.

The hall was long and another Spanish rug carpeted their steps the whole way. Doors lined the hall, and every now and then she could catch a glimpse of a fire, or a chair. Never a person though. It was as if the house was empty. The hall widened to a large room. A fireplace was on one end, circled by sofas and armchairs. Another chandelier hung from the ceiling. A staircase was on the other end, leading to a part of the upstairs that didn't connect with the front. A large, shining window took up the whole wall in front of her. The view was marvelous: A green yard, fenced in by the same gray brick wall as out front, and tall cone shaped trees. A stone path led from the house to the gate at the far end. Even from here, Leanne could see the french houses outside the gate. In the center of the huge yard was a fountain, identical to the one out front.

She became aware of people in the room besides Edgar. A tall, mustached man and a smiling woman. The man wore a white undershirt, dove gray overcoat, dove gray trousers, and fancy brown shoes. He had dark hair slicked sideways across his head, and shining brown eyes. The woman wore a peach colored dress, with lace trimming on the sleeves, neck, and around the waist. She had blonde hair and deep blue eyes. *'Please let them be nice.'* Leanne prayed softly.

WHEN THE SOLDIERS CAME

The woman smiled sweetly. "Mademoiselle Leanne Martin, I presume?" She had a high voice. Her nose wrinkled. Was there a slight disdain as she focused on Leanne's dress? Not sure. Her smile seemed genuine though. Leanne again felt self conscious, but brushed it away.

Leanne nodded. "*Oui.*"

The man stepped forward and kissed her hand. "Monsieur Ivo Lucroy. It's a pleasure to meet you."

His voice was deep, and he was smiling, but it didn't reach his eyes. Instantly Leanne felt nervous. The woman stepped beside her husband, put her hands on Leanne's shoulders, and kissed her cheeks.

"Madame Laurette Lucroy. Aren't you stunning?"

She seemed to be referring to Leanne's hair and eyes, obviously not her dress.

Leanne smiled shyly, not knowing how to respond. Nervously she rubbed her left foot against her right calf. Madame Lucroy noticed the movement.

"Ah, Dear, you must be tired."

Leanne thought for a moment, it was around noon and the walk over had been pleasant, but her head was pounding from all the crying she'd done yesterday. She smiled grimly. "*Oui.*"

Monsieur Lucroy nodded.

"Alright, you can head up to your room, Leanne, darling. Dinner happens at five. Feel free to wear anything in your wardrobe. See you then."

He turned back and walked to the sofa.

Leanne, taking that as a cue to leave, turned on her heel and disappeared back into the hall. She took the stairs swiftly and was grateful to find herself back in her room. Looking at the wardrobe she remembered Monsieur Lucroy's invitation to wear anything and interpreted this into *'Don't wear anything you brought. Wear something we approve of.'* Feeling worse than she had this morning, she laid carefully on the bed, making sure not to wrinkle it. *'Father, merci for all the blessings that Thou hast given me. I will try my best to give light to the people that dwell here. Please bless Rose, that she will find a friend in Paris. Please give Marius and Jameson Thy protection as they are fighting for Thy truth. Amen.'*

The reverberating ringing of a bell brought her sitting up in shock. She glanced at her watch as she got out of bed. It was 4:45. She made her way to the wardrobe and flicked through the dresses. Finally she found one. It was simple, but elegant. Turquoise with white lace on the belled sleeves and collar. The turquoise silk ruffled like water down to her ankles, where it covered the simple black slip-on shoes she chose. She hurried into the bathroom and quickly redid her hair. As she tied the turquoise ribbon tighter, she made her way across the landing and down the stairs. At the last few steps, she halted not knowing where the dining room was. Or the kitchen. Or wherever they ate. She stepped down slowly, trying to think where they would eat dinner. Light steps on the landing above her made her stop again. The steps continued until their owner wrapped around the stairs. It was a boy. His dark brown, slightly curly, slightly wild hair was brushed to the side falling across his forehead. Melted chocolate brown eyes lit up as they met hers. His face lit up with a smile and he gave a small chuckle.

WHEN THE SOLDIERS CAME

She couldn't help but smile. The boy was breathtakingly handsome. This was the first time she'd ever thought a boy was cute and she knew she was blushing. The boy halted on the steps, his hand on the banister.

She thought for a moment.

"*Bonjour*," she said shyly. "I'm Leanne Martin. I'm new."

She held out her hand timidly, gazing at the boy from under her eyelashes.

The boy shook his head as if to clear it, then took her hand and shook it gently. "I'm Anthony Tremblay." He smiled a little wider.

Leanne grinned at him. "It's a pleasure to meet you."

Sure enough she was blushing. She could feel the heat on her neck and cheeks.

"The pleasure is all mine." he responded.

The bell rang again. Leanne shifted to head down the hall, but Anthony didn't release her hand. She pulled him slightly and said, "It's time for dinner."

He shook his head again. "You're right. Come, the dining room is this way." He took back his hand but offered her his arm. When she took it, he led her down the same hall as she'd gone down with Edgar. He opened one of the doors to the side before they made it to the other room. The dining room was grand. A long, mahogany table ran down the center with a large chandelier hanging above it. Nearly two dozen chairs were pulled up around it with fine dishes at each place. Monsieur Lucroy smiled as they entered.

"Good, Anthony. Leanne. The last two."

He motioned to empty chairs on the left side of the table. Anthony quickly pulled a chair out of Leanne, and then claimed the one beside it.

Madame Lucroy looked at Leanne. "Let's do introductions, shall we?" Without waiting for a reply she clapped her hands once.

"Right. So Leanne, next to you, as you probably already know, is Anthony. He's fifteen. Beside him is Tristan Lafaille, He's nine."

Leanne leaned forward a little to see who she was talking about. Tristan was a small boy with happy, dark gray eyes. His hair, black as night, flopped across his head untamed. He nodded happily at her. His face was glowing with a smile, and the way he was seated so close to Anthony made her think that something was special between them. He looked like a happy boy without a care in the world. She instantly fell in love with him. She's always had an instant connection with small children. Charle Bonnet had been one of her favorites, but she had known every child under the age of six on her block.

"Then comes Marc Arries at fifteen."

Marc was a strong looking figure. His black eyes watched her carefully. He ran a hand through messy blond hair, ruffling it and making it stand on end. No smile welcomed her. He was too occupied circling his finger around his empty glass. Leanne gave him a smile anyway, resolving to stay as far from him as possible.

"Beside him is Gerta Auclair. Fifteen."

Gerta was beautiful. Sunshine yellow hair fell to her chin, framing an elfish face, small nose, and cornflower eyes. She smiled at Leanne and waved. Leanne waved back, hoping to gain a new friend, but hurried to listen to Madame Lucroy.

"Beside Gerta is Esmé Couture, she's fourteen like yourself."

Esmé was a different picture from Gerta, instead of sunshine yellow, her curls were midnight black. Esmé's eyes were a stormy gray, way different from the happy blue of Gerta's eyes. Her face was hard and scars were visible on her arms and hands. She nodded a welcome to Leanne, her eyes brightening a little. Leanne waved back, wondering where the scars had come from.

Madame Lucroy continued. "Next to her is Nathan Périer. Fifteen."

Nathan had black hair and shocking green eyes. He was well muscled. His biceps bulged in the blue, short sleeved shirt he was wearing. He gave her a wide smile as she caught his eye. She blushed and looked away, but not before catching the glint of curiosity in his eyes.

"Gael Lubar. He's sixteen."

The young man that met her eyes was a happy looking person. He had hazel hair brushed back from shocking blue eyes. A smile curved his lips. Lines crinkled at his eyes and around his mouth that Leanne guessed came from smiling and laughing. He waved and said, "Welcome." The first to speak of all of them.

Leanne grinned. "Thank you."

"Then there are the sisters, Lidia and Lovisa Glos. Lidia's almost sixteen. Lovisa is ten."

The sisters were identical, with loosely curled blonde hair and shimmering green eyes; Leanne could only tell them apart by their size. Lovisa was short where Lidia was tall. Lovisa was shivering and clutching Lidia's arm. Her frightened eyes were darting around the room. Lidia gave a quick smile and slight wave. Leanne returned it, then smiled invitingly at Lovisa, earning a half smile in return. Silently, Leanne promised herself she'd get on the little girl's good side no matter what it took.

"Then comes Leo Dupont, he's fifteen."

The boy that met her eyes didn't strike her as friendly. His face was pinched into a scowl, with high cheekbones and a small scar on the edge of his chin. His blue eyes were dark and half hidden behind black eyebrows. Black hair fell over his ears. His hands, resting on the table, looked strong and unrelenting. But as she looked into Leo's eyes, she caught a glimpse of fear and satisfaction. She was confused, those two emotions didn't really work together. She shrugged, deciding to work that out later, and turned back to Madame Lucroy.

"Last, but not least, are my children, Annabella and Delroy. Annabella is four, and Delroy is five and a half." She ended with a giggle.

Annabella was a sweet looking child with small, chocolate brown eyes and long, honey colored hair. Her face was delicate, almost like a fairy's. Delroy had his mother's blue eyes and his father's dark hair but he matched his sister in face shape. However he looked more like a woodland elf than a fairy. Leanne smiled. Looking at the little boy reminded her of Charle. She was unprepared for the wave of homesickness and hurt that crashed over her. She missed Charle terribly, along with Rose, Jameson, and Maruis. *'What had happened to them all?'*

WHEN THE SOLDIERS CAME

'Stop it.' she told herself sharply. She had to remember that Charle and Rose were gone, no use reopening the wound with wishful thoughts. That could be done tonight, in dreams.

Chapter 6

The dinner went slowly. With no talking, even a whisper was noticed. Leanne was bursting with questions, but a glance from Anthony made her believe that speaking at meals was somehow impolite. So, she decided to wait. A swift smile from Gerta and a reassuring wink from Nathan made her think that maybe she'd have friends here. Edgar was standing beside the door, his eyes scanning for any sort of trouble. House maids, like Claudia, were sure the food on the table would never run out. The lights cast glares off the plates, and Leanne lost her appetite. She gracefully refused the maid's sweet question if she wanted more, and leaned carefully against the back of her chair. Soon Monsieur Lucroy wiped his lips with a handkerchief and got to his feet.

"Alright outside. And please, no more throwing water."

He said it with a smile, but Leanne could see an angry glint in his eyes.

Esmé was the first on her feet. She wore a simple navy blue dress, nearly the same fashion as Leanne's. Hers was just missing the lace. She gave a lingering smile at Madame and Monsieur Lucroy and hurried to the door. The rest dogged her steps as if dinner had been unpleasant. Anthony lingered, watching Leanne. Slowly, she got to her feet. Not sure what to do, she glanced at her dishes sitting in a neat pile on the table. Anthony saw her confusion and gently grabbed her arm.

"Come on, Leanne." He pulled her gently.

She allowed him to lead her through the maze of hallways and rooms before coming back to the living room. Everyone was on the other side of the glass. The girls were sitting in a perfect line on the edge of the fountain, and the boys were staring at the window waiting for them. Leanne suddenly felt small and shy. Her feet paused mid step and she was left unable to move staring at the seven boys and girls. Her heart hammered painfully in her chest before leaping into her throat. Anthony squeezed her arm gently.

"Don't worry." His smile made the muscles in her legs work again, and she stumbled down the steps and onto the stone patio.

Esmé stepped forward first, her black hair blowing across her face. Her gray eyes were unreadable.

"*Bonjour*." She offered a smile. "I'm glad that you're able to stay with us."

Leanne couldn't help but smile back. "The house is grand. I've never seen a place like it."

Esmé laughed a little. "Neither had I when I first got here. Come with me, a dinner introduction isn't enough."

She looped her arm through Leanne's and dragged her to the fountain.

Gerta bounced to her feet. "*Bonjour*, Leanne. In case you forgot, I'm Gerta." Her golden hair caught the last rays of the sun as it disappeared behind homes and buildings. Her dress was of lavender silk and ruffled from the waist down like Leanne's. The bodice was tight with lace at the collar. The sleeves were puffed with more lace at her bicep. A golden necklace hung about her neck with matching earrings and bracelets.

Leanne waved happily. "Leanne." She could easily tell this girl came from money. The clothes she wore and the way she talked gave it away. This wasn't just the type of dress and jewelry someone gave her when she moved in. *Non*. This had come from wherever Gerta had come from.

Gerta grinned widely. She gave a small wave and went to talk to the boy, Marc. Lidia got to her feet pulling Lovisa with her.

"*Bonjour*. I'm Lidia. This is my little sister, Lovisa." She smiled, and Leanne felt her heart melt. The young girl was adorable with her wide green eyes and the loose curls framing her face. She could have come straight out of a story book. Something seemed off with the two. Their eyes were happy, but they held hidden pain and secrets.

Lovisa gave a half hearted attempt at saying hello but squeaked in fear as Leanne looked her in the eye. She contented herself with a quick half wave before jerking Lidia away to the lawn. Inwardly, Leanne's heart sagged. She wanted to be friends with the little girl and was disappointed to see that the girl was scared of her.

Nathan stepped forward. His steps swaggered a little as if he was used to being looked up to and obeyed. Leanne looked him in the eye as he spoke. He was handsome. "*Bonjour*. Leanne?" His mouth curved slightly at the question, but as she nodded confirmation, it widened, making his face even more handsome.

"I'm Nathan. I'm glad that you could find a place here. I hope we can become friends." He winked as he took her hand and shook it. "I'm studying medicine. What are you learning?"

Leanne ceased up with shyness.

"I haven't had schooling. My brother couldn't afford it. But I can read, write, and speak in German and Italian." she said it slowly, hoping this would please him.

Nathan gave a gracious nod. "Those are great skills."

Behind Leanne, Anthony tensed. His brown eyes darkened and his whole frame stiffened. He returned to normal as Marc stepped forward. Marc's face was dark and as he gave a smile, Leanne could tell it didn't reach his eyes; but as his eyes met hers something sparked.

"Hi."

His voice bordered on bored. Nathan gave him a dark glance before he hurried away.

Leanne pretended not to notice the look Nathan gave Marc and grinned. "Hi!" she returned the greeting.

He was a stiff person but the warm grasp in which he held her hand explained that he could be kind and friendly if he wanted to.

He looked a little uncomfortable. Leanne, unsure what to say to someone who looked like he never spoke more than three words, glanced at Anthony for help. He stepped up and looped an arm through hers. "Come, see the gardens, they're absolutely wonderful."

He led her to the right side of the mansion. Behind a large pop off of the wall, Leanne could see trees nearly as high as the roof. Colorful blossoms were shining in the deep greens. Anthony grinned at her expression. "The Lucroy's like everything fancy." He opened a small gate and escorted her through it.

Leanne's jaw dropped, bright flowers in all sorts of colors grew happily in every direction, their sparkling petals shimmered in the sinking sunlight. As the shade of the wall slowly inched itself farther into the garden, small little mushrooms began to glow. Fruit bushes and smaller trees were dotted around the winding stone path. Leanne spun, taking it all in. She stopped, looking back at Anthony. "How? It's only March, there's no way this all could be this green by now. Spring has hardly come."

Anthony gave an unconcerned shrug. "Honestly I have no idea, and frankly I don't care. Whatever Monsieur and Madame Lucroy do is up to them."

The bitterness in his voice shocked Leanne, she wondered how a person could speak so unpleasantly about another. "Why? What have they done to you? They've given you a roof over your head and three hot meals a day. What's so bad about that?"

Anthony's expression darkened. "They only do so because the government pays them to do so."

Leanne raised her eyebrows in confusion. "What's so wrong about that? They certainly have enough room. And from the looks of the house and yard, and the food we were served tonight make me think they were rich long before they were paid for taking in youth for the government. Weren't they?"

Anthony gave a smile that looked more like a grimace. "I'll tell you later." He turned for the gate. "The others are probably gone, we'd best be getting in bed."

Leanne frowned, looking at her watch. "It's only seven, surely a bunch of teenagers don't go to bed so early. What's wrong? Won't you tell me?"

Anthony colored, something fell behind his eyes, masking his thoughts. Leanne felt a ting of hurt, she didn't know why, but Anthony blocking her made her want to cry. She was about to ask him again, but paused when the gate was pushed open. Claudia was standing there, the same smile curving her lips. "It's about time you get inside, it's starting to get chilly."

She forced herself to shiver before stepping out of the way making way for Anthony and Leanne to walk by her. Anthony instantly moved toward her, a look of relief on his face, but Leanne looked back at the flowers, blinking more tears out of her eyes.

"Leanne, darling, hurry now. Best get inside." Claudia wrapped a kind arm around her shoulders before giving her a light push toward the gate.

Confused and hurt, Leanne hurried out of the garden and ran into the yard. It was empty. Frowning she ran into the house, up the stairs, and flung herself on her bed, tears rolling down her face. Something was wrong in this house, too many people being too closed off and close mouthed. She missed home, where the only secrets kept were what was for dinner and what the next person's birthday gift was. She took a gasping breath. "Jameson, I want you back! Come back, please!"

She was too scared to use the thick, silk comforter, and instead pulled one of the pillows over her head. *'Father, help. I need Thee, I can't do this. I can't.'*

WHEN THE SOLDIERS CAME

Leanne rolled over, the comforter shifted as she moved, and the pillow over her head flopped to the ground. *'What woke me?'* she wondered without curiosity.

Someone knocked on the door, their first was kind, but insistent. "Mademoiselle Martin, are you awake?'

She froze in fear as she sat up. *'Where am I?'* She looked around for some kind of answer.

"Mademoiselle Martin?" The door opened and a kind, elderly man was smiling at her. "Get ready for school."

Leanne blinked in surprise, everything that had happened yesterday came rushing back. She blinked again, struggling to digest Edgar's words. "School?" she asked, almost breathlessly.

Edgar's smile deepened. "Of course, now hurry, breakfast is nearly ready." He closed the door and Leanne heard his steps retreat.

She flung herself out of bed, a thrill running through her. School! She was going to school. She ran over to the wardrobe, wondering what one wore to school. As she was struggling to decide, another knock sounded outside. "Enter." Leanne called, barely caring who it was.

The door opened and a black haired girl stepped in. *'Esmé,'* Leanne recalled. *'Her name is Esmé.'*

Esmé smiled kindly at her. "Nathan told me you don't study anything. I interpreted this as you didn't go to school, as anyone who did would be far more stuck up than you are."

Leanne shook her head gently. "That's an awful thing to say, you're not stuck up. And my best friend, Rose, wasn't stuck up either."

"Kind of you." Esmé responded, walking over to Leanne's wardrobe and flicking through the dresses that the Lucroy's had provided. "But, though I can't speak for your friend, I've hardly had any schooling, myself. I can see how you'd think me less stuck up than the others." She picked out a peach colored dress, it was less glamorous than some of the others. It was simple, with no ruffles or lace. It looked just like one of Leanne's dresses from home, but instead of buttons on the back it had a zipper, and there was a black belt for her waist, "I think this is perfect." Esmé bent and pulled a pair of shiny, black leather, ankle high boots from the base of the wardrobe.

Leanne took the clothes. "*Merci.*" She hurried into the bathroom and began to change. "Esmé, are you still out there?"

"*Oui.*"

"Could I ask you something?"

"Sure."

"Why didn't you get a lot of schooling? If you don't mind me asking of course. My brother said it was important, and that anyone who had a chance should do it." She opened the door and stepped out, the dress was very beautiful, and Leanne loved it. The shoes were perfect.

Esmé slipped into the bathroom and grabbed a brush. "I didn't get the chance. You see, my Papa left when I was a baby and my Mama didn't have enough money to send me. She worked a lot when I was growing up and didn't really care what I did most of the time. So, when I could, I'd sneak out to the school house where other kids were learning, I'd push a window open, just a little, and I'd listen. I'd write in the dirt to practice my spelling, but I could never get the hang of reading or *mathématiques.*" She gave a small laugh as she tightened a peach colored ribbon in Leanne's hair. "That was before my

Mama died of pneumonia. And I found myself homeless at age nine."

Leanne gasped, tears filling her eyes at the prospect of being homeless. "What happened?"

"Well, I didn't want to get sent to some work house, so I lived on the street. I begged for food, sometimes took it from garbage bins if I couldn't find anything else. I got into fights over food sometimes." She showed Leanne the scars on her hands and arms. "I can fight pretty well with a knife. I lived five years on the streets, before a man found me and threatened to sue the city if they didn't do anything for me. So, they bagged me up and sent me here. Giving me a home, *oui,* but not a family. Anthony was here, along with Tristan, Gael, Lidia, and Lovisa."

The girls moved across the landing and down the stairs. "That's just awful." Leanne exclaimed after the full effect of Esmé's words sunk in.

Esmé only shrugged. "Some are luckier than others, I guess. Come on, we'll be late."

Chapter 7

Leanne had never seen so many kids so silent. Their faces were grave and sullen, some had tear stained cheeks and puffy eyes. Leanne frowned, the war had had a great effect on France. Of course it had affected the schools too. Hadn't the Bonnet's only been able to pay for two days out of the week for Rose and Théo?

Anthony was walking near her engrossed in a conversation with Tristian. The young boy seemed to be glowing. His face was washed in sunshine and his laughter rang a pitch higher than Anthony's. Esmé walked closer to Leanne talking about something called History with Gael and Lidia. Gerta and Lovsia were talking about something Leanne couldn't hear. The younger girl looked terrified. Her eyes were wide and her hands were shaking. Leanne touched Esmé's arm. "Esmé, what's wrong with Lovisa?"

Esmé paused her conversation. "Oh, her? She always looks that way in the morning."

"Why? Did something happen to her?"

Esmé shrugged. "I don't know anything about her, or Gael, or Lidia. They're really closed about themselves. All I know is that their parents died and they were sent here by the government. Gael and Lidia started dating, and both are fiercely set on protecting Lovisa." She turned away and continued her conversation.

Leanne shivered slightly when they walked through the large gates. Gael and Lidia waved nervously to them and continued walking, heading to the highschool a few blocks further. Leanne jumped when Anthony grabbed her arm. "I'll help you sign in." He waved good-bye to Tristian, who was talking to a small blonde haired boy, and walked Leanne up the broad steps. The building was huge, made of a dark red brick with polished granite floors, sweeping staircases, and never ending doors. As they walked Anthony turned to her. "You're not mad at me are you?"

Leanne faltered for a moment, words freezing in her throat. Anthony's dark eyes, trained on hers, were gorgeous, heightened by the black jacket he wore over a thick white shirt. "Uh...um, *non*. Of course I'm not. Why would you think that?" She felt embarrassed. She figured she was blushing something awful, her face felt uncomfortably hot.

She watched as Anthony crimsoned, too.

"Nothing. I was just wondering. After last night...Ah, I mean..." He hung his head. "I don't know."

Leanne smiled softly. "I understand. I'm not mad at you." She took his hand and squeezed it reassuringly before dropping it, inclining her head, and raising an eyebrow.

Anthony jumped and led her to the front desk.

"Name? Age? Schooling?"

A sharp looking woman with a severe looking face pelted her with these questions as she stood there. Leanne looked nervously at Anthony. He gave her a reassuring smile and nodded his head encouragingly. Leanne took a deep breath. "Leanne

Martin. Fourteen. I haven't had any public schooling. But I can read and write in French, German, and Italian, and I know a small amount of English as well."

The woman didn't look up but jotted down something on the piece of paper in front of her. Suddenly she looked up. Her eyes were a stony gray, and pierced Leanne when she looked into them. The woman frowned, making her look like a very disagreeable person. Her gaze trained on Anthony.

"Where are you supposed to be, young man?"

He swallowed nervously. "*Mathématiques*, Mademoiselle."

"Then what are you doing?"

"I was waiting for Leanne. I was hoping I could..."

"Get to class." The woman commanded sharply, leaving no room for argument. As Anthony scampered off, the woman returned her gaze to Leanne. "Follow me, we'll get you in class."

School was interesting, and she loved it, even if it was a little hard to understand, right up to the last two classes. The last two teachers only talked about the war. Right now it did not look good for the French. Her heart sank like a stone when the first teacher announced that it seemed most likely that Germany would invade the very heart of France and the country would crumble. She had to blink back tears when the second teacher claimed it probable that nearly three fourths of the soldiers that had been sent out would die and that half the remainder would be taken into Germany and never seen again. She was grateful for the bell that signaled the end of the school day, and ran as quickly as she could to get away from the horrible place where faith and hope didn't seem to exist.

"Leanne!"

She didn't know who was calling her, but she didn't really want to know.

"Leanne, wait up!"

Anthony huffed behind her and caught her arm. "Are you okay? You ran out so fast. How was the first day?"

"Alright; up until the last two classes." Leanne muttered. Her eyes still stung from the hot tears. "The teachers only talked about the war, and they're both set that France is going to lose and everyone is going to die," she muttered bitterly.

Anthony gave her a good natured smile. "Don't worry, *Professeur* Lagrand and *Professeur* Allard are always like that. Just ignore most of what they say. Their tests are always easy, so don't worry about it. Term ends in a few months, we'll be out of there soon."

They paused by the gate. Soon the others came out. Again, Anthony attached himself to Tristian and both were inseparable all the way home. Leanne wondered why they were so close friends. And why two good looking boys, ones that would obviously get good homes, were staying with a couple like the Lucroy's.

Leanne sank into the squishy armchair and sighed, the house was deathly quiet. Edgar had sent them to the library as soon as they got home. Leanne loved the huge room with high ceilings, a crackling fireplace, and so many books.

WHEN THE SOLDIERS CAME

Shelves ran up and down the walls, going over the mantle and the door in one continuous stream. The shiny black, blue, green, red, and yellow covers glinted in the fire's light. There were two sofas, three armchairs, and a few circular mahogany tables circled around a large Russian rug in the center of the floor. Anthony was laying on the floor, Tristan beside him, both reading a book. Glancing at the cover Leanne was surprised to see it was in German. Again a spark of curiosity burned in her, making her wish she knew who all these kids were. Lidia and Gael were whispering in the farthest corner, their words drowned out by the wireless. Nathan, Leo, and Marc were sitting on one of the sofas, their faces dark and their eyes closed. Esmé and Gerta were chatting away about some latest fashion that the Germans were creating. And Lovisa was sitting beside the fire spinning something in her hands. Leanne sighed again. "Why is it so quiet?" she asked no one in particular.

Anthony looked up, resting his cheek in his right hand. "The Lucroy's are out, the maids are working on the yard, and Edgar is in the kitchen, overseeing dinner."

"Where are the Lucory's?"

Gael walked over and sat in a chair beside her. "Madame Lucroy is at some party across town. Monsieur Lucroy I believe is at work."

"What does he do?" By the way Gael's eyes tightened, Leanne could guess that it was something awful.

"What?"

Nathan got to his feet. "He edits a newspaper. For all of France, England, and Germany." The darkness in his voice wasn't lost on Leanne.

She gasped. "Why? France is at war with them."

Leo sank further against the sofa, boredom written on his face.

"The Lucroy's lived in Germany a few years before the declaration of war. Their family is still there. They moved here because of a career growth, but that didn't change their allegiance. They still salute the German flag."

Leanne shook her head. "That's awful. Why?"

"Wouldn't you?" Lidia put in, taking Nathan's empty seat on the sofa. "Even if you move to England I bet you'd still salute the French flag. After all, you're French."

Leanne nodded reluctantly.

"The same goes for them."

"Then why are we allowed to stay here? Doesn't the Government think that it's a little dangerous to have Germans looking after us in the middle of a war with Germany?"

"They cut all ties with Germany, so they claim." Marc snorted. "But we know better."

Lovisa looked up, fear written in her eyes. "Like what's going on tonight?"

Gael made a choking noise and rushed to Lovisa's side. Leanne frowned, her brow furrowed in confusion. She looked at Anthony for explanation, but was shocked to see his face was pale and grave, his eyes darting to the others. "What's happening tonight?" Leanne asked softly, wondering if anyone would answer her.

Lidia forced a smile "Nothing. Just Lovisa making stories up in her head."

A bell rang. And Gerta jumped to her feet. "Come on, time for dinner." She disappeared followed by the others. Leanne went last, noting that all their faces were nervous and pale.

WHEN THE SOLDIERS CAME

Weeks passed, and soon there was a week left of March. Leanne walked the streets of Reims all she could, trying to get free of the strange cloud hanging around the house. Ever since Lovisa had said something was happening that night in the library, everyone except Anthony had suddenly closed up, speaking to Leanne only when they had to. Anthony went out of his way to make her feel welcome, even accompanying her on her walks when he could. Today he was a little ahead at a phone booth. Leanne waited for him to reappear.

"Good call?"

Anthony's face was shining, and the worried little furrow that had been in his forehead for weeks now had disappeared. "*Oui*. Very good. Come on." He held out his arm for her and they started walking again.

"Anthony," Leanne began, a little hesitant. "You don't have to answer if you don't want to, but what are you doing at the Lucroy's? What are any of you doing there?"

Anthony stopped, his back stiffening. A sense of panic gripped Leanne. *'Father, help him not to be mad.'* "Sorry, I didn't mean to pry."

Anthony shook himself like a dog and put back his smile. "Nothing to apologize about. You've been here a while, you deserve to know our stories. I grew up on a small farm outside Rennes. I lived with my Uncle Hugo, Aunt Chloé, and Cousin Fabian. My parents died before I even knew them. My Aunt and Cousin were killed when I was twelve. I moved to Nancy with my Uncle, before war broke out and he was sent off and I was sent here."

Leanne saw tears sparkling in his eyes, but didn't point them out. His voice was strong, but Leane felt as if he were holding information. "And the others?" she prompted, deciding to think about his story when they separated.

Anthony grinned wryly. "I don't know about Gael, Lidia, and Lovisa. When they came, they were all shy and quiet. I got them to open up a little, but I've never heard their back stories." His face was a little dark when he spoke and Leanne felt a little nervous. Anthony continued. "I don't know the others' whole stories, just the small reasons they're here. You've heard Esmé's, she told me she'd told you. Well, Gerta was orphaned when she was eight. She lost her little sister when she was ten. She was adopted by a kind man. And they had a few years together. Then war was declared and he was sent away. She was sent here. Tristan was abandoned young. He grew up on the streets his whole life. He was caught stealing and was sent here as punishment. I kind of adopted him as my little brother because he was so much like my cousin. Nathan's sister raised him. They were all going to America just before war broke out. His brother in law, sister, two nephews and one niece went ahead, promising to send him money so he could join them. He came here when he didn't have anywhere else to go. Leo and Marc are school boys. They both live in Paris, but were in Metz for school. When the Germans started invading they were sent here."

Leanne stood frozen for a moment. A lot of their stories mirrored her early life, the life she'd banished from her memory. She shivered as the thoughts and memories pressed in on her.

Anthony touched her arm. "Leanne, are you alright?"

WHEN THE SOLDIERS CAME

She nodded, swallowing the lump in her throat. "*Oui,* just a little tired is all. And sad. Your lives were ruined."

Anthony only smiled and shrugged. "Maybe, but they were ruined before the war. Let's get back."

He led her back to the gate. Claudia met them with her usual cheerful smile. "Welcome back, did you have a nice walk?"

Anthony responded eagerly. But Leanne only nodded. She felt heavy. Her heart ached to help her new friends, but she didn't know how. And she could tell there was more to the stories than what Anthony had told her. She didn't press the matter, knowing that if she wasn't to be told now, she'd learn later. But she still ached to help them, wondering what she could do for them. Silently she walked through the house and into the backyard. The sun was vanishing, and the wind was whistling softly. She sighed and walked into the small garden. The flowers had opened more, their colors deepened.

"Leanne?"

She spun around, forcing a smile. *"Bonjour,* Lidia, what brings you out here? And where is Lovisa?"

Lidia's green eyes were shiny, and she was frowning a little. "I was looking for you. I haven't spoken to you much since you've been here. I felt that I was being a little rude. I'm sorry for acting the way I have to you. I've been nervous and scared but that is no excuse for my actions. I hope you can forgive me."

Leanne's smile turned real. "Of course I can. And you did nothing wrong."

Hurried footsteps thudded across the patio.

"Lidia? Lidia, are you out here?"

Nathan's voice sounded nervous and bored at the same time. Lidia's eyes dilated and she spun to face the gate.

"Nathan, I'm in the garden! What's going on?"

Nathan rushed to the gate. "Anthony has news. We're in the library and Gael's requested you." He gave a half smile to Leanne. "*Désolée*, Leanne." He grabbed Lidia's hand and dragged her away.

"No problem." Leanne muttered to the empty gate. Something hot pricked behind her eyes. She hurried to the fountain and looked at her reflection. She still looked the same, but her face was worried. *'What is going on, Father?'* She felt something warm slip down her face and was alarmed to find herself crying. Again. She cried nearly every night. She missed Jameson and Marius and Rose and Théo and Charle. She blinked back the tears telling herself to toughen up, but it wasn't any use. She sank onto the edge of the fountain and trailed her fingers in the water. She thought about writing a letter but guessed that neither train would have gotten to its destination and she didn't know Rose or Jameson's addresses. The sun disappeared, and the silver light of the moon burst from behind a gray cloud. It shimmered on the water, but she didn't care.

'Father please help me!' she gasped. *'Please. I need Thee. Don't leave me alone, not now. Please not now.'*

After an hour she got numbly to her feet. She hoped that everyone else would be in bed. She slipped inside. Too scared to turn on a light, she fumbled down the corridor in the dark. Suddenly she paused outside a door where light showed beneath it. She cocked her head and pressed her ear to the wood. The sound of nervous and tense voices made her keen to know what was being said. Two people were arguing, their voices raising in whispers. Suddenly someone else jumped in.

"Stop it!" they commanded. It was Anthony.

Anthony glared at Gerta and Nathan from the squishy armchair he was sitting in. His jaw was clenched and his foot was tapping. Gerta and Nathan were standing a few feet apart, their hands on their hips, both faces flushed. Gerta was leaning back slightly as if getting close to Nathan was repulsive. Disgust and anger balanced on her face.

Anthony turned away from them and looked around the room, the library was hot, the fire blazing on the hearth didn't help. His face was flushed. Lidia was sitting on one of the sofas with Gael beside her holding her hand. Lovisa was laying on the floor at her sister's feet staring at the fire. Leo and Marc were playing an intense game of marbles. Each was hunched over oblivious to everything else. Esmé was looking at the bookshelves muttering under her breath. Tristan was hanging over the arm of the second sofa, a book on the floor in front of him. Anthony sighed and flipped a *franc* over and over, listening to Gerta and Nathan arguing again in whispers. He rolled his eyes and flipped the coin in sync with his foot tapping. The wireless was playing, but none of them were paying attention. Even if they were, it wasn't saying anything new or interesting. Anthony caught the coin and slipped it into his pocket. Slowly he got to his feet and walked toward the fireplace. Tristan caught sight of his face and frowned.

"Anthony, what's wrong?"

He spun to a sitting position, his face red from all the blood that had been rushing to it. He leaned over again and pulled the book off the floor. Anthony glanced at the cover. It was in German. He shrugged. He could speak and read German fluently, and sometimes he'd make remarks in the foreign language leaving the little boy wondering what he'd said.

He shrugged again. "Nothing. Oh, wait—" He paused dramatically, acting as if something had popped into his head. "—the Nazis are advancing!" He made it sound like a surprise. His eyes were wide with mock surprise.

"Ugh!" Lidia groaned. She threw her head back so she was staring at the ceiling. "We got it, Anthony. What do you want us to do about it? We've sent Paris every scrap of information that we've come across. Sadly, it's not much, but we're doing our best."

She tossed a piece of her hair over her shoulder and gave Anthony an annoyed glance.

Gael smiled. "You know, Lidia, he may have a point—"

Lidia jumped to her feet interrupting Gael. "Don't you join his side. He's been going on and on about the Germans and war. I'm getting sick of it!"

She threw her hands in the air and slapped her thighs as they came down.

"Just sick of it!"

Gael raised his hands in apology and pulled Lidia back onto the cushion. A marble flicked too hard, bounced across the rug stopping only when it bumped into Nathan's shoe. Nathan and Gerta's argument paused as he tossed it back to Marc and Leo, then it continued as if nothing had happened. Tristan was going to ask what they were arguing about, but seeing Gerta's face as red as it was, and Nathan's hands clenched by his sides, made him change his mind and he went back studying his best friend's face. He'd always thought of Anthony as an older brother and he hated seeing him mad. He gently tossed the book off his lap and stepped up to Anthony. He didn't say anything. He didn't know if he could but was content to stand beside him.

Anthony smiled at Tristan briefly before turning back to Lidia. "You can't act as if we couldn't do better. We're slacking," he pointed out.

Only a few days ago, a different agent had turned in an important piece of information that they, the ones at the Lucroy's, should have gotten. He was still sour about it. He didn't blame any of his friends, but he still wished that they were better at finding things out before someone else did.

Lidia read the look in his eye correctly and groaned again.

"It's not like the information went to the wrong place! Paris still got it!"

"Shh." Gael warned, making Lidia check her tone. She glared at him before turning back to Anthony.

"I'm tired of this. I don't mind gathering information and sending it to the capital, but staying up late just hoping we can catch something in the Reims news is foolish. Madame and Monsieur Lucroy would be furious if they found out what we were doing! Spying and giving information when we're not even under attack!" her voice rose again.

A loud intake of breath made everyone quiet. Questioning glances were thrown at everyone, but each one was met with a deliberate shake of the head. They all knew what they were doing, saying it shouldn't have shocked anyone. Anthony motioned for Lidia to continue talking and the others to act as if nothing had happened. They obliged, but were careful about what they said.

Gael moved silently to the door, he was walking like a cat. His shoes made no sound on the rug. Slowly he grabbed the handle. He looked over his shoulder. Lidia and Anthony were still carrying on the conversation as if he was still over there. Gerta and Nathan were still arguing, but their eyes were trained on him. Marc and Leo were flicking marbles back and forth, but it had been a while since one had actually made a good move. Lovisa had flipped onto the sofa, her arm across her eyes. Tristan had sat down on the second sofa with his book abandoned on his knees. Gael nodded to everyone, yanked the door open swiftly, and grabbed the eavesdropper by the arm and spun her into the room.

Leanne couldn't help the cry of shock that fell from her lips as she stopped spinning. Her heart hammered painfully. All the youth were in the room. She raised her hands to her mouth to make sure she didn't make another noise. *'Save me, Father, please. Let them not be mad!'* The older boy, Gael, had advanced while she was spinning and now one of his strong hands was resting on her shoulder. It was a gentle grip but she knew that she wouldn't be able to get it off. She waited, frozen with fear, not knowing what she was going to say. Anthony was standing by the sofa, his head cocked, his arms folded across his chest, and he was watching her with a strange look in his eyes. It was Gerta that broke the silence.

WHEN THE SOLDIERS CAME

"Leanne? What were you doing outside the door? You could have come in." She purred in a sickeningly sweet voice, ending with a smile.

Leanne noticed that the smile didn't reach her eyes.

"I—" she croaked and swallowed nervously. "—heard voices." She didn't want to lie as that was against God's word. So she decided to tell the truth.

"And...?" the one called Leo prompted impatiently. He walked over and seated himself beside the small boy, Tristan, Leanne recalled.

"I wanted to know what was going on," she ended softly, casting her eyes downward, worried that someone might read the fear that so clearly showed in her eyes.

Someone huffed angrily but she didn't see who. She wasn't sure she wanted to know. She was trembling. Her knees were knocking. Her hands were shaking and she was too scared to try and stop them. Slowly she became aware of someone standing in front of her. Fearfully, she raised her eyes. The cautious boy, Marc was his name, was standing in front of her, his face and eyes dark. He put his thumb and forefinger under her chin so she couldn't look away.

"What did you hear?"

The question came out as a growl leaving no room for lies.

"Nothing!" she cried softly, feeling hot tears in her eyes. Inwardly, she cringed. The lie tasted foul on her tongue.

Marc scoffed. "What did you hear?" he demanded again. Fire blazed in his eyes.

"Nothing!" she cried again, unable to contain the fear in her voice and the tears in her eyes. She squeezed her eyes shut, shaking.

Someone hurried over and pulled Marc away. His hand slipped off her chin and she dropped her head trying to hide her fear. The person and Marc had a whispered conversation, then the person returned. He pulled Leanne away from Gael and led her over to the sofa.

"Leanne, will you look at me?" His voice was familiar. It was Anthony again. She fearfully glanced up. His face was kind, but there was a hard resolve in his eyes. She looked back down again.

"What did you hear?" he asked gently, rubbing one of his hands down her arm.

She shook her head softly.

"Something about spying and intelligence. I don't understand it."

Again, the lie tasted foul in her mouth.

Anthony hid a smile. He knew that she understood it perfectly.

"Don't lie," he said calmly.

Leanne bit her lip. "I want to join." she whispered softly.

Half surprised by her words, instantly she knew that they weren't her words. They were *His*. She glanced quickly upward. *'If this is thy plan Father.'* She took a deep breath.

"I want to join." she said louder.

This took him by surprise. "What?" he blinked.

"I want to join. I'll do anything against the Nazis. Please."

Someone started to protest, but another person hushed them. Anthony pondered for a moment. He barely knew the girl. She could have come from anywhere. But the hard look in her eyes reminded him of himself: eager, willing, trying to find a way to be useful. He stared into her face. Gone was the frightened, crying girl from a second before. The person sitting on the sofa beside him was a fighter. A soldier. Someone that was willing to do anything.

"All right. Welcome to the French Resistance."

Chapter 8

"I'm bored." Leanne muttered.

"Shh." Anthony hissed.

"What are we doing?"

"Shh."

"Are you going to say something other than "Shh"?"

"Shh."

"Ugh!"

Anthony turned his piercing brown eyes on her. "Zip it."

She raised an eyebrow. "Anthony, whom do you *think* is going to hear us? We're eight miles out of town. There's not a person around us."

Anthony made a face and stuck his tongue out.

"You asked to come. Nathan and Marc were both willing." he reminded her like he had fifty times on the walk down.

"I thought this was supposed to be adventurous." Leanne groaned. "What are we doing out here anyway?"

Gael, laying on his back a few feet from them, raised himself on his elbow and glanced at her. "Did we not tell you?"

At first Leanne thought he was trying to make a joke, but seeing the honest confusion in his eyes made her shake her head. Anthony smiled apologetically. "Sorry, thought we did." He turned and looked back at the tree line.

Gael and Leanne looked at him, eyebrows raised. Anthony was silent for a moment, before looking back at them, a guilty look spreading across his face. "What?" He demanded, feigning innocence.

Gael choked on a gurgle of laughter. Leanne bit back a smile.

"Are you going to tell me?" she asked sweetly.

"Oh," he grinned sheepishly, his face reddening. "We're meeting up with agents from Nancy."

Just then, two men broke from the small clump of trees and made their way over to them. Gael and Anthony got to their feet, but Leanne stayed down, unsure of what was going on. She scrutinized the men: the taller one had broad shoulders and a bearded face. The smaller one hung behind the taller one, his face was shadowed, with red hair falling across his forehead. The taller one stepped up and held out a hand.

"*Bonjour*. I'm Axel Brousseau."

Gael smiled and took his hand.

"Gael Lubar. This is Anthony Tremblay. Nice to make your acquaintance."

Anthony frowned. "The other one?"

"My companion." Axel didn't give any more explanation, and his look dared Anthony to ask again. When Anthony opened his mouth Axel cut him off.

"I see you have a companion that wasn't introduced." He nodded at Leanne.

Leanne got to her feet feeling a little shy.

"*Bonjour*. I'm Leanne Martin."

She offered a nervous smile and stepped closer to Gael and Anthony, trying to hide her face in the shadows. Gael gave her a knowing look, his eyes lighting. Anthony smiled at her but quickly returned his gaze to the two agents.

"If you don't mind, I'd rather keep my companion's name unmentioned. He's an undercover agent. He'll meet with you when I can't, and if he shares his name that is what he chooses to do."

Gael nodded. "So what was it that you wanted us to pass on?"

"The Germans have toppled Nancy, Metz, and Dijon. They'll be here in a few months." It was the younger agent, his face was pinched with hurt as he spoke about his home.

Gael's face fell. Anthony looked crestfallen. Leanne bit her lip to keep herself from crying. Axel's face was grave.

"I know. It's sad news, but it needs to reach Paris. Can you see that it does?"

"*Oui*." Anthony responded, his eyes veiled. His voice was tight.

Leanne looked at him, raising her eyebrow a little. Unknown to her, the younger agent's gaze was lingering on her, his face lighting in a smile. Anthony fairly shook. Leanne stepped closer to him and grabbed his arm.

"Anthony? Anthony, are you alright?" She shook him.

He blinked. "Oh, *oui. Oui,* I am. *Merci.*" He nodded to Axel and stepped back.

Axel nodded farewell. "Goodspeed. May you make it back to Reims safely, and see that the information makes its way to Paris."

Gael nodded back and turned to follow Anthony but stopped when the unnamed man stepped toward him. Leanne barely held in a gasp, the boy looked to be only seventeen. His hair was a bright auburn in color. With brilliant, dreamy green eyes, Leanne felt herself blush when the boy looked deep into her eyes. A smile curved his lips, mirrored by Leanne. He gave her a knowing smile then turned to Gael.

"My name is Lyam. Get in touch with anyone that we know is safe and ask for me. They'll get me to you."

Gael grinned. "*Merci*. Farewell." He stepped closer to Leanne. "Ready to go?"

She watched the boy hurry after Axel. "*Oui*. He seems strange."

Gael laughed. It was a deep sound that made Leanne smile. "As are all of us. Come on, we have two hours of walking before we get back." He wrapped an arm around her shoulders and they hurried after Anthony.

Anthony paused when he heard them coming.

"What took you so long?" he demanded, tapping his foot.

Leanne was reminded of a mother scolding her child. "The agent had something to say." Leanne stated, giving him a sidelong look. "Why did you leave so quickly?" She skipped in front of him and started walking backward so she could look him in the eyes and he couldn't avoid her.

Anthony grew uncomfortable from the constant, piercing look Leanne was giving him and sighed. "It's nothing, honest."

Leanne's eyebrow arched and he knew she'd heard the lie in his voice. Unfortunately Gael had, too. "Ooh, getting a little jealous, Anthony?" he crowed, throwing an arm around Anthony, pinning him to his side.

Anthony threw him a dark look and Leanne stumbled to the side so she didn't get trampled.

"What? I don't understand."

Anthony leapt to cut off Gael.

"That's a good thing. Guy stuff, you know?" The desperation in his voice made him angrier.

But Gael was too strong and too big to be held back by a fifteen year old, even if they were the same size. "I'm talking about the way Lyam was looking at you the whole meeting." He whistled. "He hardly took his eyes off you. And I couldn't blame him, the way you were shining in the moonlight? I thought you were beautiful, too."

Leanne nearly tripped. "What? When did the meeting with the agent turn into staring at me? And I still don't understand what's going on with Anthony?"

Anthony clapped a hand over Gael's mouth.

"Just ignore it." he muttered, throwing another dark look at Gael.

Leanne shrugged and made eye contact with Gael, questions echoing in her eyes. Gael smirked behind Anthony's hand and made a dismissive gesture that told her to forget it. Leanne turned away pretending to laugh, but inside she was confused. Was Gael saying that Anthony liked her? Was Gael saying *he* liked her? She was too occupied to join the boys in their conversation, though they tried including her many times. As they neared the city they fell silent. Anthony bumped Leanne with his shoulder.

"Leanne, you okay?"

She nodded.

"You sure?"

"*Oui.*"

Anthony gave her a quizzical look. "Positive?"

Leanne couldn't help but smile, "*Oui.*"

"Are all you going to do is say *"oui"*?"

She giggled. *"Oui."*

Anthony grinned.

The others were waiting for them in the library when they got back. Leanne was careful to stay away from Leo and Marc, both had received secret news about their parents and had become snappy and mean. Lidia ran at Gael and threw her arms around him. Lovisa ran to him, too. Tristan ran to Anthony. Leanne walked through the door, shocked when Gerta and Esmé flung themselves at her, nearly suffocating her. When she could breathe again she looked closely at them.

"Why?"

She tried saying more but couldn't, the words just wouldn't come.

Esmé seemed to understand. "You're one of us. We missed you. Did you think we didn't?"

Gerta echoed her.

"I was worried sick when Gael said you could actually go. I thought Anthony was going to die."

Leanne felt her eyes well with tears. Since Jameson and Rose had left, she'd felt as if she'd never have friends again. Since coming here, Anthony had been the closest but sometimes he was a little distant and closed so she never thought they'd make it to friendship. But seeing the concern and happiness in Esmé and Gerta's eyes made her cry. *'Father, merci. Oh, merci. Thou knew what I wanted and granted it to me before I asked. Merci, Father. Merci.'* She threw her arms around the girls again. "*Merci.*" she whispered, pulling away and wiping the tears off her face.

Esmé smiled kindly. But Gerta frowned.

"For what?"

"For being my friends." Leanne choked out.

Esmé hugged her again tightly. Gerta did, too, but was crying too loudly to hear the soft word Esmé whispered into Leanne's ear. "Always."

Nathan walked over to them. "Did Axel say anything about Nazis?"

Leanne looked at the boy.

"*Oui.* Didn't Gael and Anthony tell you?" She walked over and fell into one of the armchairs, grateful for a chance to rest her aching feet.

"*Non.*" Nathan muttered, his brow furrowed.

"Oh, I will." she volunteered. "*'The Germans have toppled Nancy, Metz, and Dijon. They'll be here in a few months.'*" she quoted Axel's words perfectly, but they weren't that hard to remember, because when Leanne had heard them her heart had nearly stopped.

Nathan took a step back, his face pale.

"Is he sure? Absolutely positive that they are heading for Reims?"

Leanne nodded. "He didn't say it outright, or anything. But the look on his face when he said it made me sure that he knew it was here." She didn't have to ask why this was hard news. It meant that everyone she'd just gained was in danger, and that those she had were in more peril than they were. She blinked back tears and straightened her shoulders. She didn't want to cry in front of Anthony and the others. She'd cry later in the security of her room. She shook herself and made herself listen to what was being said. Esmé was standing by the fireplace, her face flickering unevenly from the shadows being thrown around the room.

"What are we going to do about it? There had to be something?" Her voice rose in desperation and anger. The fire reflected off her eyes, but Leanne was sure that some of the heat was burning inside Esmé, not just the fire.

Anthony leapt to his feet.

"There's nothing we can do!" he retorted. "Germany is too powerful. Their armies have destroyed cities in less than hours. They'll do the same to Reims if they think we'll fight back."

"But we have to!" screamed Marc. Leanne was shocked, Marc was usually a quiet, reserved boy. The one that listened and only voted on the course of action. If he was speaking it was because he was scared or wanted something. "Reims is our home. Even if it's our home because no one else wanted us, it's still the reason we're all together. We have to fight for it!" He turned despairing eyes to Gael. "What do you say, Gael?"

As he rose Leanne sensed that what he was going to say, she didn't want to hear it. Even before he spoke tears rolled down her cheeks and she was praying harder than she ever had. Gael's eyes were red with lack of sleep, and his face was pinched.

"I hate to say it, but there's nothing we can do." He turned saddened eyes to his friends. "As Anthony said, *'There's nothing we can do.'* There's no one here to fight. All those that were even close to good soldiers were sent away. All that's left are the elderly, the young, and the women. Even if all would fight, it'd only end in death. I'm sorry. I guess we have to hope the Germans will be lenient."

WHEN THE SOLDIERS CAME

Gerta leaned over and whispered in Leanne's ear. "I bet they aren't."

Leanne nodded with her friend. *'Father, protect us. Please, save us. And give the German people heart and Thy protection, they need it more than we do right now.'* Rumors about what was happening to the German citizens had leaked out somehow, and Leanne was worried that it might not all be fake. Anthony had warned her that it was probably a trick set up by Hitler and the other Jew haters, but she didn't see why it was such a problem to pray for them. Even if, just maybe, everything was just fine on the inside. She watched her friends argue for a few more minutes before getting to her feet.

"Good night," she muttered, hurrying for the door.

Gael paused in his argument to wave. Lidia and Lovisa smiled. Anthony frowned and followed her.

"Leanne, what are you doing?"

"Going to bed. We have school in the morning, and I don't want to get in trouble for falling asleep in class again." She skirted around him and danced across the cold floorboards toward her door.

"Leanne, I have something for you." Anthony's voice was gentle and really soft.

Leanne feared the worst. Her heart nearly stopping, she turned around to face him again.

"What is it? What has happened?"

He gave her a slight smile. It was partly sympathetic, partly hesitant.

"Anthony, what is it?"

He reached into his coat pocket and pulled out a small letter. Leanne recognized Rose's handwriting and sobbed. Anthony stepped forward, placing the letter in her hands before grabbing her shoulders.

"It was delivered this morning after school. I was waiting for the right opportunity to give it to you. I hope it's good news."

Leanne nodded through her tears.

"*Merci beaucoup.* I hope it is, too." She glanced at the letter. She wanted to open it, but she was worried it would be bad news.

Anthony watched her awkwardly for a moment before turning.

"Good night, Leanne."

"You, too." She watched him walk back to the library before running into her room and carefully opening the letter. Tears filled her eyes as she read the letter. It was just a quick little note.

Leanne,

Sorry that I couldn't write for a while. Things have been a bit crazy here. I'll send you another, more detailed letter in a few days. My Mama and Papa haven't got a job so I have to pay postage. My address is on the envelope. I hope you write soon. I love you.

Love, Rose.

Leanne blinked back tears and pulled the small letter to her chest. *"I love you, too,"* she thought. She sank on the bed and looked at her watch. It was thirty minutes 'til breakfast. She sighed. She was tired, but knew she'd never get to sleep. Her mind was racing with how close the Nazis were to Reims. Laying on the bed she wondered what Jameson, Maruis, and Théo were doing. Were they safe? Were they excited for spring and summer? Suddenly she rocketed out of bed. If Rose was settled enough to write a letter, then Jameson must be getting close. She pulled a scrap of paper and a pencil from her bookbag and knelt on the floor using the bench at the foot of her bed as a desk. She hesitated a moment, deciding to write to Rose before Jameson. She was hoping to send the letter after school.

Rose,

I was so happy to receive your letter. It brought me to tears. How's Paris? How are you fairing? Are you going to school? Or waiting for next year? Do you have any new friends? Have you heard from Jameson, Théo, or Maruis? Would you tell me if you did?

I have some exciting news: I'm going to school! It's really fun and exciting, but I can't help wondering what it was like before the war? If it's so much fun now, in war time, I bet it's amazing in times of peace. There are a few of us living here, and I've made friends with some of them. I know there are a few you'd like.

I miss you so so so much. I never realized how much I needed you until you were gone. I love you with all my heart.

Love, Leanne.

She smiled then stuck the paper in an envelope, licked the flap, and closed it. Her heart was thudding happily in her chest.

When the bell rang, Leanne ran for the doors. Her bookbag felt like it was full of feathers as she raced through the school halls. People leapt out of her way, and muttered as she sped by. Anthony was already waiting by the school gate, a smile curving his lips as she ran up.

"*Bonjour.* Are you doing something important today?"

"Depends." she said evasively.

Anthony raised an eyebrow. "Really? Depends on what?"

"Nothing. I have to get to the *Bureau de Poste.*"

"Who are you sending a letter to?"

"Rose."

"Cool, can I come?" His face was innocent and lovely at the same time.

Leanne masked her enthusiasm at his invitation and instead veiled her eyes. "If you insist."

Tristan ran up to them. "Hey, Leanne, Anthony, can I come with you?"

His eyes were bright and his face was reddened by the crisp wind that was blowing.

Anthony grinned at him and looked at Leanne. "Can he?"

"Sure." Leanne smiled.

They walked down the street chatting about nothing in particular until they made it to the post office.

"*Bonjour.*" She greeted the man at the desk. "I need to mail a letter to Paris."

The man looked up, tired and sad, "My apologies, Mademoiselle, we're unable to get letters to Paris right now. Paris has shut down anything coming into the city. Worried that a German spy might get in and cause trouble. Letters and packages are able to get out, but nothing can get in. Again, I'm very sorry." His eyes were gentle and understanding.

WHEN THE SOLDIERS CAME

Leanne's heart dropped and she blinked back tears. "Thanks anyway."

They turned and walked away. Anthony stepped near her.

"Leanne, I'm sorry. I know how happy you were to send her a letter."

Leanne felt hot tears roll down her cheeks.

"I hate war!" She wiped her nose on her wrist. *'Father, why would you do this to me? What are you trying to tell me?'* She walked back to the Lucroy's, wondering if she'd ever be able to communicate with Rose again. *'What if Jameson was cut off from her, too?'* The thought pulled her up short. "Then I'll trust God knows what He's doing. He'll sort it all out."

Chapter 9

March 31, 1944

Leanne pressed her face into the marshy, new grass in the backyard. It was crisp and cool against her cheeks. A little scratchy, but a good kind of scratchy. It had been a hard winter. A hard few years in fact. Four years had passed since she'd first come to the Lucroy's and joined the Resistance. Four years since she'd been free. Luckily, since Paris had instantly surrendered when Nazis attacked, most of the cities had been spared and the few soldiers in them were peaceful and okay to be around. Although the Germans seemed docile enough, still there was hardly any food. People were dragged from their homes, arrested, beaten, and most of the time killed...or at least never seen again. Curfew had been set. Anyone seen after hours was arrested and disappeared instantly. No questions asked. It was like living in a nightmare. The gray-green German uniform had become part of her life. She hated it. She knew, heartbreakingly, what it was like in the thick of Hitler's hate. Soldiers could break in for any reason, and usually did, but she also understood that Reims, and most of France, had it easier than most. People in Poland, Denmark, Czechoslovakia, Austria, Norway, and other small countries had been treated worse than they were.

Everything had changed when the Nazis had invaded: There was no more music, unless it was German records, and even some of those were forbidden. There was no more listening to the French wireless, only the German one, but they were all lies. As were the newspapers. There was no more laughter, everyone seemed dead. Most were, anyway. They were just waiting to be caught and finished. Almost everyone had broken a few of the new laws, but once they realized the Nazis meant business, no one did anymore. Leanne and the others were the only few left that remembered and wanted back the life they'd had before. They refused to live under Nazi rule, and proved it by risking their lives every chance they got.

There were some good things though. Leanne and Anthony smiled as she started thinking about when they began dating a year ago. It had been a little weird at first, both still shy and unsure about dating while living under the same roof. Once they started, they knew they didn't want to stop. Leanne had grown up in the few short years of war. Her young, carefree face had changed. It had morphed into an adult face with darting eyes and a worried curve to her mouth. She'd also grown more pretty. Anthony pointed that out nearly all the time, as did the Nazi soldiers on the streets. They would constantly touch her hair and face, commenting in German how beautiful she was. Luckily that had never happened in front of Anthony, and she was worried what would happen if it did. Her hair had grown to her waist, but she always kept it pulled back when she went out. Her dress had become fancy, as that was what she was allowed to wear.

As she lay on the grass she couldn't shake the feeling that something was about to happen. Something different. Something dangerous. Just then someone came running out the back door. From their footsteps, Leanne could tell it was a boy. The footsteps paused then continued slower as their owner spotted Leanne. Leanne waited a few moments before sitting up and smiling at the intruder. Anthony didn't smile back. His face was worried. Leanne jumped to her feet. "Anthony, what's wrong?"

Horrible ideas launched themselves into her head, each ten times worse than the last. She tensed, expecting something awful to come from his mouth.

Instead, all he said was: "Come with me."

His eyes pleaded with her not to ask why and the urgency in his voice pushed all questions from Leanne's mind. She found herself hurrying after him out the back gate and into the winding streets of their city. Their footsteps slapped the ground, hard. They half walked-half ran for a while, trying not to catch the eyes of any Nazi soldiers. Leanne doubled over, straining to catch her breath. Her lungs felt like ice. The cold air stung her throat.

Anthony slowed. "Leanne! Come on!" he whispered again.

"What's going on?" she demanded, panting.

She had a stitch in her side. It felt as if someone had stabbed her with a knife. She glanced around and groaned. A Nazi soldier was standing at the corner watching them.

Anthony sighed and grabbed her hand.

"I'll tell you in a minute. We're almost there."

They started moving again but this time just walking, each aware of the dark eyes trained on them. Leanne noticed the houses were thinning. They were leaving the city! This was a crime punishable by death if you didn't have a permit. She struggled to stop, casting her eyes around looking for soldiers. They had to be here somewhere waiting for people to try and leave, but Anthony was stronger than her and dragged her behind him. They snuck out of the city and she found herself on a hill. In the distance she could see Châlons-en-Champagne, the city nearest to them. It was beautiful but only because she couldn't see the bombed homes and bullet sprinkled walls and roads. After a moment she became aware of something wrong. She pulled her hand from Anthony's and took a few steps forward. Her body became cold. Her throat tightened. Her breath shuddered as she forced her lungs to fill. She raised a shaky hand to her mouth. There was smoke rising above the buildings of Châlons-en-Champagne! She could hear faint popping and booming. Gunfire!

'Father, non! Why now?' She spun to Anthony. "What...why...?" Her voice was too strained to say anything else. In horror, she turned with eyes wide and refocused back on the city.

"Nazis," he responded, his hand falling on her shoulder. "They're attacking."

She spun back to face him, tears filling her eyes. From the look in his eye she knew that nothing they did was going to stop the Nazis. They were attacking and this time it didn't seem as if anything would be spared.

Together, Anthony and Leanne made their way back through Reims. Looking around, Leanne could see that most people already knew. Even more shops were closed. Hardly anyone was out, and those that were were hurrying to their homes. Leanne swallowed nervously trying to soften the tightness of her throat. They neared the Lucroy's.

WHEN THE SOLDIERS CAME

"Are we going to fight them, too?" she asked softly.

Anthony shook his head. "*Non*. We can't. I'm surprised that Châlons-en-Champagne even tried. If we did, we'd all get killed. We might be anyway. The Nazis have been docile in Reims. They have their own quarters outside the city and they're not too strict on enforcing the rules. I'm wondering how this business in Châlons-en-Champagne is going to affect us."

Anthony glanced down at her. His eyes deepened in concern at her angry and puzzled face. He squeezed her hand.

"Leanne?" he bumped her with his shoulder. "Leanne, are you okay?"

She paused, pulling Anthony to a stop.

'Tell me what to do, Father.'

A swift and heart ripping thought immediately entered her mind. She sighed, then turned back to Anthony. "Will you come with me?" she asked, her voice low.

He raised an eyebrow. "Sure."

He was obviously confused but trusted her enough to know that she wouldn't purposely put him in danger.

She barely waited for his answer and quickly pulled him down the street. Each step formed a knot in her stomach. She didn't need the signposts to find where she was going. She'd never forget. Down the street...turn right... immediately go left...another few blocks turn right again...and stop. She paused in front of her home. She hadn't come back since she'd left that day, scared of attracting the Nazis's attention to it. Even coming here seemed to be breaking a rule. After a year of the boys being gone, the letters had stopped coming. Leanne had cut all ties to her old life, unable to bear the thought of Jameson and

Marius again. But now she had no choice. She had to make sure nothing would lead the Nazis to even think that Jameson and Marius were soldiers. Her heart felt like a stone had replaced it.

Thankfully the shop looked untouched. The clocks in the windows were ticking happily, although some were off. Anthony gasped and looked at her with a silent question in his face. Leanne decided to ignore it and took the key from her pocket from where she always kept it. She quickly unlocked the shop door, smiling faintly as the familiar bell rang gaily. There was a thick layer of dust on the table and floor. This was home. Even the smell was the same, though it had changed a little.

She stepped through the shop and into the side door. The living room was also dirty, but she didn't mind. She walked to the cabinet and opened it looking for anything that could lead the Nazis to assume that Jameson and Marius were soldiers. Maybe if she went fast enough, the memories wouldn't be able to enter her mind. Anthony followed her slowly, his footsteps hesitant at the living room door.

"Is this where you lived?"

The wonder in his voice made her want to cry, but she hardened her resolve.

"Yes." she whispered. She went on tiptoe to see the top shelves. *'Father...?'*

Her fingers collided softly with something smooth. She carefully wrapped her fingers around it and pulled it down. It was a small black and gray picture. It was of her, Jameson, and Marius. Tears filled her eyes as she gazed at two of the faces she missed most. They were standing outside the shop. She was young, about nine. With a start, she realized that it must have been when Jameson and Marius had bought the shop. The nine year old staring back at her was smiling widely, with gapped front teeth and wild, gently curled hair. Jameson was standing behind her with a hand on her shoulder. He was fourteen, but his face hadn't changed from what she remembered it looking like four years ago. He was grinning widely, a proud glint in his eyes. Marius was beside him. She was shocked at how much she didn't remember what he looked like now, let alone when he was nineteen. His hair was long. So long that his left hand was holding it out of his eyes. He was smiling, a dimple on one cheek. His right hand disappeared behind Jameson, and she guessed that he was patting her brother on the back. The picture blurred and she felt a few tears slip down her face. She studied it closer, drinking in the captured details of her brother and Marius' faces, then handed it to Anthony. His hands cradled the picture, his eyes taking in the detail of all 3 of them. He glanced up.

"This is your brother?" He pointed to Jameson.

She nodded. "*Oui.*"

"He's handsome." he commented softly, seeing the tears in her eyes.

She chuckled dryly, wiping her eyes with her hand. "Yeah, he was. My friend Rose was smitten with him. Always talking about what would happen if they got married. Of course that was back before the war."

She shrugged away the thoughts, feeling a pang as they pressed back. Carefully, she took the picture from Anthony as he handed it back to her, blinking back more tears.

She checked the rest of the stuff, but there was nothing of importance. She moved to the kitchen. It was the same as how she'd left it four years ago. Everything was put away and clean, minus the dust. She moved and pulled her jacket off the peg by the door and slipped it on. Now for the upstairs. She climbed slowly, dreading the moment when she'd have to look in Jameson and Marius's rooms. Anthony's soft steps followed her. Somehow he knew what she was thinking and stayed silent. They went into Leanne's room first. The bed was wrinkled and dusty, but everything was in its place. The small wardrobe was empty. A careful search revealed nothing, but that wasn't a surprise. She hadn't wanted to leave anything behind.

Anthony looked around the cramped room.

"I can't believe you lived in something this small." Confusion tinted his voice.

She laughed. It was nice to laugh again.

"It was home. The only thing I'd ever known."

As she closed the door, she whispered a soft goodbye. Something told her that she'd never see the room again. She took a deep breath and opened Marius's door. Someone had been in here, the bed clothes were scattered on the floor and a few things were falling from the wardrobe. She was worried for a moment, but looking around she realized that no one had been in here but Marius. Together she and Anthony cleaned up hurriedly and made sure nothing could incriminate them. Then for the final room. Jameson's door opened slowly, it was very dusty, but that was all. A shiver of guilt ran through her. For some reason, she felt bad about entering Jameson's domain without him or his permission. Every time she'd entered the room, she'd been greeted by him and it was alright. Now, without him, it seemed wrong. She moved through the room. Nothing.

WHEN THE SOLDIERS CAME

They moved back into the hallway and she sighed in relief. There was nothing that even suggested that Jameson and Marius had ever lived in the house. There was nothing of hers either. Suddenly a thought popped into her mind. She skipped down the stairs and into the shop with Anthony on her heels. The small bird clock was still in the window. She took it with a smile and tucked it into her pocket. It clinked softly against the glass of the picture. *'Merci, Father. You were right, I needed that.'* God knew that she was talking about more than the clock.

Anthony opened the door, held it for her, and slipped out. He waited for Leanne to lock the shop. Hand in hand, they walked back to the Lucroy's, neither saying a word. Leanne was lost in memories. Anthony was shocked that Leanne had grown up so poor.

Leanne walked lightly up the stairs. Her shoes clicked on the steps and her dress spun around her ankles. She opened her door and threw herself on the bed. She was bored and did what she always did when she was bored. She reached into the nightstand and pulled out two worn letters. The envelopes were creased and dirty from being handled so much. The wax seals had broken off a long time ago from being opened and closed too much. She pulled out the smaller letter. It was dated April 7, 1940.

Leanne,

Paris is strange. It's a lot busier than Reims with a lot more people. And they all seem to be in a hurry. My sister, Angelica, and my brother-in-law, Brice, are doing well. They were happy to see us, although they wished it was a happier occasion. I guess all of us do. My niece, Jemma, is so sweet. I'm happy to finally meet her. Mama and Papa are looking for apartments and a job. We're hoping that we'll be moved in before long. Charle is loving all of the excitement, but he asks for you a lot, wondering why you don't come over as often. I don't have to go to the market every day or even every other day. Angelica goes once every two weeks and is able to get food to last us the whole time. I enrolled in the school near where my sister lives. It's huge. Twenty more rooms than the one at Reims. I met a girl there. She's kind and sweet, her name is Anna. She says she wants to be my friend, and I'd like to be hers, but it makes my heart ache for you. I know it will never be anything like what we were. I miss you so much! How are you? What do you do all day? Do the people you live with treat you well? Have you made any friends yet? I hope you'll write soon.

Love, Rose.

Leanne's eyes filled with tears as she read the words over and over again. Already they were committed to memory. They had been since the day she'd received the letter. She traced over Rose's name.

"I miss you, too." she whispered, then turned to the other letter. This one was dated May 2, 1940.

Little Bird,

Denmark is a lot different than what we were told. Everyone is afraid of anyone in a uniform and it took awhile to gain the people's trust. Maruis and I are fine, although a lot of the time it's cold. Some surprising news: Théo is in our company. So at least there's a familiar face. The Nazis are surprisingly good at war.

WHEN THE SOLDIERS CAME

We've had a few injuries and only one death. Don't worry! Neither I, Théo, or Maruis got hurt. I'm counting the days until I'm able to come home again and give you a hug. I miss you, Leanne. I pray every day that God keeps you safe until I'm able to watch you myself. Keep the faith Little Bird, and know that everyday we spend apart will only strengthen the joy we feel when we return to each other. I love you. Now, how are you doing? Are the Lucroy's treating you nice? Do you have any new friends? Have you heard from Rose and her family? Are you staying out of trouble? Write soon. I'll be waiting for your letter.

Love, Jameson.

Leanne pressed both letters to her chest and sighed as she relaxed against the bed. *"I'm looking forward to being with you again, Jameson. I'm praying that the war ends soon. I love you."*

A sharp popping sound penetrated Leanne's dreams. She rolled over and tried to block out the noise, wondering why Edgar or Claudia didn't turn it off. She sat up in bed. The small bird clock on the bedside table read 6:00 AM. She groaned and rolled back over. The popping continued. This time it was followed by screaming. She grabbed her robe and hurried out onto the landing, pulling it over her nightgown. Down the hall, another door opened and Lidia stepped out with Lovisa close behind her. Even though the girl was now fourteen, she still relied on her sister and never went anywhere without her. Both were wearing robes over their nightgowns. Another door revealed Anthony. His face was grave and stern but the matted part of his hair told the girls that he'd been asleep. Leanne danced her bare feet over the cold wood floor and caught his hand.

"What is it?" she asked, though she knew what it was but was too scared to believe it. She had to hear it from him.

He frowned and rubbed a tired hand through his hair.

"Nazis. They're attacking." He squeezed her hand softly then wrapped an arm around her waist, holding her to him.

Lidia's breath caught behind them.

"That's impossible. We would have known they were going to."

Her green eyes sparkled with fear as her hand tightened over Lovisa's.

Anthony nodded sadly. "I saw them yesterday. I warned as many people as I could. I also told them not to fight for I fear that would only get us killed."

Silently, Leanne wondered why Lidia was so afraid. *'Why were her eyes so wide?'* She found herself studying the older girl, puzzling over why Lidia and Lovisa were even at the Lucroy's.

"Then why are they shooting?" Lidia demanded, placing a hand on her hip.

Anthony didn't answer, only glared. Leanne pulled lightly on his arm, keeping him from stepping forward. Lidia was annoyed at his silence.

"Well...?" She tapped her foot like an impatient mother would when talking to a reluctant, disobedient child.

Gael slipped out of another room and wrapped his arm around Lidia's waist. "He's nineteen. You're acting like he's supposed to know everything." he murmured softly.

WHEN THE SOLDIERS CAME

Leanne was shocked to see him. Ever since Gael had turned twenty he had never left the house or his hiding place unless after curfew. He was old enough to be forced into the army and he claimed he'd never fight for the soldiers that took his home. Lidia flushed apologetically at Anthony and was given a good natured smile in return. Anthony noticed that Gael's face was tight, his eyes were darting around. The arm around Lidia was tense, keeping her close and his other hand had dropped to Lovisa, pulling her to him.

A pounding on the door made them all jump. The chandelier shivered and Leanne was scared that it'd fall and shatter. The person pounded again. Anthony moved toward the stairs but stopped as someone moved out of the office. Edgar walked with purpose until he opened the door. Leanne could see four people standing on the porch. The one in front was intimidating with a high forehead, thin, black mustache, hard black eyes, and a scar running from the outside of his left eye to the corner of his mouth. There was no denying that he was from Germany. A shiny, black pistol hung at his hip and he was wearing the gray-green uniform of Germany. The red band with the swastika seemed to glow off his arm. Its presence seemed to fill the house with evil. The four silver diamonds on his shoulders identified him as a Kapitän. The one behind him had two silver diamonds, an Oberleutnant. The man looked to be in his early thirties. He had shining blonde hair falling from underneath his green cap and sparkling blue eyes. Another swastika was on his arm. The forty year old man beside him had only one silver diamond, a Second Lieutenant. He was tall with thick shoulders, hard gray eyes, and black hair. His cap was tucked under one arm, the arm with yet another swastika. The last had no diamonds, he was just a regular soldier. He was half hidden behind the Oberleutnant, but Leanne could see frightened brown eyes, and short reddish-brown hair. Taking a second look, she could tell that he wasn't a German but she couldn't decide which country he was from. The Kapitän nodded at the Oberleutnant. The man smiled and took a step forward.

"Open your doors, ve're moving in." His German accent was strong.

Leanne rolled her eyes and glared.

Edgar nodded. "Of course, monsieurs."

He waved a hand and invited the men in.

"I apologize in advance. The Master and Mistress of the house are still in bed. Would you like to wait in the living room while I tell them you are here?"

The Oberleutnant translated and the Kapitän nodded. Together the four men filed into the house and disappeared down the hall following Edgar. Leanne and Anthony exchanged glances. Lidia broke the silence.

"I think it'd be best if we all got into proper clothes? We don't want the Germans to think us disrespectful."

She turned and strode into her room, dragging Lovisa with her.

Gael watched her. "Sometimes I wonder what she thinks about. You'd think we were going to a fancy breakfast with the Nazis."

Anthony chuckled. "Well, if we're going to get any information from our four guests, then I guess we'd better make a good first impression." And with that, he too, disappeared into his room.

WHEN THE SOLDIERS CAME

Gael glanced out the window. The small beam of stars shimmered faintly, drowned out by the bright stabbing glare of street lamps and lights in windows. Leanne waited for him to say anything, but he didn't and soon left. She bit her lip. *'What is going to happen now?'* Nazis were in the house and it didn't seem like they were leaving anytime soon. *'Father, protect us until we find a way to escape. Please, Father, save us all.'* She walked slowly into her room and locked the door behind her with a muffled click.

"*Bonjour.*"

The French greeting sounded dull on the foreign tongue, but again part of the normal, everyday life now. The *Kapitän* bowed in half and offered a large smile. Leanne curtsied and forced a smile in return. She regretted following Lidia's advice and found herself wearing a fancy white dress with blue trimmings and lace. The eyes of the Nazi soldiers had hardly left her and she was beginning to feel uncomfortable. The Oberleutnant stepped forward.

"Sorry. Ve're not very good at French."

Leanne recognized him as one of the soldiers that guarded the city walls. She knew who he was because of information that had been smuggled in. A group of soldiers had been sent to Paris, under special orders. The Oberleutant was supposed to go with them, a high honor, something that he didn't bother to keep a secret; until his papers had been mixed up with some younger soldier, and he had been sent here. He was sullen and angry about it, and usually took it out of citizens that were unfortunate to cross his path.

Monsieur Lucroy stepped in. "No need to apologize. Some of the youth speak German." He nodded at Leanne and Anthony. Both of them cast a glance at each other before smiling fakely at the Nazi soldiers.

The Oberleutnant raised his eyebrows in surprise.

"Really?" He smiled and addressed them in German. "It's a pleasure to meet you both, I'm Oberleutnant Devid Vetter. This is Kapitän Wolf, and Second Lieutenant Schmidt."

"*Hallo.*" Anthony responded curtly. His eyes darkened.

Leanne forced another smile. "It's a pleasure to meet you," she retorted in French. She didn't do anything to hide the contempt in her eyes, and knew that the Overleutnant could see it. She was glad he did. She also noted that the young soldier in the back wasn't introduced. He seemed to be trying to disappear.

If Devid seemed offended, he didn't show it. He turned back to Monsieur Lucroy.

"Is it possible that ve may be escorted to our rooms?" He laughed softly for no apparent reason but was soon joined by Madame and Monsieur Lucroy.

Leanne glanced at them, wondering why they were laughing, but didn't say anything. Anthony stepped sideways until his shoulder brushed hers.

"I think the stakes have been raised," he muttered out of the corner of his mouth.

"What are you talking about?" Leanne mumbled, picking at a piece of lace that was scratching her forearm. She couldn't hear any noise outside and knew that the Nazis had finally stopped shooting. At least that was good.

Anthony stared at her, his eyes serious.

"The Lucroy's have sided with the Nazis."

Chapter 10

It had only been a week since the Nazi soldiers had invaded the Lucroy's house but it felt like months. They instantly had enforced their rules and control on all those that lived there. Leanne felt as if she was in a prison. She wasn't allowed to talk to Anthony, Tristan, Nathan, Lidia, or anyone else. Hurried hellos and slight waves were passed back and forth as they passed each other, but there was always a fear that Kapitän Wolf and Oberleutnant Devid would catch them and punish them. The house maids and Edgar seemed to bear the brunt of the German's anger. They could often be seen with a new bruise or cut. Through it all, Madame and Monsieur Lucroy turned a blind eye. They enjoyed the Nazis and didn't find any fault with them. Leanne didn't understand that. Even though it was dangerous, she continued praying. And spying. Everything she found out she would store in her memory until she could add dates and places to her small book that she had hidden behind a loose baseboard in her room.

The city suffered more than ever. The Nazis, docile for four years, were now arresting people for no reason and shutting them into trains and sending them off to Germany. A strict curfew at 5:00 had been set. Anyone seen out was shot on sight instead of being sent in for questioning. Even worse, the Nazis were sweeping the houses looking for more soldiers. Their main targets were boys that had grown up since they'd first invaded. Gael had become someone of the past, Leanne didn't know where he spent his time, only that he'd never been seen around the house. She'd even looked for him before, but with no luck. She kept a prayer in her heart for his safety just like she did for Jameson, Marius, Rose and Anthony.

She stepped up the stairs lightly with the silver tray covered in tea, cakes, and scones balanced expertly on one arm. She didn't like climbing these stairs, the Nazis had taken over this part of the house. The landing was huge with polished oak floors and marble pillars and walls. It looked like a second living room. A wide floor-to-ceiling window took up one wall. Looking out, she could see the backyard. This one must be right above the window downstairs. A fireplace burned brightly in front of her, even though it was hot outside. This time, it was a British rug that covered the floor but instead of sofas and armchairs surrounding it, there was a large, oak table with a dozen chairs around it. Kapitän Wolf was at its head, with Devid on his right and Lieutenant Schmit on the left. The unnamed soldier was standing with his back towards Leanne. His head was hanging as he stared at something on the table. Devid stopped mid sentence as he noticed Leanne. She smiled and moved forward.

"The cook sent tea and things. She thought you'd like to take a break." She placed the tray on the table beside the unnamed soldier. He cast her a sidelong glance and quickly averted his eyes. Leanne thought that strange, but didn't press the matter.

Kapitän Wolf smiled at her. "How thoughtful."

WHEN THE SOLDIERS CAME

His eyes remained dark and unkind.

As Leanne set out the teacups and plates of scones and cakes, she stared at the table. In the center was a map of france. She could see Reims, Nancy, Metz, Châlons-en-Champagne, Paris, and a few other cities slashed with a red line. Small figures of soldiers were on the map, all their faces pointed to the bottom of France. Leanne poured the last cup of tea and put the pot back on the tray.

"*Adieu*." She forced a smile.

She hurried out of the room and down the stairs. She didn't notice the figure walking up and gasped as they bumped into each other.

"Sorry."

Anthony caught her arms to steady her. "*Non*, my fault." He stepped back a bit. "You okay? You look a little pale." His hand rested on her cheek.

She cast a nervous glance back the way she'd come.

"I can't tell you here. Come to my room tonight, I'll tell you everything."

He frowned. "Don't get caught, Leanne," he whispered. "Be careful." He gave her a quick, tight hug.

She smiled. "When am I not?"

He chuckled softly. She stepped out of his arms and continued down stairs. "See you later."

Anthony checked his watch for the fifth time. It had only changed one minute. He groaned and leaned his head against the cold wall of the alley. He was supposed to meet

Leanne ten minutes ago but he couldn't leave. Not yet. He scowled as he waited. He caught his stiff collar and rubbed it between his fingers trying to distract himself. Something moved in the alley across the street and he instantly became alert. It was a shadow, a little bigger than himself. It slipped from the alley and disappeared in another shadow. Anthony watched its progress with keen eyes, his heart picked up pace. Fear and expectation mixed in his mind, making him lean forward and then back quickly. Suddenly, the shadow straightened and became a man. He was standing in the faint light of a barely lit street lamp. His eyes flitted back and forth looking for Anthony, but Anthony wasn't going to reveal his hiding spot until he had been given the signal. He sank against the wall, crossing his arms over his chest. The man seemed to decide the same thing and slowly knelt to tie his boot giving a low whistle that wavered between two notes. Anthony grabbed a smooth rock and tossed it, aiming for a bench a little ways down the street. The man's head shot up at the noise and he slipped noiselessly into the shadows of Anthony's hiding spot.

"I thought you weren't here," the man whispered softly.

He had bright red hair concealed beneath a dark rimmed hat and shining green eyes.

"I almost left."

He slipped his hands into his coat pocket, scrutinizing the young man in front of him. He was panting slightly. His eyes darted around, worried that he'd been seen.

Anthony scoffed and rolled his eyes, "I've been here for fifteen minutes, it's *you* that should be glad that *I* didn't leave." He shifted his position until he was comfortable. Inside, he sighed with relief. He hadn't wanted to go back with the explanation that he was late for no reason at all.

The man struggled to hide a smile at Anthony's apparent unconcern. "Wow, Gael told me you took your job lightly, I didn't know how light." He hid a smile behind a dirt stained hand.

Anthony scowled. "I don't take it lightly. I'm completely alert."

He yawned. "Have anything to report, Lyam?" He cocked his head at the man.

Lyam grinned a little. "Didn't know you knew my name," he muttered.

"You know mine." Anthony responded curtly.

Lyam opened his mouth to reply negatively, but seeing the calm, unsurprised look on Anthony's face, thought better of it. Why deny the truth? After all, they were on the same side. He sighed, "*Oui*, I do."

Anthony cracked his neck.

"So, anything to report?" he asked again.

Lyam nodded. "*Oui*." He was reluctant to tell what he knew. Best to put them on their guard.

"The Nazis are on your trail. They're looking for you, Marc, Lidia, Gerta, Tristan, all of you."

Anthony sat up straight, fear rushing through his body and freezing the blood in his veins. "How do you know?" he asked, breathless. He felt as if he'd fallen from a high tree. He couldn't drag in air.

"One of our agents intercepted a report to Kapitän Wolf. It told them to arrest anyone they thought of as spies and send them to Germany. Also a phone call was listened in on from

Oberluetnant Devid to some *Oberst* in Germany stating that he has good reason to believe that a few youths staying in the same house as he and Kapitän Wolf are spies. He didn't elaborate, but even if he had, we wouldn't have gotten it. Our agent was dead when we arrived. It was a good thing that the information he overheard was patched through to us." His face was grave as he thought of his dead companion. True, he'd never met the man, but he was a countryman and fighting for the same thing.

Anthony sighed, his expression pained for multiple reasons. "I guess that means we're going to have to go into hiding."

Lyam nodded. "The resistance has already gotten that ready. A train leaves bright and early Saturday morning at 4, It's heading for Épernay. From there, you'll have to get to Paris. I have a letter from the resistance that you're to give to the prime minister. He's in hiding, but it shouldn't be too hard for you all to find him. After he reads the letter, he'll get you onto a train to Lille, where a British ship will pick you up and take you to England. There you'll be safe."

Anthony found a few holes. "How will the British captain know we're the right youth?" he demanded, unwilling to lead his girlfriend and friends into a faulty trip that would most likely end in arrest.

Lyam smiled. "You don't miss much. I have two other letters for the captain and King George VI." He pulled the three thick letters from his pocket and handed them to Anthony. "Good luck." He got to his feet and disappeared down the street.

Anthony waited for a few moments before following. His heart was heavy. *'What was he going to tell the others? What was he going to tell Leanne?'* The thought pulled him short. Leanne was determined to stay here until her brother came to retrieve her. She'd take a lot of convincing. A gunshot echoed through the quiet street. Anthony jumped, his thoughts shattered in an instant. He examined himself, no wound. Searching the street, he saw the shadow of a man fall with a low groan of pain. He sprinted carefully over to Lyam.

Lyam was breathing shortly, his chest barely filling before releasing. Anthony dropped beside him. "What happened?"

He forced his voice low, but already felt tears burning in his eyes.

"Sniper." Lyam panted, his hands pressed against the right side of his chest. "Go, Anthony, get out. They're probably still around." He pressed his right hand against Anthony's chest, trying to push him away.

Anthony looked around. He couldn't see anyone, but there were a lot of shadows that could conceal anything. He turned back to the dying man.

"I'm sorry," he cried, feeling tears roll down his face.

Lyam managed a pained smile. "It wasn't your fault. Just make sure it doesn't happen to you. *Au revoir.*" His eyes became fixed on the cloudy, dark night, and his hand slipped from Anthony's chest.

Anthony slowly got to his feet. He wished there was a way he could get Lyam's body back to his family, but knew that if he tried he'd be putting himself in even more danger. He cast a last look at the peaceful face, guessing that Lyam couldn't have been more than a year or two older than himself. He turned and hurried off, putting as much distance between him and the sad, gory scene as possible. He wanted to wipe the tears off his face, but his hands were slippery with blood and he didn't want to smear it on his face. He looked around cautiously making sure there were no soldiers around; then looked at himself. There was a bloody handprint on his shirt. He'd never be able to lie out of that one if he were caught. He slowed to a walk, knowing he was nearing the Lucroy's house. He hadn't thought this far. *'How am I supposed to get inside?'* He couldn't be seen, covered in blood like he was; so getting one of the maid's attention was out of the question. He turned away from the gate and went to study the wall. He hoped he could climb it. He wiped his slippery hands on his pants and grabbed the wall. The chinks between the bricks made it easy, and soon he was over. His hands were skinned and bleeding in a few places. *'Well, at least it's my own blood.'* He snuck to the front door. In other circumstances he'd go through the back, but his room was more accessible through the front. He didn't dare touch anything, but he peeked through the windows, hoping that no one would see him. He had no luck. A pale face was watching. The dark gray eyes lifted in shock when they saw him. The thirteen year old boy ran to the door and opened it. "Where have you been?" Tristan cried, softly. He grabbed Anthony's arm and pulled him inside. "Leanne has been frantic with worry about you! She's raging on and on about how you've been taken by the Nazis!" Tears were sparkling in the youth's eyes.

Anthony clapped a hand over the younger boy's mouth. "Shh."

Tristan shook his head to dislodge the hand.

"Why are you covered in blood?" He stared in shock at the bloody handprint on Anthony's chest and the blood smears on his pants.

"Not now, Trist. Come on. Where's everybody?"

WHEN THE SOLDIERS CAME

Tristan didn't hesitate. "Kapitän Wolf, Oberluetnant Devid, and Lieutenant Schmit have all gone to a meeting across town. The other soldier is in his room. Everyone else is in Leanne's room...where you're supposed to be." He jabbed an accusing finger at Anthony.

Anthony raised his hands in apology as he started up the stairs. He used the lion knocker to get Leanne's attention. Her white face peered around the door.

"Anthony!" She flung the door open and threw her arms around his neck, "Where have you been?" she cried. "I was so worried." Silently. *'Merci, oh merci, for keeping him safe, Father. Merci.'* She leaned back to make sure he was unharmed and her mouth fell in shock seeing his shirt and pants.

Anthony held her. "You shouldn't have been," he assured her before she could point out the blood. He gave her a look not to mention it and received a dark look in return. He looked around her room. When Tristan said everyone, he meant everyone. Nineteen year old Gerta and eighteen year old Esmé were talking in hushed whispers seated on the rug. Nineteen year old Leo and nineteen year old Marc were near them throwing in a comment now and then. Nineteen year old Nathan was pacing back and forth. Twenty year old Lidia was seated on the bench at the foot of the bed, Gael's arm around her shoulder. Lovisa sprawled across the bed. They all looked up when they heard Leanne's voice. Anthony was kind of shocked to see Gael. He was pale from not being in the sun for a while, and his eyes were darting around like he would run at the smallest amount of noise, but his jaw was firm and his posture was stiff.

Gael got to his feet. "Anthony, you owe us all an explanation." He stared at him, his face darkening.

Anthony took a deep breath. "I met with Lyam. He's dead." His voice broke. Lidia gasped in horror and raised her hands to her mouth. Gerta blinked back tears and Esmé turned away quickly.

Leanne uttered a cry of shock. *'Father, non!'*

Lyam had been their main contact. He'd met before with each one, and had held a place in each of their hearts.

Gael returned his gaze from Lidia back to Anthony. "How?"

"German sniper." He held a hand to forestall any other questions. "The Nazis are on the hunt for French spies, and I've been given enough evidence to suggest that we're their next target. We've been given orders to flee the city and, in the end, the country." He pulled the letters from his coat pocket and handed them to Gael.

The older boy glanced at the names. "When do we leave?" he asked softly, his voice quiet.

"Saturday." Anthony cast a look at Leanne. Her face was stricken, with tears tracking down her cheeks, but as she met his eye she nodded slowly.

"*Non!*" Lidia jumped to her feet. "You're acting as if we have no choice. Well, I promised my parents I'd look after Lovisa, and I'm not dragging her across the country to some foreign land again! Forget it! I'm not going!" She sat back down and crossed her arms.

Everyone exchanged glances. What did she mean by again? But Lidia wasn't explaining. Lovisa was staring at her sister in wide-eyed surprise, her mouth open to protest.

WHEN THE SOLDIERS CAME

Gael walked to Lidia's side. He seemed unfazed by the fact she'd used "again" in the way she did.

"Lidia, please. They're hunting me! They're hunting Lovisa. They're hunting you. If they find us they'll send us to Germany." He clutched her hand, but she pulled it away.

"I don't care. Lovisa is my sister. All I want for her is to have a good home, and she can't do that in a foreign country without me." she huffed.

Leanne stepped toward her. "Lidia, if you were to leave, then you could wait for the war to end and come back and claim her. I'm sure the Lucroy's would be happy to look after Lovisa while you're gone." She glanced at Anthony, both of them knowing that the prospect of the Lucory's looking after Lovisa were the same as all of them living through the war. Lovisa opened her mouth to disagree, but was cut off again.

"*NON!*" Lidia screamed, "Never! I'm never going to leave my sister, and I'll never leave France!" She stormed out of the room and they heard her door slam.

Chapter 11

Leanne knew that Gael was trying to reason with Lidia, but everytime she asked how it was going she was led to believe that Lidia wasn't going to change her mind. As she passed by Tristan she commented on it.

"I don't think Lidia's going to come with us. She's too scared and nervous. Nothing anyone says about it seems to make any impression on her; she's still just as stubborn." He shrugged sadly.

'Father, soften her heart, please.'

Tristan looked toward the stairs where Lidia and Gael's angry, whispered conversation could be heard faintly.

"If Lidia doesn't go, she'll be sent to Germany nonetheless. Hasn't anyone told her that?"

"I mentioned it twice today and three times last night. I don't know how many times Anthony and Gael have said it." she sighed. "I just wish she'd listen." She bit her lip, wondering what they would do if Lidia wouldn't come.

"Who would listen to what?" Devid's heavy accented voice sounded behind them and he smiled as they turned to face him.

Leanne thought frantically for an excuse.

"Claudia!" she invented on the spot. "I was wishing she'd listen to our pleas to use the sugar ration tonight in a pie." *'Sorry, Father,'* she thought. Guilt flooded her mind at the lie.

Tristan nodded, jumping on the random reason.

"That's right!" he smiled widely.

Leanne watched the Nazi's face. *'Were we too obvious? Were we trying too hard?'* Devid's smile faltered a little at their sudden and out of the blue enthusiasm. He quickly hid it.

"I wish she'd listen, too. I haven't had a good pie since I left home." He turned and disappeared into the corridors of the house.

Leanne released the breath she didn't know she was holding.

"I can't wait for tonight," she whispered. It was Friday, and they'd made the plan to leave late that night so they'd have no chance of missing the train on Saturday morning.

Tristan smiled.

"Me, too. But we don't know what's waiting for us out there. Nazis occupy almost everything from the border to the coast." He threw his hand in the air. "Once we disappear we're automatically going to be pointed out as the spies. The Nazis won't rest until we're all on a train to Germany." His happy eyes had lost their glint.

Leanne smiled sadly with him.

"I know. But being hunted has to be somewhat better than standing in the wolf den just waiting for the pounce." She raised an eyebrow and gave him a side-long glance, "You've given this a lot of thought for a thirteen year old."

Tristan nodded grudgingly. "I guess. Anthony asked me too."

WHEN THE SOLDIERS CAME

They hurried off hoping that no Nazi soldiers had an unpleasant task to make them do.

Gael groaned in frustration and flopped onto the bed. They'd been arguing for three hours and still Lidia wouldn't change her mind. He kicked his legs back and forth and picked at the comforter. A small, tentative knock sounded on his door. He sat up, his heart jumping into his throat. Before he could hide, Lovisa's frightened green eyes peered around the door.

"Gael?"

He smiled in relief and beckoned her in, his heart rate dropping back to normal. "Come on, Lovisa."

She closed the door softly, hurried to him, and climbed beside onto the bed. "What's wrong with Lidia? She's not happy with you. Did you break up?" Tears sparkled in her gentle eyes.

"*Non*." He responded quickly. But the question tugged at his mind. *'Would they?'* He wasn't going to stay here, that was obvious, but if Lidia didn't come with them, then they'd have to break up but he didn't want to. He loved her.

Lovisa's lips puckered. "She loves you, Gael. And I love you. I don't want you to go. We've been through too much!" Thick tears rolled down her cheeks.

Gael took a deep breath. "I love you, too, Lovisa. And I don't want to go, but I have to. You're safe here, but Lidia, the others, and I are not. If we don't go we could be in serious danger."

She wiped her cheeks with her palm. "I'm going too. I don't want you and Lidia to get hurt." She slipped her hand into his.

He smiled. "I know, Sweetheart. But Lidia won't come with us." He was amazed how the fourteen year old girl sitting in front of him was the same little girl he'd protected from the Germans.

Lovisa struggled to keep her tears in check. "But she has too."

"I don't, Lovisa, and I won't." Lidia's sharp voice came from the doorway.

Gael looked up quickly. Lidia was in a simple blue dress; it was beautiful. Her arms were crossed and she was leaning against the door frame. Her green eyes were rimmed red with tears, and her hair was clouding around her face. She glared at her sister and boyfriend.

"I'm not going. I love Reims; it's my home." She took a deep breath. "Lovisa, come on. It's almost time for dinner." She turned and disappeared.

Lovisa hesitated for a moment, then threw her arms around Gael's neck. "I love you." She slipped off the bed and hurried after her sister.

Gael sat in silence for a few minutes. "Well, I tried." He waited until everyone had gone to dinner before slipping into the attic.

Anthony made sure to eat slowly, he knew that any change in speed would be noticed by the Lucroy's, or the Nazis. Over his plate, he caught an intense glance from Leanne. He raised an eyebrow in question and reached for his glass. She jerked her head slowly in the direction of Lidia. Lidia's face was heavy with makeup, but he knew what she was hiding: red rimmed eyes and tear tracks down her cheeks. Her posture was perfect, but he could see the painful slump in her shoulders, the pained look in her determined green eyes, the sagging in her stiff chin, and every now and then the dark glare aimed at her sister.

Nathan leaned toward Anthony.

"We're going to have to leave fast." he whispered out of the side of his mouth, giving reason to his actions by reaching for the salt shaker.

"I know." Anthony muttered back, knocking the salt a little closer to Nathan's stretching fingers.

"*Merci*." He smiled as he took the salt. As he moved his arm back to his place, he secretly dropped something on Anthony's plate then went back to eating as if nothing had happened.

Anthony, worried that it might be seen if it sat on his plate for too long, used his fork to slide the small piece of paper off the plate and onto his lap, where it was quickly transferred to his pocket. Marc, a few seats down, noticed the small exchange and shot a questioning glance at Anthony, who chose to ignore it and keep eating. Anthony's mind burned with confusion and curiosity of what the small paper held but forced it under control. He'd open it later, in the secrecy and security of his room.

Madame Lucroy looked up suddenly. "You are all quiet tonight." She put on a kind smile. "Has something happened?"

Her tone invited them to speak so Gerta decided to answer for all. "*Non*, Madame Lucroy, we're just tired after playing in the garden all afternoon." She gave a sagging look and turned sleepily back to her food.

"Oh, that seems so unlike you all. I know how much time you spent inside today. And Kapitän Wolf said he noticed you, quite a few times, in the library."

Gerta's eyes widened in fear, and she turned in mute appeal to the others. Esmé, seeing her friend's plight, stepped in. "Well that's strange. Gerta and I were in the garden for half the afternoon and took a walk until dinner. She couldn't have been in the library. I wasn't in there today and I've been with her all day." She jerked a thumb towards Gerta and then smiled innocently at Kapitän Wolf. "Perhaps you made a mistake."

"Perhaps." The Kapitän answered, giving a slight smile to the girl, but his eyes remained dark and hateful. He used his fork to push the food around on his plate. "Monsieur Lucroy," he said suddenly, turning from his food. "I was wondering if the boys could come with me tomorrow. I have an errand I need to run and I would appreciate some help."

"Why certainly." Monsieur Lucroy answered, placing his fork on the napkin beside his plate. "Which ones would you like? I'm sure they'd be delighted to help you." He glanced at the boys, his look telling them that if they weren't delighted then they'd better get there quickly.

"How about these three?" he answered, pointing to Anthony, Leo, and Nathan. He turned to them and shot them a winning smile.

Anthony felt as if the bottom of his stomach had fallen out. He clutched at his glass and forced himself to drink so he didn't say something out of line. Out of the corner of his eyes he saw Leanne's face drop and Leo's shaking hand return his fork beside his plate. Nathan was the only one that looked calm. Anthony and the others could guess why the Nazi leader needed the three boys. They were nearing the age to become soldiers, so if they left, they wouldn't be returning. He cast a glance around the table again. Everyone was eating slowly, trying to stop the tears from sliding out of their eyelids. Leanne swallowed nervously as she picked up her glass with a shaking hand. Her eyes met his and filled with tears. He turned away quickly.

Nathan smiled at the Kapitän. "I believe that I speak for all of us when I say we'd be delighted to accompany you. Hopefully we can be of some small service to you." He took another bite of the roll in his hand.

Kapitän Wolf stared at the young man. "My thanks." He turned back to his food, not saying another word.

Anthony shot Leanne a worried look. She'd recomposed herself and smiled at him briefly then struck up an intense conversation with Gerta, Marc, and Tristan. Leanne made sure to keep the conversation rolling with no end in sight. She kept at it until Monsieur Lucroy dismissed them. As they all hurried to the door, Anthony made sure he brushed shoulders with Leanne. She turned with a questioning glance. He slid a small note he'd written under the table into her hand. She disappeared out of the door with a swish of her aqua-colored dress and was out of sight before Anthony could shoulder his way after her.

Leanne carefully examined the small slip of paper in her hand. It was so small with only a few words on it.

My room. 12:00. Don't be late. Important. Anthony.

She tapped her foot as she looked at the words. What could be so important? They were supposed to be leaving tonight, anything that needed to be shared could be done on the train. She glanced at her watch. It was only 9:00. That left three hours. She took a turn about the room, glancing for anything of hers. She sighed when she found nothing and threw herself on the bed. It bounced slightly. She sighed again and pulled a small book from underneath her pillow. Why wait for 12:00 in boredom? Time could be spent in such better ways.

The small alarm on her watch pealed loudly, shocking her out of a sound sleep. She hurried to quiet it. Her head cocked, listening for any sound that might warn her someone heard the alarm. When no sound came, she slid off the bed, slipped her slippers on, placed the book carefully on the bedside table and snuck out into the hallway. She came and tapped on Anthony's door. It swung open on silent hinges. His pale face met hers for a fraction of a second before he seized her arm and spun her into the room. She gasped as she stilled her spinning. "Anthony," she demanded in a whisper, "what's going on?" She raised her hand to her head trying to dispel the headache that she knew was coming.

Anthony caught her free hand and pulled her to the bed.

"Sorry, I just had to talk to you." He pulled a small envelope from his pocket and gave it to her.

She opened it and gasped.

Marc,

Lidia has made up her mind on staying. Any attempt to change it results in anger and stubbornness (from both of us). I believe that we need to leave even later than planned. Although I believe Lidia will keep our secret, there is a chance she might reveal where we're going in hopes that the Nazis will have mercy on her and Lovisa. I don't believe she told them that I'm here, but I'm not betting on it. I saw her talking to Devid after dinner. I didn't hear what they were talking about, but I'm sure it wasn't good for us. If Lidia did betray our plans, then the Nazis will be ready to take us at 2:00. I say we wait two or three hours and then hustle to the train station just as the train is about to pull out. It's risky, but if we barely make it then the Nazis have no chance of getting on behind us. Please let me know what you think, and share this with the others. I know Anthony and Leanne will have good opinions of what to do. Everyone meet in my room around 12:30 and we'll discuss our next plan.

Gael

Leanne frowned. "Why? Lidia was such a good friend. What happened?" Hot tears burned behind her eyes but she blinked them back. Now was not the time.

Anthony shook his head. "I don't know. But it's nearly 12:30. Are you coming to the meeting?" The hopefulness in his voice wasn't lost on Leanne.

She gave half a smile. "It seems like I don't have a choice. Gael's counting on me and you to show up. If we don't, I hate to think he'll turn to Tristan as the next planner."

Anthony scowled. "Tristan is a good kid, he has amazing ideas."

"I'm not saying he doesn't. His ideas always border on death." She shrugged as she turned to the door. "I'm going. Are you coming?" She grinned invitingly.

Anthony sighed. Her brown eyes filled with hopefulness and Anthony knew that he couldn't say no. Besides, going to this meeting meant spending more time with her, so he wanted to go, too. "I don't have a choice either." He got to his feet and walked toward her. She grinned and held out her hand. He captured it and opened the door. Together they stepped out onto the landing, making sure their shoes didn't hit the ground too hard. Even in a house this big, they couldn't be sure if someone was listening.

Chapter 12

Gael frowned as everyone filed in. His heart thudded as the door closed without a sound. He knew that the door closing had just severed the chance of him and Lidia ever getting back together. He'd spent a part of the afternoon pleading with her, begging her to reconsider. He'd even cried a little. But he'd accidentally pushed her too far and she'd snapped. She'd whirled on him.

"Get out!" she'd cried, pointing at her door. "We're through! We're over! I'll never speak to you again!" She'd spun back around, throwing her hands to her face. He'd waited, hoping that she'd turn around and tell him she was sorry, but when thirty minutes had passed with no change, his hope had begun to ebb. He'd made sure they were alone in the library after dinner so they could hopefully work it out. She hadn't said a word and he knew deep down that she never would. They were done.

He took a deep breath and looked at the three girls and five boys. They were all watching him with confused eyes. Gerta took a step toward him and placed a soothing hand on his forearm.

"Gael, is there anything I can do to help?" Her lips curved a little in compassion.

"*Non. Merci*, Gerta." He gave a sad, but thankful, smile.

She smiled at him as she returned to her seat. Gael glanced at them all again. "I don't need to tell you why we're here. You all read my note. What do you want to do?"

Leanne spoke first. "I agree with you. Leaving later is the best thing we can do. It's risky and there's a chance we miss the train, but we can always walk if we do miss it. Or try to find another way. If we leave at 2:00 and get caught, then there's no starting over. We won't be able to just go with a different plan. We'll be stuck, heading to Germany, for some fate that's probably worse than death."

She took a deep breath, letting her words sink in. They didn't actually know everything that was happening in Germany. The Nazis controlled their wirelesses and newspapers, but everything they'd heard didn't sound good.

Anthony nodded his head. "I agree with Leanne. Three chances are better than one ending."

Gerta and Esmé both muttered consent, but Leo and Marc got to their feet. Marc was the first to speak.

"What if it's a trick?" His eyes were dark. "I've been wondering how the Nazis knew where Anthony and Lyam were meeting. I believe, and Leo agrees with me, that there is a spy in our midst." He eyed them all with a scrutinizing glance, the anger and distrust in his eyes clearly readable. Leo stood by his side, his arms crossed, equally watching them all.

Tristan jumped to his feet.

"No one even knew Anthony was meeting with Lyam. We were all pretty shocked when we found out! And we're all spies. Duh!"

"Shut it!" Marc snapped. "You should zip it and let the older kids talk."

WHEN THE SOLDIERS CAME

Tristan crimsoned and dropped his head, tears filling in his eyes. Anthony opened his mouth to defend Tristan, but Nathan beat him. Nathan marched up and slammed his palm into Marc's chest.

"Don't you talk to him like that! He's got every right to be here and speak his mind!"

Leo jumped to defend his friend. "Don't you boss him around!"

Gerta hurriedly got to her feet. "You have no right telling Nathan off like that!" Her voice was high.

Surprisingly, it was Esmé flying to her feet next and defending Leo. "Don't yell at Leo like that. He could easily snap you in half!" Fire burned in her dark eyes. Her fists clenched by her sides.

Leanne blinked in surprise not knowing who to defend and who to attack. Anthony wasted no time however, and was quick to tell Esmé off.

"He could not! And he doesn't have a right to speak to Nathan or Tristan like that!"

Gael looked at Leanne. "What happened?"

He'd watched the whole thing but couldn't understand what was going on.

Hurried footsteps outside the door sounded, but those in the argument were too occupied to notice. Leanne looked up sharply.

"Shh!" Her heart raced as she imagined a group on Nazi soldiers on the other side of that door.

Gael noticed the steps too and lurched to his feet. "Shut it!" His eyes blazed with fear and he searched the room for a hiding place.

By the time they all heard him and quieted down, it was too late. The door knob was turning. Leanne watched with horror as it twisted first one way, then the other. Slowly it opened. Lovisa slipped through the door, her worried eyes scanning the room. "Gael!" she whispered happily. "I was worried you had already left." She ran to him, throwing her arms around his waist. A look of relief flooded his face. Lovisa looked into his kind, compassionate eyes.

"Lidia told me that we were leaving. The Kaptin," she faltered a little on the accent, making it sound wrong, "told us that we'd be given a fine home in Germany for the work she did for the mother country. I believe she told them about your plans to escape." Tears slipped down her face, pouring off her chin. "Gael, don't let them catch you!"

His face was hard. "Don't worry about it." He frowned. "Do you believe me now?" he asked Leo and Marc. Both were at a loss for words. He turned back to the girl clinging to him. "Do you want to go to Germany?"

"*Non!* I don't want to leave you!"

He placed a calming hand on her shoulder. "You're coming with me. Come on! We'll meet you at the train station at three." He took Lovisa's hand and walked out of the room. Their footsteps were nearly silent.

Leanne looked at all of her friends. They were standing across from each other. Marc was glaring at Tristan who was staring sadly at the floor. Nathan glaring at Marc. Leo glaring at Nathan. Gerta glaring at Leo. Esmé glaring at Gerta. And Anthony glaring at Esmé. "You all had better be ashamed of yourselves. Is that any way to treat your friends?" Something hot pricked behind her eyes but she blinked it back. "I hope you'll all come. See you at three." She turned and half ran to the door with her hands at her face and disappeared behind it without a sound.

Anthony dropped his eyes. The anger melted off him like a bucket of cold water leaving only shame. "I'm sorry, Esmé. I shouldn't have," he offered, looking her in the eye.

"I forgive you." Esmé whispered, tears filling her eyes. "And I'm sorry, Gerta."

The apologies and forgiveness ran down the line until it got to Marc. His eyes stayed angry and unsorry at the boy sniffling in front of him. Tristan raised his eyes. "Sorry, Marc." he whispered softly, a small bit of hope kindling in his eyes. But it was soon quelled by the angry fire burning in Marc's eyes.

"Marc!" Gerta whispered fiercely, confusion tinting the words.

"*Non!*" Marc returned haughtily, his gaze remaining on Tristan.

"Marc." Leo leaned toward him. "Just do it!" he whispered softly. "They'll never let you leave if you don't."

Marc glared at Tristan. "Sorry," he snapped savagely, making the boy retreat a couple of steps. And before Tristan could forgive him, he stormed out of the room, leaving the others in a stunned silence.

Anthony hurried and hugged his young friend. "Don't worry about it, Trist. I'll see you later." Then he slipped from the room, hoping to get a few hours of sleep before having to catch a train.

Leanne crouched in the shadows. Gael and Lovisa were on her right and Nathan and Gerta were on her left. Tristan and Anthony had just disappeared in the night. A few minutes before them, Marc, Leo, and Esmé had tiptoed away. Leanne had her eyes trained on the house. The flashing lights and confused mumble of voices told her that their absence had been discovered. She could see Lidia on one of the balconies. Even at a distance, she could see the tears in Lidia's eyes and on her face. Lidia was missing Lovisa, and she seemed determined to find her. Her eyes had been raking the shadows searching for movement. Leanne leaned toward Gael. "She's not going to move. We're going to miss the train if we linger any longer." She shook his arm. "Send Lovisa with Nathan and Gerta, I'll run with you. I'll go slow at first, and once Lidia sees you she'll believe I'm Lovisa. We're almost the same size. We'll slip into the streets and alleys until the train is about to leave, then we'll get on it while it's gathering speed."

Gael frowned. "It's risky, but the only plan we have." He turned and told the others. "Nathan, you guys need to wait until the Nazis come after us then you and Gerta help Lovisa get to the train station. You should have a head start but be careful. There are more soldiers on the roads."

Nathan nodded and gently took Lovisa's shaking hand. "Come on, we'll get you safe." Reluctantly, Lovisa released her hold on Gael and allowed Nathan to pull her to him.

Gael returned his gaze to Leanne. "You ready?"

"*Oui*." She buttoned her jacket and got ready to run.

"Now!" Gael grabbed her hand, dragged her bodily to her feet, and set off running down the street.

WHEN THE SOLDIERS CAME

Leanne pretended to be struggling, as if her legs were shorter and she wasn't as quick. They hadn't even reached the other side of the street before Lidia's cry of alarm echoed in the dark night.

"There they go! Gael! Lovisa!" she screamed their names, her voice shrill and painful on their ears. "Come back!"

Gael tugged on Leanne's arm. "Come on!" he screamed unnecessarily loud for the sake of those in hot pursuit. "Lovisa!"

They kept running. Leanne knew that she'd have to keep running slow on purpose so Nathan, Gerta, and Lovisa could make it safely to the train station. A German voice called behind them. "Halt!" But they didn't stop.

For half an hour they ran until Gael nodded to her. Together, they put on speed and darted into an alley. As they emerged, a gun went off. Gael screamed and stumbled. Leanne spun around to see Gael stagger, blood dripping from his thigh. She gasped as she steadied him.

"*Non!* Gael, please! Can you make it? Gael!" *'Father, help!'* she silently pleaded. Frantic she looked at his leg, luckily the bullet had gone all the way through, but it left a gaping hole in his thigh.

"*Oui*." he muttered. "But only if we hurry." She clutched his arm until he was steady. He ground his teeth and squeezed his eyes closed but willingly started moving when Leanne gave a slight tug on his arm. She hadn't seen where the shot had come from and no one had shouted a warning, but neither of them stopped to look around. After a few minutes Gael cried out and slumped to the ground, his leg buckling under him.

Leanne dropped to her knees beside him. "Gael?" She shook him. "Gael! You have to keep walking. I can't do anything else to help you!"

His eyes fluttered open and he smiled weakly. "Just help me up." he panted, his head sagging. "I can make it, just help me up."

German boots thundered down the roads and alleys, their cries bouncing off the houses and stores lining the streets. Gael staggered forward. Fear and pain flashed in his eyes. Leanne wrapped her arm around his chest and let him lean against her. "We're almost there. I can see the train station." Desperation sank into her voice as she struggled to keep Gael upright.

A shrill whistle went off, screaming loudly. Smoke and steam launched into the air, the smoke barely visible in the graying sky. The white steam stood out like a searchlight. "It's leaving!" Leanne cried, taking a few lurched steps. Gael gasped in pain, but held tighter to her arm.

"Help me." he muttered, his breath heavy.

She looked sadly at the train getting ready to move. "We'll never make it!"

He jerked her around and looked her in the eye. "We'll make it. Give me a push and I'll run as fast as I can." He pushed her lightly toward the train.

She swallowed nervously, clutched Gael's hand tighter, and ran. Her dress whipped about her legs, causing her to reel and struggle to catch her footing. Now it was Gael's weak hand steadying her. His face was pinched in pain, but he was standing solidly. She gave a quick smile and took off running again. The train whistled again, the chugging and clacking of its wheels sounded strangely loud, as if they were the only things making noise in the world. Leanne used her free hand to brush sweat and hair from her eyes.

"Come on, Gael! We can do it!"

His panting and gasping sent pain to her heart. "Come on! So close!"

"Halt!" a voice cried, followed by rushing and pounding steps. Leanne stole a glance over her shoulder, hiding a gasp as the Nazi soldiers closed the distance.

Another voice rang out. "Faster!"

Leanne looked forward, her heart leaping at the voice. Anthony was standing on the platform of the caboose, his left hand clutching the railing. His right stretched painfully far, reaching for them. Shots fired; their loud screams made Leanne and Anthony flinch. The bullets sang as they whistled over Gael and Leanne's heads. Anthony ducked a few times, wincing as the bullets crashed into the wood railing, throwing splinters in all directions.

"Hurry!" Anthony screamed, panic filling his voice.

Leanne screamed in pain as a bullet ripped through her upper arm. Her hand jerked and she almost lost grip on Gael. Gael groaned in pain and anger, making Leanne close her hand quickly. Gale stumbled but she kept a firm grip on his hand making him keep moving. They were gaining on the train, but it was slowly speeding up. Leanne bit her lip. *'Father, give me Thy strength and I will succeed.'* With an anguished cry, she launched herself and Gael forward and clung to the cold, slippery hand that was reaching for them. Instantly the hand slid down and caught her wrist, clinging to her.

Anthony groaned. His arm and shoulders were crying and burning in pain as they were stretched. His foot slipped, sliding on the slick metal platform. "*NON!*" he cried, struggling to regain his balance and hold onto Leanne's wrist.

Leanne cried out again. Her wounded arm screamed in protest as she struggled to keep hold of Anthony and Gael. "Someone help!" Anthony screamed over his shoulder, his teeth ground against each other in pain. "Please!"

Leanne's hand slid slowly, each centimeter making both of them try clinging tighter. Anthony's tear stained face lifted until he was looking into the despairing brown of Leanne's eyes. Both were panting with effort and both knew that Gael and Leanne couldn't keep running forever.

"I'm sorry, Leanne!" Anthony cried, hoarsely, more tears tracking down his face.

He looked over Leanne's shoulder and focused on the Nazis. They were no longer running, only following at a slow pace, knowing that once Anthony let go, it would send Gael and Leanne tumbling to the ground, possibly killing them on impact. It would be easy to get them after they fell, and they were content to walk after the runaways. Anthony cried in agony again as it became Leanne's fingertips he was clutching. Her hand was clammy, but warm against his skin.

Leanne gasped in pain, her arms were burning. Hot blood dripped down her arm and soaking her sleeve. Everything was in sharp focus: her hand slipping from Anthony's. Gael's hand tightening in hers. The tears in her and Anthony's eyes. The warmth of where they were touching.

Gael was panting, his legs tiring as he struggled to keep up with the fast moving train and Leanne. Blood had soaked his pants, warming his leg. He was hyper aware of Leanne's hand tight in his. He knew that if she released Anthony, she'd never let go of him. Swift, light footsteps sounded in front of them and Gael heard a pained cry and looked up to see Leanne's hand slip out of Anthony's. His eyes widened in surprise as he saw another, quicker hand shoot out and catch Leanne's wrist before she tumbled to the tracks. He raised his eyes and gasped. It was Lidia holding her, unwilling to let them go. "What—?" he panted.

"Don't speak." she commanded sharply. Anthony regained his balance and caught Leanne's hand again, below Lidia's. Together they hauled Gael and Leanne aboard.

As they crashed to the platform, Leanne whimpered softly. Anthony crawled over to her and pulled her into his arms being careful to avoid her injured arm. She gulped down air.

"Gael? Is Gael okay?" she gasped as soon as her lungs filled with air.

Anthony looked over, Lidia was stroking Gael's hair away from his eyes. He was semi-conscious, his breathing slowly evened out. Anthony nodded.

"For now. How about you?"

She nodded as her eyes closed, her head falling onto Anthony's shoulder. *'Merci Father, I am forever in thy debt.'*

"I'm better now," she stammered.

Then she passed out.

Chapter 13

Lidia steadied Gael and they followed Anthony closely as he staggered down the hall. Leanne was lying in Anthony's strong arms, and he was careful to keep her from slamming into anything, usually taking the hit on his shoulder instead. They slipped through the car, hoping no one saw them. As they neared the end, Lidia opened the door and they jumped into the freight car. Gerta jumped to her feet and ran to them, tears shining on her stricken face.

"What happened to you?" she cried at Gael and Leanne. "We were so worried!" She noticed the blood spilling from Gael's leg and Leanne's arm and cried out again. "What happened?"

Gael sighed wearily and stumbled a little, his face was sweaty and pale. Lidia held him tightly so he didn't fall over. Leanne twisted in Anthony's arms, her eyes fogged with pain and lack of sleep. "Nazis. How's Gael?"

Anthony squeezed her gently. "He'll be alright. Lidia?"

Leanne sagged in his arms, slipping unconscious again.

Lidia looked up. "He's okay, for now. Where's Nathan?"

Nathan got up from his spot on a crate and moved over to them after hearing his name. As he neared, he didn't need to be told what he was needed for. After examining Gael's leg, he bit his lip.

"He'll live, but best if we get him to a doctor as soon as possible. There may have been something on the bullet."

Anthony nodded gravely. "Will you check Leanne?"

Nathan moved over to them. He tried to look at the wound, but the dress's sleeve was in the way and he took out a knife. Anthony caught his wrist.

"What are you doing?"

Nathan saw his concerned expression.

"Nothing. I'm going to cut her sleeve to see the wound." He cut the dress over her shoulder and exposed the wound. It was already shiny and red, with blood pooling out and sliding down her arm.

Anthony, however, wasn't looking at the wound. His eyes were drawn to the pale skin of her shoulder and arm. A blush rose in his cheeks and he quickly looked away. Gerta saw his face.

"Anthony, will you get me a blanket from one of the crates? She's shivering."

Anthony, thankful for the interruption but nervous to leave her, hesitated. Nathan nodded. "That would be most helpful. And one for Gael."

Anthony opened his mouth, saw Leanne's shoulder again, closed it and nodded.

"Be right back."

After digging through a few crates he found what he was looking for. Making his way back to Leanne, he was pleased to pass Gael. He took the second blanket from his arm and gave it to him.

WHEN THE SOLDIERS CAME

"*Merci*, for getting her here." He shot a glance at Leanne. Gael shook his head slightly.

"No, she did it all. I owe my life to her. I would have been caught by Nazis if she hadn't pulled me along." Pain flashed through his eyes.

Anthony smiled and knelt beside Gerta noting that Leanne was awake and a snow white bandage was now covering her shoulder and upper arm.

"Here." He handed Gerta the blanket and took Leanne's hand. "Are you okay?"

A small smile curved her lips and she squeezed his hand weakly. "I will be. I have an amazing doctor and an amazing boyfriend." She squeezed his hand again with weak fingers.

Gerta laid the blanket out and set about making a comfortable bed. When she said she was ready, Anthony gently picked up Leanne and settled her. A few gasps and squeaks of pain slipped through her white lips but she never cried out.

Gerta nodded as Leanne gave another small smile.

"You should sleep if you can."

They were silent for a moment, then Leanne stared at Gerta beside her. She'd tucked her hair into a white bandana, but a small piece had escaped, falling into her determined blue eyes. Leanne found herself wondering who she was. She knew she was good in a leadership role, and she came from money, and the small bit that Anthony told her years ago; but she didn't know about her full past. Or where she came from. Also, if she was rich, why was she somewhere like the Lurcroy's during the war? She decided to ask her.

"Gerta, what's your story?" she asked, slurring the words a little.

"Hmm?" she glanced up. "What?" A small smile curved her lips.

"Your story?" she prompted again. Anthony looked at Leanne with a sense of worry.

"Oh." A small flicker of pain danced in her eyes, and Leanne noticed a bit of sadness in her smile.

"I grew up in Limoges. My Mama died when I was two, giving birth to my baby sister Alice. My Papa died from sickness six years later, leaving me, my older brother and sister, and younger sister to look after ourselves. My sister got married and then died in a house fire. No survivors. My fourteen year old brother died in a car crash a day later. Alice and I were sent to an orphanage. Everyone wanted Alice, but I wasn't needed. Why take an older girl when you can have a young one that'll be able to help the same amount but eat less? Everyone tried adopting her, but I refused, threatening to run away with her if they tried to take her. She was the last part of my family. The best thing I had. The warden saw my plight and decided that if folks wouldn't take me, they couldn't have Alice. I should have let her have a home." Tears filled her eyes and her voice dropped to a whisper. "After two years of us being there, the flu swept in, sickening most of the little children. Alice died the next Monday morning. She was buried behind the orphanage with three others. I was devastated. I was allowed a month to spend time at her grave every day before I was put on a train and sent to an orphanage in Amiens. I was scared. I was only ten and already my life had been destroyed. I made up my mind that I wasn't going to any orphanage. As soon as I felt the train stop, I ran away from my escort and disappeared. I lived three days on the run before I was found by a rich bachelor. He talked to me as we were walking to the police station, and he asked me if I wanted a home. I told him that I wasn't ever going to go to an orphanage and he asked if I'd like to live with him. It was more that I could hope for. He took me in, and I became his daughter. When the threat of war came, he took me to Reims hoping to dodge the draft that was in Amiens. We weren't that lucky. They found him and asked him to go, even though he didn't really have a choice. He sent me to the Lucroy's with the promise that he'd come and get me after the war. I'm hoping that he lives." Her breath caught and she turned away, hiding the tears in her eyes.

Anthony placed his hand on her arm. "I'm sorry."

She smiled again. "It's hard, but I get by. What happened with you?"

He turned quickly, tears filling his eyes. Leanne perked up. She had constantly asked him about his past but he never gave in. He'd only shared a small bit here and there. She half expected him to be silent, but he shocked her when he spoke.

"I grew up on a small farm outside Rennes. I lived with my Uncle Hugo, Aunt Chloé, and Cousin Fabian. My parents died before I even knew them, so I don't really miss them. Thieves broke into our home when Fabian was ten and I was twelve. We'd been out picking berries and we returned to find our fields, house, and barn on fire. Screaming was coming from the house. Fabien ran forward, dropping the bucket he had been holding. I cried for him to stop and tried to grab his arm, but I missed. He ran into the house and it collapsed a few seconds later."

Anthony's voice caught and he dropped his head. Leanne's hand tightened around his own. He looked at her. Her eyes stared into his, giving him strength. "I believed them all dead," he continued huskily, "but as I was watching everything I'd ever known turn to ashes in front of my eyes, a hand was placed on my shoulder. I turned and saw Uncle Hugo. He'd apparently been out plowing in the new field when the fire happened and hadn't noticed the smoke until it was too late. Together, we salvaged what we could. We buried Fabien and Aunt Chloé's bodies, and left, unable to stay where the memories were. We moved to Nancy, but we'd only been there a few years before war was declared. Uncle Hugo was sent away, and I set off in search of a place to live. I stumbled on a Government employee and then was sent to the Lucroy's. A few days later I was given a letter from a very kind soldier. He explained that Uncle Hugo had been killed. *'He died a hero.'* I was told, but I didn't care. I wanted him back. I didn't want the badge or the medals, the congratulations and the apologies. None of them would bring back the only Papa I'd ever known. I was alone. And I didn't think I'd ever have another place to call home, or a family; but then you all came into my life. Showing up one at a time. At first I hated you all, not understanding who you were...until Tristan came. He reminded me so much of Fabian that I was unable to hate him. Everything he said and did reminded me so much of Fabien that I devoted myself to him. He became my family, filling part of my heart that had been completely empty since Fabien, Aunt Chloé, and Uncle Hugo died. Apparently Tristan needed me as much as I needed him, and we became inseparable."

He ended, feeling the tears running down his face. Even now, the faces of Fabien, Aunt Chloé, and Uncle Hugo swam in his mind. Fabien: Laughing and smiling as he darted around

WHEN THE SOLDIERS CAME

in the grass. Aunt Chloé: Grinning as she called the into come eat; dancing barefoot in the kitchen as she made cookies or some other amazing dessert. Uncle Hugo: Staring into his face. Telling him to be strong. Boarding the train. Giving a last wave before disappearing forever.

Anthony bit his lip to keep from sobbing. He was now gripping Leanne's hand rather firmly, but she didn't mind. She was sorry for him and wanted to help in any way she could. Someone stepped forward and hugged him. It was Tristan. His face lit up as he caught Anthony's grateful eyes. Leanne watched them, wondering what the boy's story was.

Tristan caught her looking and his smile faded.

"I never had a family." he whispered. "I grew up on the streets since I was 5. At 9, I was caught stealing and was going to be sent to some work place until I could pay for what I took, but the judge decided to be merciful and sent me to the Lucroy's instead. He told me and the Officers that war was coming, and I deserved a second chance. I met Anthony and he was the big brother I'd always wanted, later he told me that I reminded him of his cousin. That started our friendship." Tristan's eyes were shiny, but he was smiling. It seemed like nothing that happened could break his spirit.

Anthony turned to Nathan. "Yours?"

Nathan smiled grimly. "I've lived in Reims my whole life. I was raised by my older sister. Our parents had died in an accident. My sister, her family, and I were going to go to America, we were going to be free. We were going to have a fresh start. But then the war came. My brother-in-law only had enough money for himself, my sister, and my two nephews and one niece to go. They'll send me a ticket when they get the money, they promised, and I'll join them in America as soon as possible."

Leanne wasn't shocked, that hadn't differed or gone into more detail of when she'd heard it the first time.

Esmé walked over and sat beside them. "I heard what you were talking about." Before anyone asked she continued. "My Papa left my Mama and me when I was two, I don't remember him at all. My Mama became sick and died when I was eight. I spent five years living on the street, eating scraps to survive. After a while someone took me in, decided they didn't want me, and threw me out again. I was found, sent to an orphanage for a year, and then to the Lucroy's." she said sadly. Leanne didn't listen for hers, she already knew it and was too pained to listen to it again.

Everyone else came over, they looked at Marc and Leo. "I think it's your turn." Gerta whispered.

They shrugged and Leo smiled. "I lived in Paris until I was ten, then my parents sent me to a boarding school in Metz. I spent a few years there then came here, to Reims. Marc had the exact same experience. When war came, we both got letters from our parents telling us to go to some man named Lucroy. Here we are." Again, both shrugged.

Leanne turned her head away from them, jealousy burning in her chest. It was hard not to be jealous, Marc and Leo had everything she wanted, whole families. They took them for granted, and it seemed ungrateful to Leanne how they talked about it. Her eyelids felt heavy and she struggled to stay awake.

Lidia had her arms folded, and when everyone turned to her she dropped them, tears sparkling in her eyes. "Lovisa and I grew up in Pinsk, Poland." Her eyes were downcast. Everyone was captivated. None of them knew anything about them. "Gael, too." she continued. "He was just my best friend then, but he's the reason Lovisa and I got out of there alive. He found us and took us away, leaving Pinsk a few days before it was invaded. My parents had called him crazy and had refused to come, telling me that if I was going to take Lovisa then I had to look after her. So I took her and Gael led the way. We hurried to the coast, but before we got there Germany invaded. We'd gotten on a ship that was heading to Denmark, but a German ship was pursuing us, and the ship ran to France. We disembarked at Lille and traveled the country, settling in Reims. After a month or so we started dating, and we've all been together ever since."

Everyone was quiet, that meant Gael, Lidia, and Lovisa had been chased and hunted before by the Nazis, and if they were caught, they'd be killed as traitors. Poland had been under Germany's control for five years now, and everyone that left was killed. Gael was old enough to be one of Germany's soldiers, and they would say he deserted from the army, a crime punishable by death, even if he had left before the Germans had fully occupied Poland.

Leanne moved her head restlessly until she found Gael, he was laying on his side, his leg heavily bandaged, he was sound asleep. She spun her gaze until it landed on Anthony. "Goodnight." she muttered softly, giving in to the calm sensation of sleep.

Only then did Anthnoy look out the window, it was getting lighter, but was still dark. He rubbed the back of his hand down her cheek, then brushed a piece of hair behind her ear. "Goodnight."

Leanne woke after a while. She tried to get back to sleep, but it seemed to evade her, everytime she got close, her arm would burn and she'd wake again. The small boxcar was filled with heavy breathing, so she tossed and turned carefully. Making sure not to jerk her arm or disturb Anthony who was sleeping close by, his hand holding hers. The murmur of voices caused her to still. She painfully looked around, catching sight of Gael and Lidia. Lidia was kneeling beside Gael, her face pinched in guilt and hurt as she looked into Gael's eyes.

"Lidia, why are you here?" The accusation in Gael's voice was low, but discernible. Leanne held in a gasp at hearing his voice like that.

Lidia raised red rimmed eyes. "Because I realized I was being selfish and stubborn. You were only trying to help me, like you did before. And I love you." she added softly. "Oh, Gael, I've always loved you. I was frightened, I didn't know what to do." Tears shone like drops of moonlight as they rolled down her cheeks. "I'm so sorry, Gael."

Gael seemed to relax and Leanne saw tears sliding down his face. "I love you, too, Lidia. But how did you get here? Leanne and I saw you on the balcony."

She took a sad breath. "After I sent the Germans after you I realized my mistake. I saw Nathan, Gerta, and Lovisa leave for the train station. I was about to call the Germans when I remembered what you told me that night in Pinsk when I told you about watching Lovisa." She looked down sheepishly, tears rolling down her cheeks.

Gael smiled. " '*I'll do whatever I can to save Lovisa, nothing will ever get in my way. Even you, Lidia.*' " he quoted. "That?" he asked softly.

WHEN THE SOLDIERS CAME

"*Tak*. I realized how stupid I'd been. You were trying to save Lovisa and I was only getting in your way. I was the one that was too scared to leave the home we'd made. And you were doing your best to keep the promise you'd made me that night. So I slipped out of the house and ran to the station. At first Anthony wouldn't let me on, convinced the Nazis had sent me and were getting ready to ambush the train. Then the train started moving and I panicked. He agreed to let me on, but I don't think he trusts me anymore." She hung her head, shame and regret coloring her face.

Gael smiled softly. "That's Anthony for you. I'm glad he's that way, I know he'll do anything to protect us. And for the record, I never stopped trusting you." He caught her hand and pulled her down until his lips pressed against hers.

Leanne rolled over again, embarrassed that she'd eavesdropped on their private conversation. But a part of her was glad, she was happy that they'd made up. She gently squeezed Anthony's hand and finally fell asleep.

Chapter 14

Leanne muttered softly as she opened her eyes, the bright sunlight shone through one of the slanted boards on the side or the freight car. Where was she? She couldn't remember what had happened. Someone beside her rolled over and propped themselves on their arm. Leanne turned to see who it was, but cried out as hot pain shot through her right arm, tears filled her eyes. The person touched her left shoulder and held her down. She blinked through the pain and noticed it was Anthony. His reassuring smile was gone, replaced by fear and concern. It was a little odd seeing him like that, but she dismissed the thought. There was probably a good reason for it. She went to move again to look around her, but Anthony's strong hand kept her down. "You've been shot, Leanne. Don't move. We'll get you help at Épernay."

She sighed as she laid back against the blanket acting like a pillow.

"What happened?" she asked. Her head felt fuzzy making it hard to think straight.

Anthony turned quickly. "You don't remember anything?" The concern in his eyes touched her.

"I remember shouting and gunshots, but other than that I draw blank." Her eyes widened as she tried to remember.

"It's okay. You got shot in the arm. I'm surprised you made it to the train." His eyes glossed over and Leanne knew that it must have been painful to watch.

Suddenly the night flooded her mind. She gasped and again tried sitting up, only to be stopped by Anthony. "Where's Gael? Is he okay?" She couldn't disguise the panic in her voice. *'What if he'd died?'*

Anthony nodded. "You both were running for a while. Lidia came out and helped me pull you both up. But don't worry! You're both safe now. I won't let anything happen to you." He touched her face with his hand. It was cold, but soothing.

"Between you and God I don't have a doubt." She gave a small smile, but it faded as Anthony turned away. "Anthony, what did I say?"

His face hardened. "You said God was looking out for you. Well, Leanne, He's not! There is no God! Only people who are very, very good at twisting lies to seem as truth. We've had this conversation for the past two years! When are you going to give up this stupid notion of God!"

Leanne recoiled, hurt flowing through her. "I know there is a God." she whispered shakily, growing more confident as she went on. "And He loves you Anthony Tremblay. He will help you whenever you ask for it, believing you will receive it. He knows you, Anthony. He knows that you're struggling. Turn to Him, ask for help. You will get it."

Anthony set his jaw, unwilling to answer.

"You can ignore me right now Anthony, but you'll never be able to ignore God for long. One day…one day, you'll go home and then you'll see Him and you will no longer be able to ignore Him."

WHEN THE SOLDIERS CAME

"Go home? My home is France, and your so-called God let it get destroyed!"

Tears flooded her eyes, despair sinking into her heart. "*Oui*, home!" she cried, trying to contain her tears. "A place for all of his children. A place where everyone can live together forever. I will be going there when I die. I will stand before my Father and He will judge me according to my life here on Earth." The tears slipped down her face. "I'll get to see my Mama, my Papa, and my little sister," she sniffed. "And I hope you'll be there with me. Anytime you need someone to talk to, Anthony, I'll *try* and be there. But God will *always* be there. Trust Him."

They fell silent for a while. Anthony looked back at her.

"You had a little sister?"

Leanne nodded, wiping her eyes with her fingertips. "*Oui*. Sophie. She was two years younger than me."

Anthony slid closer to her. "You were semi-conscious when we shared our life stories; what's yours?"

The memory was so long ago that it no longer hurt to talk about it. It only left a dull ache, as if something were missing. "I was six. Sophie was four. Jameson was eleven. We lived in Caen. Mama and Papa were downstairs with Sophie. I was upstairs in my room; Jameson was telling me a bedtime story. The Orne River flooded; gallons and gallons of water poured onto the streets. Our house was right on the water's edge. My parents started yelling and Jameson grabbed me and jumped out of the window, landing on our neighbor's bottom roof. The water shattered our windows and poured into the house, filling it in a matter of seconds. Jameson carried me across rooftops until a boat came and picked us up. The water took a while to drain, and it was three days before we could get into our old house. Mama, Papa, and Sophie were all dead. It was said they died instantly, the water was so heavy. Jameson and I were sent to an Uncle's house in Riom. Our uncle hated us and felt as if we were burdens. Jameson decided that he could care for me better than our Uncle, and so we ran away after two years. Our money ran out at Rouan. We were stranded and hungry. There we met Marius. He was eighteen and ambitious. He fed us and then asked Jameson if he wanted a job. Jameson was eager, and together they started planning a business. As there was already a clock shop in Rouan, we headed off into other cities. Sometimes we'd get business, other times no luck. Finally, when I was nine, we settled in Reims. Marius said it might not be permanent, but I was too excited about finally having a place to live. Business was really good. After almost everyone had a watch, we set about making repairs. Reims became home." she ended, giving a sad smile. "I sometimes wonder what my life would be like if Mama, Papa, and Sophie were still alive. I think it would be fun having a sixteen year old little sister," she sighed.

The train shuddered as it continued on its path. Leanne peered from her position through a gap between the boards. Anthony noticed her gaze and got to his feet, glancing out another gap. Her life story raced through his mind. She was a lot like him. She'd lost everything, too. He forced himself to look outside. The green landscape was covered with shimmering sunshine, sending blinding light across fields and forests and mountains. Shadows fled on swift wings, straining to escape the bright light of the glowing sun. Majestic birds flew through the sky; their wings helped them defy the laws of gravity. The train sped by small villages and farms. Horses and cows grazed peacefully in green and gold fields. Workers close to the tracks looked up, watching the speeding machinery flash beside their fields. The small houses were quaint, with perfect little curls of smoke and always a guard dog sitting on the porch wagging its tail. As he watched, Anthony felt pride for his country fill his chest. He loved France. As they passed by bigger towns, his chest seemed to have the air sucked right out of it. Signs of war were evident everywhere. Bombcraters punctured the earth leaving ugly, brown dots in fields and meadows. Trees that had grown happily for years were scarred and leaning in strange directions. As they passed through the towns, evidence was even greater there. Houses were falling apart; their furniture was thrown out in the yards. More bomb craters dotted the street and bullet holes sprinkled walls and walkways. People were walking hurriedly, their heads down, uncaring about others on the street. Nazis were goose stepping down the roads in columns. Their boots echoing loudly down the streets. The train stopped a few times, but no one came into the freight car.

Leanne captured Anthony's hanging hand. "Seen anything interesting yet?"

"Minus Nazi soldiers by the hundreds? *Non.*" he replied sadly. "Gael's awake." he added, seeing a slight movement from the older boy. He was half distracted, and decided to not talk about home anymore. He was also still sore about what Leanne had said about God. *'There was no God!'* he cried in his head. *'If there was He would have protected my Aunt, Uncle, and Cousin. He would have saved France from her enemies.'* He vowed never to talk about God again, no matter how much Leanne brought it up or wanted to talk about it. *'God never did anything for me, why should I believe in Him?'*

Leanne looked over her shoulder. Gael struggled to sit up while Lidia struggled to hold him down. She could see the frown creasing his lips, the sweat on his forehead. She sighed. "I feel horrible, we were supposed to get here safely." She bit her lip. "It's all my fault. If I would've run faster, they would never have gotten a clear shot."

Anthony pulled his eyes from the landscape and followed her gaze. Even though he was still angry from the argument, he wasn't mad at her. He dropped her hand and wrapped an arm around her shoulders.

"It wasn't your fault. It would have happened if you were there or not. Just forget about it, Gael doesn't blame you and neither do I."

Leanne noticed that he'd made sure not to mention God at all and she felt a pang of sorrow strike her heart. She loved Anthony. And she loved God. She didn't want to pick between the two of them but inside she already knew what she'd pick if she had to make the choice. Oh, how she hoped Anthony would be able to forgive her if she ever made that choice.

Someone slipped beside Gael, and placed their arm around his waist. It was Lovisa. Her soft smile convinced him to stay down.

The train lurched to a stop, screeching as its wheels ground together. Anthony took a quick glance at the station sign. Épernay. They were here. He turned to the others. "Get up!" he cried softly. "We've got to go!" He gently took Leanne in his arms. She bit her lip and tears filled her eyes, but she didn't make a sound. Leo and Nathan moved to help Gael. Any minute now, someone might open the sliding door and get a glimpse of them all. Marc and Gerta were the farthest ones, and as the others slipped through the door, the freight car was flooded with light as the sliding door opened. In unison Gerta and Marc dropped to the ground, crouching behind a crate.

Nathan, the one at the side door, shrank back. His eyes widened in fear as he met Gerta's frightened eyes. *'Go,'* she mouthed, giving a slight wave away. *'Get out of here.'*

When Nathan hesitated, Marc added his glare to Gerta's and finally Nathan disappeared. German voices filled the boxcar. Some barked orders in clumsy French while other men climbed in. The crates shifted as they were unloaded. Gerta looked at Marc. "Get in one," she whispered, barely above her breath. "Hurry."

Marc went to protest then changed his mind. Carefully, with Gerta holding the lid, he flipped into one of the crates and vanished from sight. Gerta crawled to another one, farther away. Her dress snagged, and her small squeak of fright was louder than she'd intended. The hubbub of voices silenced and French and Germans alike shot searching looks at each other. Gerta leaned back carefully and unhooked her skirt. She cursed herself for making noise in such a dangerous position. Silently, she finished her journey and flipped slowly into a crate.

A French man, sent by the others, saw her out of the corner of his eye. He turned to tell the others, but paused. If the person was hiding from the Germans, then they meant no harm to those in Épernay. He shrugged and started back to the front. One of his comrades looked at him. "Anything?" he asked softly, hiding his moving lips from the German officers standing behind them.

"*Non,*" he replied, grabbing another crate and sliding it off the freight car into the waiting hands of two other men.

Gerta took a deep breath and held it as long as she could. It was so dark she couldn't see what was in the crate with her. Someone moved it and she shoved her hand to her mouth to keep from crying out. The crate slid along the ground, then dropped. Her heart leapt to her throat and she whimpered softly. The crate thudded and stopped moving. Silently, she shifted until she was comfortable. '*Where were the others? Did they get somewhere safe? Did they get caught?*' The thoughts raced around in her head. She didn't know what to do, so she waited, listening to the pounding of boots on the station platform.

Anthony crouched tensely at the entrance to the dark alley. His back, legs, and neck ached from his position, but he didn't dare move. He was too frightened. He turned and watched Leanne who was waiting, tense and confused. Her head leaned against the stone of the building shadowing them. She opened her eyes and turned to face him with something unreadable in them. Behind her, Nathan and Leo were gripping Gael's waist and arms, straining to keep the young man from falling to the stone ground. Lovisa was clutching Lidia's hand behind him. Tristan and Esmé were both jumbled together behind the sisters. Leanne jerked suddenly and cried out softly as her arm bumped against Anthony's. Anthony clapped a hand over her mouth, a little too late. A man turned and caught sight of them. His eyes widened slightly, but he remained aloof walking in their direction. He crossed the street and stopped in front of them.

WHEN THE SOLDIERS CAME

"My name is Andre Jules. What are you doing here? You look like you're running away."

Anthony frowned, unsure of how to answer. He glanced at the man. "Why should we trust you?"

Andre's face looked worried. "Why are you here? And why is there no trust in this city anymore? Please, just tell me who you are."

Anthony blinked. Then looked at the others, Nathan and Leo looked ready to run, and the sisters were tense. He glanced at the man, yeah, he could easily take him out if needed. "We're running from the Nazis." he hissed, keeping his voice low.

Andre's eyes lifted in surprise and joy, "Paris told me you might be by. Follow me. One at a time," he whispered and then sped off.

Lidia hesitated, then slipped out and followed the man before anyone could tell her not to. They waited tensely, wondering if Andre was going to turn Lidia over to the Nazis. Suddenly, he reappeared and took Lovisa. Next Esmé. Tristan. And finally it was only Leanne, Gael, Leo, Nathan, and Anthony. When Andre returned. he frowned. "You'll have to stay here until dark. Don't worry, it's in an hour or so. Stay out of sight. Don't make a noise. I'll come and get you when it's safe." He turned to walk away.

Anthony bit his lip. "Wait," he cried desperately. "There's two more of us, but they got stuck in the train." He didn't know why he thought Andre could help, but he had to try. If Andre was willing to help them, then he'd have to have a way to find Gerta and Marc.

Andre's eyes filled with pity. "The train you were on left over an hour ago. Your friends either got off, got captured, or are on their way to Dijon. I'm sorry." He shook his head to dispel any more questions and melted away, wrapping his coat around himself.

Anthony sank to the ground, and pulled Leanne onto his lap as he blinked back tears. *'Where were Gerta and Marc?'* he thought, brokenhearted.

Leo and Nathan helped lower Gael. His face tightened but his lips remained closed.

Time passed slowly. Nazi soldiers marched down the street, their thudding footsteps sounding strangely loud in the coming dusk. The sun sank lower and lower, throwing shadows on the wall and sending people hurrying to their homes. Gael and Leanne slept on and off, but each time they went unconscious, they muttered painful cries and moaned. Finally, Anthony and Nathan decided letting them sleep wasn't the best idea and would shake them each time they looked close. Anthony started counting civilians passing by to spend time. He reached thirty-four by the time Andre reappeared. He was dressed in a dark trench coat with a dark hat pulled low over his face, shading a thin black mustache and fear filled gray eyes. He didn't say anything but turned back around and walked off. The boys got to their feet and walked hurriedly after him, working together to keep the two wounded ones from unnecessary pain. Andre led them to a small house. He ushered them upstairs and into a room. Locking the door, he departed. Anthony was quickly seized and drawn farther into a small, but comfortable room. Tristan grabbed his arm and dragged him to one of the walls. "In there." he pointed at the wall.

Anthony gave his friend a sidelong glance. "Where?"

Then the wall opened, revealing a spacious room beyond.

WHEN THE SOLDIERS CAME

"There." Tristan smiled, shoving him lightly in the back to get him going. He stumbled into the room and was hugged from behind by Tristan, unable to contain himself any farther.

As Anthony laid Leanne down, he spun to Nathan.

"Where are they?" he demanded.

No one had to be told who he was talking about. Nathan, the last one that had seen them, dropped his head sadly. "I don't know. I didn't see them get off the train." He struggled to keep his voice level.

Leanne tossed her head. "They'll be okay. Gerta and Marc can take care of themselves. Don't worry." She smiled a little, gritting her teeth in pain.

'Father please watch over them. Thou knowest where they are, thou can do all things. Keep my friends safe, please.'

Pounding on the downstairs door made them all quiet. Andre opened it. "Good evening. This is a pleasant surprise."

A small, indiscernible voice spoke urgently.

"I see. Come in, upstairs, first door on your right. You'll find it easy enough." Then the door closed and steps sounded on the stairs. Behind the hidden door, Nathan listened as someone crossed the room and started feeling the back wall. The small door opened, and a startled gasp came from the newcomer. Nathan grabbed her hand and yanked her through the door.

Chapter 15

The girl was small, barely bigger than Lovisa. She had black hair and dark brown eyes. Her face was pale. The dress she wore was torn and so dirty no one could tell what color it had started out as. She was panting as she looked at them all. A thin, scuffed trench coat was wrapped around her, and she was hugging it against herself as if she was scared it would be taken from her. Leanne was the first to speak. "Hello. I`m Leanne. Who are you?"

"My name is Rébecca." Her eyes dropped and she shivered slightly.

Leanne offered her a smile. "How old are you?"

"Sixteen," she answered shyly, keeping her eyes downcast.

"What are you doing here?" Nathan prompted, his eyes wide at the thought of the small girl actually being sixteen.

"Hiding." she responded softly. "Like you all."

"Why are you hiding?" Leo interjected, sounding irritated.

"The Germans are hunting me." Rébecca growled, her voice dangerously low. "I assume it's the same for you?" Suspicion glowed in her eyes.

Her question was aimed at Leo, but Anthony answered.

"*Oui*. Why are they hunting for you?" His tone was kind, like a worried parent.

Rébecca's eyes flicked toward him. "I'm a Jew." She slipped off her coat, revealing the gold band on her arm, the star of David seemed to pop off the fabric. "Aren't you all?" Fear filled her voice, and she recoiled, wrapping her arms around her chest and hugging herself.

"*Non*." Lidia whispered. "We're spies. Hated by the Germans. They're chasing us so they can send us to Germany."

A knock on the door made them all jump.

"It's me," Andre spoke softly. "I have food."

Nathan opened the door and took the basket Andre handed in.

Andre whispered over his shoulder. "I suggest you get some sleep. You'll have to leave tomorrow." Then he left.

Nathan handed out rolls, cheese, and a flask of water. After they ate their small meal, they settled down for the night. Nathan checked on them, making sure they had enough room and were comfortable. Then he bent down to check on Gael. His leg was swollen; the wound rimmed with purple and black blood. Nathan's face dropped and he squeezed his eyes closed. He didn't know what to do. He rebandaged Gael's leg and made him comfortable. Gael didn't open his eyes, but a mumbled *merci* slipped from his hot lips. Nathan smiled sadly, then went to Leanne. She was in better shape. Her wound was still clean, just looked angry.

Night passed quickly, bringing morning faster than they wanted. Rébecca woke first. Her deep eyes took a while to adjust to the darkness of the room. She glanced around at the others, sleeping peacefully. Her gaze rested on Gael. His eyes were open, but glazed and unfocused. His face was dry, but from here Rébecca could see that he was burning with fever. His head was rolling from side to side, and small gasps of pain escaped his lips. Slowly, Rébecca got to her feet, tiptoeing across the sleeping figures, and knelt beside the boy. As she reached for his hand, someone's hand shot forward and caught her wrist, making her squeal in fear. She turned and saw concerned deep brown eyes and brown hair. The boy's face was handsome, but creased with fear. She backed off, trying to draw her hand back, but the boy held on tightly. He sat up and frowned.

"What are you doing?"

She opened her mouth to answer, but changed her mind and instead asked, "Who are you?" Again she tried pulling away from him, but she found the grip unrelenting.

"My name is Anthony. And you didn't answer my question."

"I was just checking on him. I didn't think it would be a big deal." Her fear started to ebb, being replaced by anger. She glared at the boy. "Release me!" she demanded, jerking her hand again. Anthony did as told and Rébecca slipped backward, almost crushing someone sleeping. "Why would you do that?" she screeched in a whisper.

Anthony raised an eyebrow. "I thought you wanted me to let you go." Rébecca huffed and turned away, folding her arms across her chest. Anthony glanced at Gael, his eyes had closed and his breathing had evened out, but he was still hot. He looked back at the angry girl. "I'm sorry. I shouldn't have. I was just scared and nervous."

She turned and smiled at him. "Where are you headed?"

Anthony smiled back. Although she would have never admitted it, Rébecca thought the boy looked cute when he smiled. Anthony absentmindedly brushed a lock of hair off

Leanne's forehead and behind her ear. Leanne turned fitfully, a soft moan escaping her mouth. Anthony winced at the sound. "Paris." His hand moved back to Leanne's cheek and started drawing patterns on it, she sighed softly but kept sleeping.

Rébecca gasped. "The Germans are there. It'll be dangerous for you."

Anthony chuckled. "Better than staying here, waiting to get found. Where are you going? There's not a lot of places that are safe."

"Toulouse. I heard that there are people, most of them Jews, and French soldiers. I've heard the soldiers have been sent there by the Government to keep us safe. They're going to defend the city and they'll take in other Jews. I believe I"ll be safe there," she ended softly. She turned and tiptoed away, her footsteps making no noise.

Leanne muttered, and instantly Anthony bent over her, whispering small words of comfort. One by one the others opened their eyes, blinking in the darkness to adjust their eyes. As Gael was waking, a small knock sounded on the hidden door.

"Get up. I have breakfast, then you have to go."

Andre's voice was strained. Anthony thought that curious, but decided that he was under a lot of stress. He took the small basket and handed out the food. It was the same as yesterday, but seemed to taste worse.

They ate hurriedly. Anthony shoved some food into his coat pocket, hoping Leanne would be able to eat when she woke. Nathan motioned for Lovisa and Lidia to leave, then Leo to help him with Gael. Tristan left next followed by Rébecca and Esmé. Anthony slid out next, slipped face-first back in, and pulled Leanne with him, careful to avoid her arm. Andre came in, his face was shaded by another dark hat. "Out the back door. Run to the station. There is a train going around noon. It'll make a stop, but then head to Laon. Good luck."

He turned to leave.

"Wait!" Anthony hurried to stand up. "Is there a doctor here?"

Andre frowned. "*Oui*. But he'd throw you to the Nazis before you could even ask for help. He's one of them."

Like the night before, he vanished quickly, melting into the walls and rooms of his small but spacious house.

Anthony glanced at everyone, forcing the despair he was feeling from his face. They were all waiting for someone to tell them what to do.

"Let's get going. We don't want to get found."

As the others filed out of the room, moving carefully, Anthony stepped up to Nathan. "What about Gerta and Marc? If we leave them we'll never find them again."

Nathan sighed sadly. "I know. But there's nothing we can do about it. We've got to get going." He turned and hurried down the stairs. Anthony followed suit.

Out in the muddy streets of Épernay, Anthony felt vulnerable. Leanne was walking shakily beside him. He clutched her upper arm, worried that she'd blackout. Even here in the back streets, he could hear the stamping boots of German soldiers marching down the streets. Rébecca's wide eyes scanned the streets. "I have to leave you. The train that you're taking is heading in the wrong direction. *Adieu*." Then she faded into the shadows. No one spoke.

Anthony faltered for a moment, then turned around. "Come on."

They snuck through the alleys and dark streets, taking pains to remain silent and unnoticed. After a few minutes, someone screamed and the thudding of heavy boots rang loudly in the small town. People shouted, some in fear, some in joy. Anthony looked around, but the people that were guiding the Nazis weren't pointing at them. "Gerta. Marc." he whispered under his breath. Making a quick decision he turned to the others. "Nathan, lead the others away. Leanne, come with me." He tightened his hand and ran off into another alley.

Nathan watched until they disappeared and then turned on his heel. "Hurry. We have to get to the train station."

Unseen by Nathan, Tristan slipped off after Anthony and Leanne.

The alleys twisted and turned, usually ending in the brilliant light of the main streets. Anthony was quick to correct his running and made sure he stayed in the shadows pulling Leanne right on his heels. The screams and cries of the townspeople and the deep calls of the Nazis were an excellent guide. Leanne halted as they neared the center courtyard of the small city.

"Anthony, what's going on?" she panted, she jerked her arm from his hand and clutched at the stitch in her side.

"The Nazis are chasing someone, I believe it's possible that it's Gerta and Marc." Anthony answered, walking slowly.

'Father, non.' Leanne prayed silently. *'Please, non.'* She was so worried that she was unable to speak.

WHEN THE SOLDIERS CAME

The houses fell away and they stood staring at a courtyard. It was wide, with flat cobblestones on the ground and large houses and buildings curved around it. Nazi soldiers were ringed in the middle; their two captives crouching and trying to hide in plain sight. One was a girl, and the other was a tall man. Anthony breathed easier. It wasn't Gerta and Marc.

He turned to go when Leanne caught his arm.

"Rébecca." she whispered, eyes filling with tears.

Spinning around, Anthony saw that the girl was indeed the Jew they'd met. Her face was scratched and even more dirty than it had been before. Blood dripped off one of her elbows. Her eyes were white with fear. Her hands were clenched into tight fists. Her hair was frizzy and falling out of the small ribbon she'd tied it back with that morning. The man beside her was dressed in a trench coat with a hat pulled low, shading his face. His gray eyes and black mustache were barely visible: but they both recognized him as Andre.

Anthony watched in horror as the Germans knocked their prisoners around. The people of Épernay had gathered, some calling insults at the prisoners, others crying into handkerchiefs or coat collars. A German voice rang out, speaking in a very good French accent. "Shut up!" Instantly the crowd stilled. The speaker was addressing the crowd, his face hidden. "These are traitors to the *Führer*! The man has hidden spies against the great mother country, and the girl has believed that her rebellion will help you, but they have both been caught!" The man's eyes burned with anger and hatred. His hands clenched by his sides, spittle flew from his mouth. The people nearest him backed away a little. "France is gone! You will turn to Germany to rule you! The mother country will defend you and protect you from the wicked lies that are being shared by England, Russia, and everywhere else! You are nothing! Your country has abandoned you!" As he spoke, the Nazi soldiers spread out behind him, keeping Rébecca and Andre in front of them, slowly shoving the two prisoners against the back of a building.

Rébecca's eyes hardened. "You lair!" she screamed, flinging her head back she glared at the Nazi leader. "You have no idea! France is strong! Even now our men and boys are on the battlefields! They are fighting you and your country! We will win!" Her high voice carried over the silent courtyard, she turned and addressed the crowd. "Do not give up! Please! France needs you! Help us!" she screamed.

A Nazi soldier rushed forward and struck her on the mouth. She spun and fell to the ground. The leader turned, and Anthony heard Leanne gasp. His own breath left him as he looked into the face of the German. It was Devid, the Oberlieutenant from the Lucory's. Devid's face was satisfied as Rébecca got to her feet, spitting blood. "*Bereit!*" he shouted.

Soldiers in the line raised their guns. Rébecca's eyes widened as she stared into the empty faces of the men who held the guns. She brushed pieces of hair away from her face, clearing her vision.

"*Ziel!*"

The guns cocked. Rébecca lifted her hands to shield her face. A small whimper escaping her white lips.

"*FEUER!*"

The guns coughed as they spat bullets. Rébecca and Andre jerked and flinched as the bullets sprayed. Both sagged to their knees, then fell lifeless to the ground; their bodies thudding softly. Blood pooled around them, coming from the many ripped places in their arms, legs, and chests. Women in the crowd screamed. Men stared aghast. Children started crying. Devid nodded slowly, his face twisted angrily.

"That is what happens when you defy Germany," he howled. "Everyone get to your houses!" He turned to the row of soldiers and shouted. "Soldiers! Find the ones we came for! I know they're here!"

Anthony stared aghast as he looked at the two bodies laying on the cold cobblestones of the courtyard. Leanne broke down in tears. Rébecca's face was turned toward Leanne. Blood dripped from her mouth. Her empty eyes stared at Leanne, begging for help that no one could give. Tears slid off her cheeks onto the ground beside her.

Leanne stared at Rébecca's body, watching blood spread around her. *'Father take her to thy kingdom. Give her love. Give her peace. Give her a home. Give her the safety and security she didn't have on Earth.'*

Anthony wrapped a hand around Leanne's left bicep.

"We need to leave. They're coming."

Chapter 16

Anthony and Leanne hurried through the streets. Relentlessly, behind them came the sound of heavy, stomping boots. Tears sparkled in Leanne's eyes. She dashed them away angrily. She didn't really know Rébecca; but she had stood for their country. She had defied the Nazis to their faces and had paid the price with her life. Leanne struggled to swallow the lump in her throat. She stumbled and was caught by Anthony's steady arms. Neither spoke as they ran, looking for the train station. Épernay seemed determined to keep them from their destination, spinning in circles and throwing them in plain sight of anyone on the streets. Stumbling, they finally heard the shrill whistle of a train. Relieved, both turned and headed for it. As they clattered onto the platform they skidded to a stop. Shocked at what they saw.

Gerta gasped as she ground herself to a stop. Her boots slid on the polished wood, throwing her off balance. Marc caught her waist and steadied her. The train was gleaming in front of them; its engine was throwing smoke and steam and whistling every now and then. The windows were washed spotless. But neither of them were looking at the train. Anthony and Leanne had just appeared on the other side of the platform. Gerta threw herself forward and ran to them, opening her arms wide.

Anthony smiled widely and caught Gerta in a hug, spinning her around. Marc was next. "Where have you both been?" he cried, releasing Marc.

Gerta turned from hugging Leanne. "We got stuck in the train so we crawled into crates and were unloaded. We spent the night in the boxes, not knowing where we were or where you all were. Morning came and we got out and started searching for you all. When we couldn't find you, we made up our minds to come to the station, hoping you'd leave on a train."

Pounding footsteps made them all look up in surprise, but they smiled when Nathan and the others appeared. They all hugged one another, squealing in relief.

Anthony frowned. "Where's Tristan?" He scanned the faces, searching for the happy, glowing face of his little friend.

Nathan looked around him. "I don't know. I thought he was right here."

Gael opened his eyes slowly.

"He ran off," his voice was low and pained, "after you." He sighed and pointed at Leanne and Anthony.

Anthony stepped back, stricken. Leanne caught his hand, worried that he'd fall over or run away.

"But he wasn't there!" Anthony cried. "I never saw him!" He turned to Leanne, despair filling his eyes and voice. "Did you?"

"*Non*," she breathed softly, clutching Anthony's hand tighter. Her eyes searched the platform.

WHEN THE SOLDIERS CAME

'Where is he, Father?'

Gerta choked back tears. Esmé spun on her heel, searching the platform for the boy that had a special place in their hearts. Leo looked around too, his face drawn in worry. Nathan stared at the ground, tears pooling in his eyes. Lovisa and Lidia both started crying, hugging each other. But it was Anthony that took it the hardest. He released Leanne's hand and fell to his knees. His eyes blurred as tears, falling thick and fast, cascaded down his cheeks.

"Anthony!" a faint voice cried. "Anthony!"

It sounded like the wind, but an octave higher.

Anthony raised his head, staring in wonder at his friends. Each one met his questioning glance with a shake of the head. He got to his feet, searching.

"Anthony!" the wind called again.

"Tristan!" He could barely see the form of the boy running toward him. "Tristan!" He ran forward, his arms opening, even though they were far apart.

"Anthony!"

The cry turned to relief. Tristan's face was tear streaked, his eyes wide with fear. Anthony sped up, unable to reach his friend fast enough. All of a sudden he stopped. Something was off. Tristan ran to him, his eyes blurring with tears. Anthony took a few steps toward him. "Trist?" The air felt heavy, and dark. Anthony looked around, an unexplainable pit of fear tightened in his stomach and chest. A form stepped out of the shadows behind Tristan. The boots. The uniform. The hat. The face was shaded, but Anthony could see the lips curled in a sickening sneer. Anthony's eyes widened.

"*Non*," he whispered. "*Non*. Tristan!" he screamed.

Tristan glanced over his shoulder, fear made him double his pace; but there was nothing he nor Anthony could do. They were ten feet apart. So close. The crack of a pistol shattered the air.

"*NON!*" Anthony screamed, watching the boy jerk, then tumble to the ground. The train whistled and its engine started. Anthony hurled forward, scooped up Tristan, and ran blindly to the train. The cries of the others drove him on. The pistol cracked again and again. Bullets buried themselves in the smooth wood of the platform, raising splinters. Tristan lay limp in Anthony's arms, his head rolling, arms and legs flopping. Hands reached down and drew Anthony up onto the train. Nathan wrapped both boys in his strong arms and pulled them into the safety of yet another freight car.

Anthony dropped to his knees placing Tristan in front of him. Everyone stared in confusion wondering if Tristan was okay. They all seemed scared and kept their distance...except Leanne. She knelt beside them, tears falling down her cheeks, her hand landing on Anthony's thigh. *'Father save him! If it be thy will save him!'* She blinked back the hot tears filling her eyes.

Anthony carefully arranged Tristan on a pillow, letting the boy rest. Tristan clutched at his hand. "I love you," he whispered, his eyes filled with fear.

"I love you, too, Trist. Now go to sleep." He put his hand under Tristan's back to slide him farther onto the pillow, but paused as something hot and slippery wet his hand. He drew it back, staring in horror at the scarlet liquid sliding off his fingers. "Tristan?" He raised his stricken eyes to the boy laying in front of him. Leanne gasped in horror.

The boy gasped, his face twisted in pain. "I love you." he repeated.

"*Non. Non.* Come on, Trist. It's going to be fine." He clung to the small hand in his. "It's going to be just fine."

Tristan gasped. "I love you." He stared into Anthony's eyes.

"*Non.* Don't say that. It sounds like goodbye."

Tears blurred his vision. He bit his lip to keep from crying out.

The small face lit with a smile. "I love you." The pain and tears in his eyes lessened.

"Don't!" Anthony cried, hanging his head. "Please, Trist. I need you."

"Don't forget me, Anthony." His voice was lower than a whisper, and ended up mouthing the words. The small head fell to the side. His hand went limp, blood slipped from his mouth and down his cheek. Leftover tears rolled slowly down his temples and fell into his hair.

"*Non.*" Anthony clutched the small hand sliding from his grip as he gazed into the sweet face. He stopped at the eyes as the life left them. "*Non.*" he whispered again. "Tristan, look at me." He cupped his hand around Tristan's small cheek. "Look at me." He wiped away the blood, gently caressing Tristan's face.

The young teenager didn't respond. Anthony swallowed painfully. "Tristan, look at me!" he cried, the tears falling down his face. "Please! Look at me!" He shook the small body. "Come on! Please! Please!" His heart burned. His chest throbbed.

Tristan didn't move. The smile remained on his face, but his eyes were hollow. Empty. Lifeless. Turning the boy over, Anthony could see the small bullet hole in the base of his neck, even if a doctor had been there, there would have been no chance of saving him. It was a miracle that Tristan had woken up at all. Anthony placed his hand over the hole and rolled Tristan back over. He dropped his head onto the boy's stomach. "Please," he whispered. "Come back. Come back." He threw his hands over his head and sobbed. "It's not fair. It's not fair. Come back. Come back." His voice broke and he sobbed harder. Leanne moved her hand and rubbed Anthony's back, unable to keep her own tears in check.

Nathan stepped over crates toward Anthony, Leanne, and Tristan. His face was full of worry. He froze in shock at the scene.

"*Non*." he whispered. "It's not possible." Hot tears filled his eyes, making sight impossible. He felt his way forward, falling on his knees beside Anthony and Leanne. "What happened?" he cried.

"Devid." Anthony sobbed. "I know it was him. I know it was. He shot Tristan. He took Tristan from me." He remained kneeling, clutching the small body. His tears trailed off his face and landed on the boy's coat, making dark imprints on the fabric. "I won't forget, Trist. I'll never forget," he whispered, seeming to forget that Nathan was there. He turned and buried his face in Leanne's unwounded shoulder. Leanne ran her hand through his hair, murmuring words of comfort. Her eyes met Nathan's. Slowly he got to his feet, understanding the small plea in her eyes.

He turned and made his way back to where the others were sitting. Gerta looked at him, her face anxious with worry.

"What happened?" she asked, springing to her feet.

Nathan took a heavy breath. "Tristan's dead."

WHEN THE SOLDIERS CAME

Gerta sank back down, her hand thrown up to her mouth. "*Non*." She looked down in shock, her mouth falling open. "*Non*. He was fine! I know he was!"

The others looked down, tears falling down their faces. "He is now." Gael responded heavily.

Tears filled everyone's eyes. Lovisa burst out sobbing. "How?" she cried. "How?"

Nathan shook his head. "Nazis." Was all he said before laying down and refusing to say anything more.

Anthony looked at Leanne. "Can you leave me alone for a minute?"

He hated asking her to leave, but he had to.

She smiled sadly. "Of course." With tears in her eyes, she got up and left. Walking slowly between the crates, she pressed her hand to her mouth to keep from sobbing loudly in case someone was asleep.

'Father take the pain, I can't hold it. Please take it from me. Let me know Tristan's with you.' A sudden warm feeling of peace ran over her, warming her from the inside out. *'Merci, Father.'*

Anthony looked at the boy in front of him. "I'm so sorry, Trist. I love you." He got to his feet and hurried away. Slipping from the freight car, he made his way to the back of the train. The ground was moving a little slower back here, but still too fast. Everything was moving too fast! Anthony buried his face in his hands, hiding the tears in his eyes. *'It's not fair!'* he thought bitterly. *'It's so not fair!'* Without warning, images of Tristan filled his mind: The boy laughing, smiling, playing. Sitting down with another book to get lost in. Staring with confusion when Anthony made a remark in German. The happy relief in his eyes when he'd seen Anthony waiting on the train station platform. The way his arms had fallen open, getting ready to hug him. The soft spoken *"I love you"* that he'd said.

Anthony sobbed, trying to get rid of the images. His friend was haunting him, and he hated it. He dropped to his knees and clutched at the railing like a lifeline. He felt as if he were drowning.

Leanne watched painfully from the door. Her arm throbbed and burned, but it wasn't anywhere near the pain in her heart. She watched Anthony, the one she'd looked up to, broken and in pain. She didn't know how to help him. She moved to disappear back through the door, but her shoulder bumped against the wall, and she couldn't help but gasp. Anthony turned at the noise. Leanne watched fearfully, wondering if he'd get upset about her following him. But his eyes were pained and empty. He held out his arms, tears dripping off his chin. Leanne hurried to his side, threw her good arm around him, and held him as he cried. She rubbed his back and pressed her cheek to the crown of his head. "I love you, Anthony," she whispered softly.

He didn't raise his head. "I love you, too, Leanne. Don't leave me. Don't ever leave me."

Leanne held him tighter, she was aware of the strong muscles of his arms around her waist, the soft fabric of his shirt. "I'll never go anywhere. I'll be by your side, always. And so will God," she whispered.

Chapter 17

Two hours passed on the train, but still things seemed dark. Anthony stared blankly out of the small hole in the planks, watching the land blur. Leanne sat beside him, one hand on his back, the other gently clutched his hands on his lap, silently mouthing a prayer. Everyone missed Tristan greatly. It seemed as if the heart of everyone had been ripped out, but they were all still in danger, and seemed resolved not to give into their grief. Leanne whispered hymns and small prayers every now and then, asking for help.

Leo, trying his best to keep his spirits high, was trying to get them all in a good mood again; asking each girl if they wanted to dance and the boys if they'd want to throw a knife or search through the crates. Each question was met with a '*non*' until finally Esmé had agreed to a dance, and wistfully they started. Soon enough, everyone joined in, laughing, clapping, and stopping their feet in time to the song Nathan was humming. All except Anthony and Leanne, both stayed where they were, content with watching the flitting landscape pass by.

The train coughed smoke and steam and the brakes squealed and threw sparks as they ground against each other. Very slowly, the train screamed to a stop. The city was a middle sized town. The peaks and roofs of the houses glimmered in the evening light. Gael looked up. His eyes were bloodshot and puffy from crying, but there was a determined glint in them.

"Where?" He nodded at Marc who had a map spread across his knees.

"La Ferté-Sous-Jouarre. Some city near Meaux and Paris. Another few days and we'll be in Paris...and then free." His eyes grew wistful.

Leo hopped over to the window. "I don't see any Nazis."

"It doesn't matter." Nathan said sternly. "We're staying on the train." His voice was dark.

"That's impossible." Lidia gasped, leaning over to stare at him. "The man in Épernay said it was going to Laon. That's far away and bound to be crawling with Germans being so close to the border." She raised her eyebrow as if daring Nathan to argue with her.

Nathan tossed his head as he took in what Lidia said. "I know," he muttered at last, "but I don't think La Ferté-Sous-Jouarre is a place we want to stop at. I say we go to Laon and then catch a train to Paris."

"*Non*." Gerta pulled herself to her feet. "That's way too risky. Better to stay here in La Ferté-Sous-Jouarre, catch a ride to Meaux, then another to Paris. And if that's not possible, then we walk," she stated matter of factly.

Gael sighed and dropped his hand into his hands. "We have to go somewhere. I think that staying on the train is way too risky. We also have no way of knowing if La Ferté-Sous-Jouarre is overrun with Nazis. Another possibility is to wait for the train to leave the station and then jump off, hoping no one sees us." He grimaced as he thought of the difficulty that option might be with his leg.

WHEN THE SOLDIERS CAME

Esmé shook her head. "Gael you could never walk that far. I'm surprised that you're even up and walking around."

Gael shook his head hard. "I can do it. But, I'll leave it up to you guys. Are we staying here or getting off?" He glanced at them all, wondering what they'd decided.

Nathan voiced his opinion again only to be shot down by Lidia. The others broke out in argument. Leo turned to the two figures seated beside each other. "Anthony, what do you say?"

Anthony's pain twisted eyes raised sadly and met Leo's. "I want out of here as fast as possible. I vote get off here and hitch another ride."

"Leanne?" Leo continued.

She gave half a smile. "I vote with Anthony." He squeezed her hand, cautious of her arm.

"I'd say that settles it." Leo turned to the others. "Don't you?"

Nathan turned away, anger rippling across his face. Gerta, who'd agreed with Nathan, frowned. The others nodded, giving their agreement.

"Alright then." Gael got shakily to his feet. "Disembark."

They tumbled out. Gael had struggles with the stairs and Anthony and Nathan helped him down. Anthony looked at the group before him.

"Leo, do you want to go in the station and find out a little about this town?" He glanced at Gael; his face was soaked with sweat and his eyes were bright, but he was forcing a smile. "And try to see if there's a doctor that will help us. I'm worried for Gael." He turned to Leanne, her face was clear, but everytime she moved her arm a bit she would grimace. "And Leanne." he added, returning his gaze to Leo.

Leo nodded and headed for the doors. The handles were cool to the touch, and he shivered. Wrapping his coat tighter around his shoulders, he shoved through the door and stepped inside. The station was grand with a glass domed roof and marble floors, or it would have been, if half the roof wasn't missing and the floor wasn't stained and ripped up in places. A rotund man raised his eyebrow when Leo walked in. He had no hair on his head, but a thin black beard and mustache, with gray streaks in it. He smiled.

"You look like you're running away."

He said it like a question, but Leo could tell he knew the answer.

"*Oui*. From Nazis." he answered, darting his eyes around, fear pulsing through his veins.

The man gave a slight smile. "Don't worry, *Fils*, no one here would even dream of giving someone over to those thieves. You're safe. Anything I can help you with?"

Leo bit his lip, nervous to speak to a stranger, then he thought of the others. "I need a place to hide. Me and a few friends. Oh, and a doctor."

The man nodded. "I'm Monsieur Blanc. Get your friends here. You'll be able to hide in the attic. And the doctor here is a close friend of mine. I'll contact him and ask if he's willing to help."

Leo smiled and ran back to the platform. The others were hiding in the shadows. "Come on. I found a place to hide."

Leanne glanced at him. "Are you okay?"

Leo nodded, but didn't say anything. Gael got to his feet, his face pale, his breathing heavy. Lidia took one side of him, draping his arm over her shoulders. Nathan took the other. Anthony pulled Leanne into his arms and held her tightly. Slowly they moved into the station and up the stairs. Gael's steps staggered, sweat poured off his face, his lips pursed in pain. Leanne was awake, but her eyes were bright with fever. Anthony pressed the back of his hand onto her head, quickly he pulled it back, her skin was burning. He held her tighter, fear gripping his heart. Leanne read the fear in his eyes and slid her hand down his arm. "Anthony, I'll be fine. Don't worry about..." She coughed, her whole body shaking.

Anthony stopped moving as she coughed. When she stopped he looked into her eyes. "Leanne, I'm worried about you."

She laughed, but struggled not to cough. "I'm fine. Just feeling a little off, don't worry, I'll be okay."

"Liar." he muttered, reaching the top of the stairs.

Leanne looked around, wondering where they were going to go now. A creak made them both look up, Nathan's face was smiling at them upside down. "Come on. Anthony hand her to me."

Anthony leveled Leanne and pushed her upward. Nathan caught her left wrist and pulled her into the dark square behind him with Anthony shoving her from below. After a few minutes, Nathan reappeared hanging lower than before. Now he was bent double from the waist down.

"Here." He stretched his arms down.

Anthony reached up and grasped Nathan's wrists. Someone unseen was pulling Nathan and soon they both were in the darkness of the attic. Some shadow closed the trapdoor before a flashlight flipped on.

Leanne was leaning against a dusty, sloped wall. Dust was floating through the air, only visible in the beam of the light. Other than that the room was completely dark. She looked around but was unable to see anything. Anthony crawled over to her, sneezing and coughing from the dust. Gael was leaning opposite from them, coughing deeply. Lidia crooned and fussed over him as she checked his leg. Gael softly shoved her away, sliding his leg painfully away from her. Lovisa crouched in the dust beside the trapdoor, the flashlight at her feet. Leo, Marc, Esmé, and Gerta were having a small conversation beside the wall behind the trap door.

Leanne dropped her head onto Anthony's shoulder, her eyes half closed. Anthony ran a hand down her face; it felt like fire. He quickly moved and looked at her arm. It was infected. He could see it as soon as he moved the bandage. It was purple, blue, and green, with scarlet-black blood swelling and spilling from the ragged hole in her arm. He recoiled and looked away.

"Leo? Leo?" he called in a whisper, trying not to wake Leanne who'd finally fallen asleep.

Leo looked up and crawled over. "What?" His face was dark.

"Is there a doctor here? Is he going to help?"

"*Oui*. Monsieur Blanc said he'd talk to the doctor. Don't worry Anthony. We'll get them both help. Neither will die." His eyes were calm and comforting. A reassuring smile curved his lips.

Loud thudding and raised voices halted all conversation. The shattering of glass and splintering of wood made all of them wince and flinch. Leanne tossed in feverish sleep. Opposite her, Gael was doing the same thing. Their faces were filled

WHEN THE SOLDIERS CAME

with pain, and small gasps and moans of pain escaped their white lips. Lidia gently slapped a hand over Gael's mouth. Anthony did the same to Leanne. Just as their hands were about to silence the sleepers, a cry of pain came from Leanne; echoed by Gael. All the others paused in horror. The sounds from downstairs ceased. No one dared to breathe. Anthony wrapped an arm around Leanne's shoulders and cuddled her to his chest. Her cries ripped into his heart. An indiscernible voice spoke, then heavy footsteps sounded on the stairs.

Esmé watched her friends' worried faces. Each had fear in their eyes. Each was frozen in horror. She frowned, wondering what they were to do. Suddenly, she knew that not all of them would get out of here. The Nazis were on the main level, arguing with the station master, and no one would be able to leave until they found what they were looking for. She took a deep breath, making up her mind. Unnoticed, she crawled to the trap door. Silently, she pulled it up. Blinding light flared into the attic. A small, muffled gasp came from Lovisa and she hurried to close the door, but not before Esmé had swung down and dropped out of sight.

Esmé landed softly on the ground. The planks squeaked under her boots. She knew the risk she was taking but was willing to try if it meant saving the others. The footsteps mounted the stairs, trying to be quiet, but was too loud for someone that was listening for it. She took a deep breath and hid in the shadows, waiting for the opportunity. The officer stepped onto the landing. The light in his hand scanned the room. As he turned the flashlight, Esmé gasped softly. It was Devid. His face had been chiseled into something hard, but his blue eyes and blonde hair made him unforgettable. Another soldier came from behind him. It was the soldier from the Lucroy's. The one with red hair and brown eyes. His face was scared and half hidden in the shadows. The soldier leaned toward Devid.

"They're not here." His voice was low, and he spoke in French with the faint trace of a foreign accent.

Devid scowled. "I'm not saying that the ones that ran away from us are here. But possibly others. Our spy reported some activity. We will find the reason someone is hiding here."

The other soldier matched his scowl.

"It'll never work. Those kids are too smart for you. Ha! All of France is. You'll never win."

Esmé was shocked. She'd never seen a German acting against his country. She dared a look, but it was still the two German soldiers. Devid stood slightly in front of the other. Devid let loose a bark of harsh laughter.

"Maybe France, but certainly not Poland. You all fell on your knees as soon as we landed." He lightly slapped the soldier on the cheek and walked toward where Esmé was hiding.

She drew back, stifling a gasp. The soldier was Polish; just like Lidia! And Lovisa! And Gael! A thudding noise drew her senses back to the dark room. Devid was knocking on the walls and stamping on the floor. Periodically, his eyes would dart to the ceiling as if he was going to check if it was hollow or not. Esmé took a deep breath knowing now that it was for the best that she was the one that had come from the attic. She'd been mean and hostile when the Nazis were at the Lucroy's. None of them had ever gotten a close look at her. She'd use that for her advantage. She took a deep breath, whispered a soft goodbye to her friends, and darted out into the open, charging for the stairs. The Polish soldier and Devid gave cries of alarm but she was already down the stairs, her boots thudding heavily, her dress wrapping around her legs. She made it to the second level before rough hands imprisoned her. She stared around in shock. Five gray-green clad figures ringed the room followed by the Polish boy and Devid. She focused on him, noting a satisfied glow in his eyes. She bit back the scream of fear that built in her throat as she anticipated what was coming.

Anthony glanced around the dark room, lit in a ghostly light by the flashlight. The cries and quick footsteps from downstairs made him wary. Silently, he counted those around him. Leanne...*oui*. Leo...*oui*. Lovisa...*oui*. Gael...*oui*. Gerta...*oui*. Lidia...*oui*. Marc...*oui*. Nathan...*oui*. Esmé...*non*! He bolted to his feet. A cry of anguish slipped from his clenched throat. *Non!* Everyone was giving him strange looks. *'Esmé.'* he mouthed. Suddenly everything slipped into place. The strange lifting of the trapdoor. The cries. The footsteps.

Esmé had sacrificed herself for them!

Everyone in the attic, minus Leanne and Gael, gasped and raised their hands to their mouths. The dusty room went deathly silent as all were straining to hear what was happening downstairs. Voices were rising, one an octave higher than the others. A man screamed in rage. Another echoed in despair. Then a gunshot, followed by a muffled thud. Anthony looked around in shock. Lidia's red rimmed eyes met his, confirming the thought that was running around in his mind. Esmé had laid down her life for France. The kind girl, the one that had only wanted a family from life, was dead.

Chapter 18

Devid put the smoking pistol in its holster at his hip and stared at the slumped form of the girl on the floor in front of him. Her last moments had been spent defying him, staring him down and screaming insults. That didn't sit well with him. He scowled at the Polish soldier staring at him.

"Get rid of the body." He turned to walk away.

The soldier hurried after him.

"You shouldn't have done that. She could have been useful."

"Shut it, Albin. I don't need you telling me how to do my job. Especially since you owe me."

Albin snorted. "I don't owe you anything."

Devid's face distorted into rage. "You owe me your life!" he screamed in the red haired soldier's face. "And don't ever forget it!"

Albin took a step back.

"No, I don't. I was perfectly happy to die when you all invaded Poland, it would have been easier. I even wish that you had not interfered. Better die in Poland as a free man than be in a Nazi's debt!" he spat.

Devid's face hardened, his mouth a white slash across his face.

"I wish I hadn't either."

"Then kill me," Albin muttered, a hard determination glowing bright in his eyes.

"I can't," Devid retorted. "You know I can't."

A smug smile slowly crept across Albin's face.

"You've grown fond of me. How sweet." He gave a sassy grin, clapped his hands behind his back, and turned to the other soldiers. "You heard Kapitän Devid! Get rid of her!" He spun back to Devid. "It still feels weird calling you Kapitän. I don't like it." His face relaxed into an easy grin.

It felt odd to Devid, too. His sudden promotion seemed to be masking something horrible, something that still remained unseen. But he couldn't help but smile at his Private's happy face.

Albin was still talking.

"Why did you kill her? And the two in Épernay? I'm starting to think you are having too much fun with this."

Devid turned a weary glance at the young soldier. "Not enjoy. Just duty. Both were traitors to Germany and the *Führer*. It's my job. As it is to find the other French dogs that are hiding somewhere from here to Lille. Tell the troops to move out! We get back on the train as soon as we can."

He walked powerfully from the room, but his commanding walk masked worried thoughts. When Albin brought up the deaths of the young woman and middle aged man it sent a pang to his heart, but it also resurfaced a memory he was trying to forget: how he'd killed the little boy, Tristan, at the train station. Tristan had been a cute boy, one that he shouldn't have killed. But now that he had, he made sure to keep it a secret from Albin, knowing full well that the young soldier would freak out if he ever heard.

Albin stared after Devid, wondering what could be running through his mind, before spinning on his heel and calling orders to the soldiers behind him.

Leanne groaned and tossed fitfully. Her arm was burning and tears rolled down her cheeks. Anthony had told her an hour earlier about what had happened to Esmé. The burning in her arm wasn't anywhere near the burning in her heart. She'd given a small prayer of blessing and goodbye to Esmé, but the aching was still there.

She felt lonely and instantly looked for Anthony. He was gone. She flipped her head side to side looking for him, but to no avail. A man had been checking on her every now and then. Something had been put on her arm which had cooled the pain for a little while, but now it was back, seemingly worse. She groaned and struggled to sit up, but fell with a gasp back onto the table she was laying on. Someone moved into her line of sight. Lidia's pale, red rimmed eyes sought hers.

"Leanne, how do you feel?" Lidia placed a calming hand on Leanne's uninjured arm.

Leanne took a deep breath. "Hurts. Where's Anthony? How's Gael?"

She could tell by the pain rippling across Lidia's face that it was bad. Tears filled Lidia's eyes and she struggled to keep back the sobs. "Anthony's right outside. He'll be in in a moment."

She turned away, brushing feather soft fingers across Leanne's cheek.

Leanne struggled to touch Lidia's hand. "Gael?"

Lidia sadly shook her head, sobs shaking her body. "The doctor says there's hardly a chance of him surviving. The wound got infected, worse than yours. If he doesn't keep still for a while then...then..." Tears ran down her face as she sobbed uncontrollably.

Leanne tightened her grip. "Then we stay here for a while. Gael won't die. He's too strong. Don't worry, Lidia, he'll be fine." She wished the burning in her shoulder would lessen so she could give Lidia a hug.

Lidia gave a half smile, struggling to swallow her sobs. "You can't stay here. Not after what happened with Esmé. Anthony's getting ready to leave."

"He can't leave me! I won't—He can't!" Tears started pooling in her own eyes. Fear of being left behind surpassed the pain in her arm and she struggled to get up.

Lidia smiled sadly again, pushing Leanne back onto the bed. "*Non,* Leanne, he's not going to leave you," she whispered. "He's going to leave me and Gael. We're staying here. You're all going on without us, including Lovisa." She dropped to her knees and broke down in tears. "Take care of her, Leanne, please! Watch over Lovisa for me!" She dropped her head onto the table and sobbed. "She likes you a lot, even if she doesn't show it. She's scared and fragile, but she trusts you. She respects you. Please, Leanne, please."

Leanne clutched the older girl's hand. "I will. Don't worry, Lidia, I will."

WHEN THE SOLDIERS CAME

The door opened and Anthony walked in. His face was set, and he didn't bother with words. He scooped Leanne into his arms and turned to walk away. "Farewell, Lidia." His voice cracked. "I hope...I hope Gael gets better. I hope you can find a better life here. Good luck." He turned and strode away. Leanne peeked around his arm, catching a swift glance of Gael, pale faced and unmoving, lying on a table in a room similar to the one they'd just left. Her heart thudded painfully as they left the room.

Lovisa met them at the train car door, her hands on her hips, a determined curve to her mouth. "Where's my sister? And Gael?" Her eyes peered around, but quickly returned to Leanne's face.

Leanne struggled out of Anthony's arms and hurried to the girl, unable to stop the tears from falling.

"I'm so sorry, Lovisa! Gael's in danger, he could die if he moves! Lidia's staying behind with him! I'm sorry!" she cried. She pulled the small girl to her chest with her good arm.

Lovisa stood in shock, not comprehending the swift flowing words. She shot a pleading glance at Anthony. He didn't speak and instead brushed past Leanne and Lovisa with tears in his own eyes. Lovisa stared at him, then at the young woman holding her, then at the sparkling train station. Fear gripped her and she struggled out of Leanne's arms. "Where are they?" she demanded, stamping her foot in anger.

Leanne bit her lip, holding in another sob.

"They're staying behind." she explained slowly, tears rolling down her face.

Lovisa shook her head. "Lidia would never leave me!" She stomped her foot again and turned to run onto the station, sobs shaking her shoulders.

Nathan appeared and caught her arm. Leanne took a tentative step after her. "Lovisa, it's not my fault."

Gerta walked toward her, her face red and blotchy and her eyes puffy.

"It's okay, Leanne. She'll get over it. Come on, you got to get some sleep. We're going to Lille."

Leanne's head shot up. "What about Paris? The Prime Minister?" She turned to look over her shoulder at Nathan and Lovisa.

Anthony touched her arm making her look at him. Gravely, he shook his head. "*Non*. Nazis have been at every spot we've stopped. I have a feeling they know where we're going so we're not going to Paris after all. We're going to Lille right away. We'll mail the letter to the Prime Minister when we're in England."

Lovisa was sobbing in a corner. Nathan was rubbing her back and muttering to her under his breath. Leo and Marc were sitting sullenly in the back, their faces shadowed. Leanne turned her gaze back to Anthony.

"You're sure this is the best idea?"

Anthony rubbed a hand through her hair. "I'm hoping it is. What do you think?" He moved a little to look at her.

She snuggled closer to his side. "I'm with you, wherever. I believe it's the safest, and surely it will get us out faster."

WHEN THE SOLDIERS CAME

The train started to move, the boards shook and shivered. Many of them nodded off quickly after such an eventful day. Night fell outside. The sky remained empty. Starless.

Leanne squeezed Anthony's hand and crawled over to Lovisa, hoping to quiet the sobs that echoed in the empty boxcar.

Nathan had long since fallen asleep, along with Gerta, Leo, and Marc. Anthony could barely make out Leanne's soft voice as she whispered to Lovisa. Soon she started to sing, it was a famous lullaby called *Berceuse de Brahms*:

Bonne nuit, cher trésor.
Fermez les yeux et endormez-vous.
Laissez votre tête s'envoler, au creux de votre oreiller.
Un beau rêve passera et vous l'attraperez.
Un beau rêve passera et tu t'en souviendras.

It was a weird song, but it was peaceful and soon Lovisa was sleeping soundly. Leanne looked up and caught Anthony's eye.

"It's strange," she muttered, stroking Lovisa's hair. "We've grown up with French lullabies. She's grown up with bombs and gunfire." Tears shone in her eyes. "How can anyone do that to another person? How could anyone let that happen?"

Anthony shook his head, looking at the small figure curled into a tight ball beside Leanne's legs. "I don't know. I wish I had the answers. But I don't." He calmed himself by holding Leanne closer to him. "Leanne, do you think anyone else will die?"

She turned away, her brown eyes sparkling in the night.

"I don't know. I hope not. But we can never be sure right? I guess we have to trust in God."

Anger boiled in Anthony. "Again with God! Are you sure He even cares? If He does then why did He let Tristan and Esmé die? How could He take my parents? And my family? Did I do something to offend Him?" Tears slid down his face and he cursed himself for being weak.

Leanne was hardly shocked at his sudden outburst.

"Anthony, it's nothing you did. That's not how God works," she answered thoughtfully. "God's testing you. He needs to know if you're strong enough to keep believing in Him even if the world is breaking."

Anthony scoffed. "The world *is* broken. It'll never go back to what it was. The sooner we accept that the better off we'll be." He laid down and closed his eyes.

Leanne frowned. She opened her mouth to reply but thought better of it. Instead, she closed her eyes and laid down allowing the train to rock her to sleep.

Chapter 19

Leanne could smell the ocean before she saw it. The salty tang was in the air mixed with fish and seaweed. She hesitated on the train step. Lille was so different from the France she knew. The Nazis were desperate to keep hold on this city. She looked around and could see at least ten different buildings crumbling to the ground. Bullet holes and bomb craters were in every direction. The people were running by, never lifting their eyes off the pavement.

'Father, help me help them.'

Anthony grabbed her good arm and pulled her off the train.

"Let's try the wharf first. That's where the captain should be."

Lovisa was still crying, her hand clenched Nathan's. Leo looked tense. His eyes darted every which way as if he was looking for someone. Marc and Gerta were carrying on a whispered conversation. Anthony was still steaming from his conversation with Leanne. *'If there is a God, then He would care about His people more than this. He would have killed Hitler in his youth. He would have saved us from the tyranny of Germany.'*

Anthony turned and walked purposefully toward the gate motioning for the others to stay behind. As no German came to stop him, he disappeared behind the city walls. After five minutes, Gerta set out after him. Her ruffled dress was hidden beneath a trench coat. Lovisa refused to leave Nathan, so they walked in together. Marc went next.

Leanne looked at Leo. "Are you okay? You look a little pale."

"*Oui* I'm fine. Now get going." He pushed her roughly after the others.

She hurried through the thick walls and melted into the shadows, looking over her shoulder, a little hurt. Anthony was waiting for her, his face determined.

"We have to find a place to stay. All of us walking to the wharf together might draw attention. Might as well turn ourselves in if we do that. Come on," he added, seeing Leo come through the walls.

Anthony turned and sped off through the streets. At each corner, they would stop, decide a direction, then set off again.

Leanne couldn't help but compare this city to Reims. In Reims, there was content and happiness. Or there was before the Nazis had fully attacked. Even in the occupation, there was still happiness. This gray town seemed to have never belonged in peace time, its buildings all looked old and destroyed, as if they'd always been that run down. And surely the people never knew peace, their faces were tight but kind of relaxed, as if war was something normal to them. Children were begging on the streets, their clothes in rags, their faces gaunt and hollow. Nazi soldiers were standing on each corner, their guns held in front of their chests, their faces hidden by their wide brimmed helmets.

'Father keep us safe, let us be able to get out of here.'

WHEN THE SOLDIERS CAME

She looked around for men and women. She saw plenty of women; their hair tied back from their faces, their arms wrapped around themselves as if trying to hide. But where were the men? The only males she saw were the Nazis. She hurried forward and plucked on Anthony's sleeve.

"Where are all the men?" Even in Reims there were still older men and men unfit for the German army.

Anthony looked around. "I don't know, but that's not our problem right now, is it?"

Leanne blinked. "It is. As you, Nathan, Leo, and Marc are standing out like swans in a pond of ducks. Every Nazi eye has followed you guys. Mark my words...they know we're here."

Anthony scoffed off her warning and waited until she got back into her spot in line before sneaking a glance around. Sure enough, the two Nazis on the other side of the street were watching them intently. One nudged his companion and whispered something. The companion nodded, evidently confused. Anthony cursed silently, but continued forward. A warm, May night was falling fast and the people were hurrying to their homes. Nazis were having fun stopping people, harassing them, and then following them to see if they made it indoors before curfew. Anthony saw a soldier eyeing them and turned into the nearest building. The top half was falling apart but the bottom was still intact with quite a few rooms that he could see. He hurried back out, and motioned for everyone to get inside. The soldier stepped forward as Marc disappeared with Anthony and Leanne still outside. The soldier was young, about the same age as Anthony. "*Hallo, gute Nacht, nicht wahr?*"

Leanne swallowed nervously. Even though she understood everything the soldier had said, she decided to play innocent.

"What? I'm sorry, I don't understand what you're saying."

The soldier cocked his head, evidently wanting her to understand him. "*Gute Nacht, finden Sie nicht?*" he repeated, his eyes on her face.

Anthony grabbed Leanne's hand. "Let's go. Curfew is coming." He turned to go inside.

"Halt." The soldier raised his hand, palm out, fingers together. "Vhere are you going, *gnädige Frau und Herr?*"

Anthony shot Leanne a worried look. *'Oh, God, if you really are there then help!'* he cried silently. Suddenly words flooded into his mind.

"*Bonjour,*" he answered calmly. "We were heading into this building for the night. We were trying to get home, but the sun set faster than I thought it would. I'm Monsieur Bonsete and this is my wife, Paulette. Monsieur, please. If we don't get inside, we could get in trouble." He wrapped his arm around Leanne's waist and pulled her into him.

The soldier's brow furrowed. "You live here?" His accent tinted the words.

"*Non. Non.* We don't have enough time to get home. Please, Monsieur." Anthony cast his eyes about as if worried for his safety.

The soldier stepped back, dropping his hand.

"Alright, go inside." He turned and walked away.

Anthony felt weak, his head pounded. But his prayer had been answered and he knew it.

Leanne clutched his arm until they were safely behind the door.

WHEN THE SOLDIERS CAME

"Anthony, that was amazing!" She threw her arms around him. "I can't believe you just did that. I thought for sure we were going to be arrested."

Anthony hugged her back. "You were right," he responded, somewhat dazed.

Leanne frowned. "Right about what?"

Anthony leaned back until he was looking into her eyes. "There is a God, and He is watching over me. I didn't know until I just asked Him for help. And He answered.

Leanne's eyes filled with tears and hope. "You believe me?" A smile curved her lips. "You really do? And when did you ask?" Her face became a little skeptical.

Anthony sighed, "I didn't know how else to get the soldier away, I was out of ideas. So I prayed for help. God gave me the words to say, and it worked. Leanne, you were so right, I'm sorry I doubted you. Do you forgive me?"

Leanne dropped her arms from around him, giving a small smile. "*Oui*, I do."

Leanne lay for a while unable to sleep. The pounding of German boots echoed in the streets of Lille. She couldn't help but shed a few tears at the thought of leaving her home country, possibly never to return. As she cried, she suddenly thought of Jameson and Marius, and Rose. More tears filled her eyes. *'What had happened to them? Was Marius and Jameson still alive? Was Rose married and happy somewhere off in Paris?'*

Anthony rolled over and clutched her hand. "Leanne, what's wrong?"

"Nothing," she responded heavily. "I'll be alright, don't worry about me."

Anthony sat up. "Liar. What's wrong?"

"I miss them!" She cried softly, burying her face in her hands. "What if my brother is dead? What if Marius is captured? What if Rose is married?" she wept bitterly. "I'll never know! I'm leaving France. What if I never find out about my family and friends!"

Anthony wrapped his arms around her shoulders and pulled her into him. "It'll all work out. God has a plan, doesn't He?"

Leanne sniffed and wiped her nose on her sleeve. "*Oui,* it's just that I'm scared of leaving France. I've never done it before. It seems strange."

Anthony was kind of shocked. He rubbed a hand down her back. "Just think of it as an adventure. And I'll be by your side the entire time."

"I know. I'm sorry."

"You never have to be sorry to me, Leanne. Never. I understand. Now get some rest, we should be leaving in an hour or so."

The air was heavy. Dark clouds filled the sky. Anthony stared at the frothing, gray water. The waves rolled heavily before crashing onto the docks making all the boats shiver violently. His stomach rolled with the ocean. He glanced around. The city lay in darkness. The last bit of sun was swallowed up in the thick clouds. He looked down at his clothes, he knew he should be thankful for the disguise as it would make sure he wasn't recognized and killed, but wished that it'd come from somewhere other than the rubbish pile. He wore a stained and tattered brown shirt, ragged trousers, and a jacket riddled with holes and a scarf that smelled awful. Leanne had carefully given him makeup, turning his hair black, and giving him the look of a starving person. He had to walk stooped and broken, as if he had been spared from the army on account of a broken leg. He snuck onto the wharf and across the water stained planks. A man watched him carefully, then stepped forward. "You! Lad! Where are you heading?"

Anthony tensed. The voice wasn't speaking German or French, it was some other language. *"Je rentre à la maison. Je me suis fait prendre après le couvre-feu. S'il vous plaît, ne me dénoncez pas!"*

The Englishman frowned. "I don't speak that bloody tongue of yours," he whispered violently. Thinking for a moment, he took a chance. "Where are you going?" he asked again, changing his language to German.

Anthony responded in kind, repeating his statement. The Englishman laughed deeply. His face was kind and weather worn with lines around his eyes from smiling and squinting into the sun. He wore a blue coat, but a band with the Nazi swastika was on his arm. Anthony's eyes drew to the slip of scarlet fabric again and again. The English captain saw the fear in his eyes and clapped a calming hand on his shoulder.

"Fear not. If I could tear it off I would."

"You're not of the Nazi party?"

"What you ask is treason." The captain pointed out.

"Maybe. Is the wind fair? The sea high?" Anthony looked at the angry water as he spoke, hoping that he'd guessed right.

The captain bit his lip. "*Ja,* the wind is fair and not too slow. But for your other question...No, the sea is not high." He looked at the swirling water. "It was high but an hour ago." He steered Anthony onto the deck of a ship. "I wasn't expecting you so soon," he murmured in English, then switched to German. "I thought you were some beggar." He took in Anthony's attire. "You are great with disguises."

"*Merci.* Now...here." He pulled the worn letter from his coat pocket.

The captain took it with a coarse hand and opened the flap. "You are not the only one?"

"*Non,* Sir. My girlfriend and five others accompany me. We are being hunted ruthlessly and have already lost two members to death, and two others to dangerous wounds. We would be very obliged if we could set sail at the earliest time."

The captain nodded. "Come at midnight. The sea should be lower with a quick wind. I shall get you all to safety."

Leanne clutched Lovisa's hand and together they walked swiftly toward the docks. Unable to see anything in the black out, they went by sound, listening to the water dashing on the planks and rocks. The others weren't far away. As they neared the ship, Leanne paused, fear rooting her feet to the ground. Lovisa tugged at her hand. "Leanne, come on! We have to go!" she whispered earnestly. "Please!"

Leanne shook violently. "I can't." She ripped her hand from Lovisa's weak grip. *'Father! I need thee! Give my thy strength! Please, Father!'* A stronger hand closed over her wrist and dragged her forward. Anthony had come to pull her aboard.

"Halt!" The German voice was strong and loud. "Halt!"

Fear drove Leanne's legs quicker. Anthony was running. She was running. Lovisa was running. As they neared the ship, Anthony started shouting.

"Get ready to pull out! The Nazis are on us!"

Gerta and Nathan were rushing from a different direction. Leo and Marc from another. The captain was watching with horror from the gangplank thrown from the ship to the dock. A cry of despair made Anthony and Leanne turn. Gerta and fallen, and Nathen with her. Soon, they were surrounded. German voices screamed at them to lay down and not move. Anthony jerked Leanne and Lovisa forward. As they neared the ramp, the captain stretched down his hand, and grabbed Lovisa. "Come on, Darling, let's get you safe." He raised his eyes and locked onto someone behind them. Quickly he jerked Lovisa onto the ship, giving a warning cry to Leanne, who was trying to get up the gangplank, and Anthony, who was waiting for her to board.

Anthony looked over his shoulder, and gasped. Leo had stopped running and he held a smoking pistol. Marc was sprawled on the ground at his feet, blood pooling around him.

Leanne gasped. "Leo?"

Leo leveled the pistol. "Anthony, Leanne, dismount. Captain, give me the girl."

Anthony threw himself forward, upsetting the plank and causing Leanne to tumble to the dock. The captain gave a yell as the ship pulled away from the dock which had been held fast by two ropes, one on the stern and the other on the bow. Anthony turned to face Leo who was quickly walking toward them. He reached out and punched Leo in the face. He quickly pulled a knife from his coat. He ran the length of the ship, severing the stern rope. As he made his way to the bow, a cry made him halt. Leo was standing again. Leanne was on her knees in front of him with his arm around her neck and the pistol at her head. Anthony was close enough to cut the rope but he stood frozen. He stared at Leo.

Leo smiled viciously, blood spilling from his mouth and newly crooked nose.

"Anthony, you cut the rope, I'll kill her. Drop the knife into the water. Now!" he screamed. The Nazis were quickly crowding around them, their eyes amused at the scene in front of them.

Leanne's eyes met Anthony's. *'Trust Him.'* she mouthed, glancing upward. *'Trust God.'*

Anthony slashed with the knife and watched with satisfaction as the rope severed and fell with a splash into the water.

"God is good." He dropped to his knees and waited.

Leo cried in anguish. Lovisa screamed over the sound of the wind and water. Nazi soldiers ran forward and roughly grabbed Anthony, throwing him to the deck in front of Leo. Angrily, Leo threw Leanne from him and buried his foot in Anthony's face.

"You will regret that. I'll never let you forget it!"

"*Sohn, hör auf.*" A figure broke off from the group of soldiers and stepped forward placing a hand on the angry boy's shoulder. "He'll regret his actions in *Dachau*."

Fear shot through Anthony. The man was Devid, and he'd called Leo his son. Devid knelt and brushed his hand across Leanne's face, then slapped her. "Albin!"

The red-haired soldier stepped forward. "*Ja*, Kapitän?"

"Take them all to the train. It leaves for Germany at dawn. Kaleb." He turned to Leo. "Go with them, my son. You've done Germany a great service. You will be rewarded handsomely." He turned and walked away. "I'll meet you there."

The Leo they knew smiled again. His chest puffed slightly. "You heard my Father. Now!"

Anthony was yanked to his feet and his hands bound behind his back. Leanne beside him. Marc was pulled into a sitting position, his face was pale and worn. Blood soaked the front of his coat. Gerta and Nathan were dragged over. Anthony looked around at his friends. Leanne met his eyes, her confident smile was gone, replaced with terror. They had been found. They were going to Germany.

Chapter 20

Leanne rolled over and groaned. Every muscle protested and burned at her slight movement. Her hands were numb as the flow of blood had been cut off by the rough shackles tight around her wrists. The rough boards were uncomfortable. She struggled to sit up and gasped. The healing her shoulder had gone through was coming undone. Blood slid down her arm. Nazis were standing guard around the small shack she was laying in. She shivered. Even though it was spring, it was still frigid. Someone approached. The door was thrown in and Leo, or Kaleb as he was actually known, was standing there. The ripped and tattered clothes he'd been wearing for the past few weeks were replaced. Now it was a German uniform. The swastika danced on his arm. A pistol sat snug on his hip. He smiled sadly at her.

"You know, I did like you." He dropped to one knee. Unlike the other Nazis, he seemed uncomfortable standing above her.

She scowled. "You were never on our team, were you?"

"France is lost. You really bought my story? A rich school boy stranded in Reims?" He laughed brokenly. "My heart belongs to Germany. My Father initiated me into the army and

I infiltrated France easily. And your little spy ring. If Anthony wasn't so noble, I would have succeeded in getting you all."

Leanne caught a bit of joy at the words. She was really confused.

"What about Gael and Lidia?"

The question burst from her before she was able to stop it.

Kaleb half grinned. "Others may lie to you, but I know it would benefit me nothing. Lidia waited two days for Gael to heal before dragging him onto a train and disappearing. I heard she made it to England. I hope she finds her sister, if a submarine doesn't sink Lovisa's ship first." He got to his feet. "I'm sorry, Leanne. I wish I could spare you from this, but Father believes that you deserve it. And I have to agree with him. Goodbye." His eyes were slightly shiny, but when Leanne looked closer all she saw was anger.

Leanne shook her head. "I don't need your pity or your mercy. God's mercy is enough for me. Though you send me to my death, God is with me. If I die, I will be back in his arms. I hope one day I can forgive you, Leo or Kaleb, whichever you prefer. God still loves you, and I know I should love you because He does. And I want you to know that I will—in time. Goodbye."

Hurt and embarrassed, Kaleb turned and strode from the shack. Albin stepped toward him. "Father is on the platform, Kaleb. Go, before he gets upset." He turned to walk away.

"Brother!"

Albin turned and stared at his half brother. "What, Kaleb?"

"How's Mother?"

Albin smiled. "Worried about *her* son, but otherwise fine."

Kaleb ran forward and matched his gait with Albin's. "Do you still fancy yourself Polish? After all, Father is German."

Albin grinned. "*Tak*. After all, I'm only half German, that means I'm half Polish."

"Why?" He skipped beside his older brother. "Why would you even want to admit to being half a Pole?"

Albin glanced at his younger brother. "I'm Polish and German, I take pride in both."

"Are you saying you aren't on our side?" Kaleb's face pulled into a frown.

Ablin placed a hand on his brother's shoulder. "I'm on both sides brother. Evenly split. I'm with Poland, but I'm also with Germany."

Kaleb shook his head. "I thought they were going to kill you for being half German? They would have, too, if Father hadn't intervened and saved you."

"They were." He patted Kaleb's back and made him take a few steps, "Those in Germany were also going to kill me for being half Polish. I don't belong in either. But I trust both."

Devid was waiting for them. His face lifted in a harsh grin as he looked at his sons. "Kaleb, I'm very proud of you. Your mother has missed you these past four years. You are to accompany me back to Munich, for a while before I send you to your brother. Albin, go with the train. Make sure the prisoners get handed to the officer of *Duchau*, personally. They are traitors to the *Führer*. I want them treated as such." He turned and strode away.

Albin watched as his brother shifted uncomfortably. "You okay?" he asked.

"Yeah." Kaleb threw a confused glance over his shoulder, staring at the small group of shacks five feet away from each other. Marc was in one of them, probably trying not to bleed to death. Kaleb swallowed painfully.

Albin nudged him. "Feeling a bit conflicted?"

"*Ja.* I got to know them, they were my friends." In truth the only two he ever felt really close to were Marc: Who'd probably never speak to him again. And Esmé: Who was now dead, killed by his Father.

He blinked back tears and turned from his brother.

Albin watched him. "You know, I wasn't going to tell Father about you all leaving."

"You weren't?"

"*Nie.* Until you told me to. I could tell you were confused and conflicted. Your voice was shaking. Why?"

"I didn't want to tell you. I was going to run with them. I could have too. I could've not contacted you at all. I could have run away." He took a shuddering breath. "If I'd done it, I would've contacted you to tell you I was in England. What would you have done?"

"I would've found my way to you. Both of us are being used, you know that." The train blew its whistle as the sun shone over the mountains, its warmth instant and soothing. Albin threw his arms around his brother. "*Bądź bezpieczny.* I love you. See you after all this is over."

Kaleb nodded, then looked over his brother's shoulder. Leanne, Anthony, and the others were being pulled from the shacks. Each one's hands were bound. Anthony's face was bruised and bleeding. Leanne's face was worried and panicked. Marc was leaning heavily on the soldier leading him, his hands pressed to his stomach. Gerta had a bruise darkening on her jaw and she was slightly limping. Nathan was walking confidently, but with fear shining in his eyes.

Albin pulled open a boxcar door, helped the prisoners into it, and unlocked their bonds. Albin mounted the passenger car steps. As he closed the door, he turned and waved farewell to Kaleb. The train whistle pealed and pulled out of the station.

Leanne rolled over and crawled to Anthony. The boxcar was empty except for them and sodden straw. It smelled awful. Anthony looked up and pulled her to his side.

"Leanne, are you okay?"

She nodded silently. He glanced down at her and saw tears rolling down her face. He brushed his thumb across her cheek, lingering a little.

"Leanne?"

"I'm fine," she muttered, leaning against his chest. "How are you? How's your face?" She winced as she looked at it. His eye was bruised and half his mouth sagged.

He caught her hand and squeezed it gently. "It's good, I just have a headache. How's your arm?"

She rolled her shoulder and slightly winced. "Okay. It smarts now." She glanced around the drafty boxcar. "Anthony, are you scared?"

"*Oui.*"

"How far away is *Dachau*?"

"Well," he pondered for a moment. "From Lille to *Dachau* during times of peace is about seven hours to a day, but in war time I just don't know. We may be picking up other prisoners; it could be weeks before we finally get there."

Nathan looked up from where he was sitting. "What day is it?"

Leanne cocked her head. "June 1st."

Anthony leaned his head back against the wall. "We should get some rest."

One by one, the others fell asleep. Leanne glanced around, a feeling of panic eating at her heart. She brushed the tears off her face and got to her knees restlessly. *Father, I need thy help. Thou knowest what's going on. Thou knowest we're in big trouble. Father, please help me. Help Anthony. Help Gerta, Marc, and Nathan. Give us the strength to stand up for what is right. Give us the strength to stay strong in the trials that have been given to us. Please Father, I'm scared. Help me, please.'* The train jerked suddenly, causing her to slam to the ground. She raised her head dazedly. *'Father, help me trust you.'*

The train slowed to a stop, screeching as the wheels ground together. The door was thrown open and the red haired soldier from the Lucroys stepped in, a depressed sag to his mouth. He nodded slightly and sank to the ground by the door, his rifle laying across his lap. Another soldier followed, sitting on the other side.

Leanne sat, paralyzed with fear, until Anthony's hand slid into hers. She looked over and offered a half smile. Anthony squeezed her hand and pulled her to him. "Go to sleep, Leanne. I won't let anything happen to you."

Chapter 21

The train ride was long, bumpy, and uncomfortable. Leanne couldn't ever remember a time when she wished she was home more than now. They were all given a slice of bread and a cup of dirty water a day. Other than eating and slight conversation, the days were spent dreaming about food, warm clothes, family, and freedom. Sometimes there were nightmares and sad thoughts about where they were headed. Rumor had it that *Duchau* was a horrible place and anyone who was sent there didn't return.

After the fifth day on the train, Leanne was leaning against the wall when a commotion made her look up. The train had been paused for over three hours because of a delayed bomb on the tracks. It didn't seem to be moving any time soon. The Nazi soldiers were having a whispered argument. The red haired soldier, Leanne heard him called Albin, was trying to keep his comrade, Dirk, from leaving the train. "Don't get off. *Proszę.*"

Leanne blinked at the unfamiliar word that wasn't German, which both soldiers had been speaking. It wasn't French or Italian either.

Dirk was struggling to get the door open as Albin tugged on his arms, ripping and pulling him away.

"Get off!" Dirk screamed. "I'm not dying for your stupid prisoners! I'll just be in the next car!" He jerked the door, making Albin groan.

"It's not about the prisoners! You were asked to guard them. You were placed in the boxcar with them! That means you stay with them!" Albin tugged the door back.

Dirk frowned. "Let's get out of here! We could die!"

Just then there was sudden pounding on the roof. Both Nazis dropped to the ground, throwing their arms over their heads, one screamed *feindliches Flugzeug.* Enemy aircraft.

The others woke and sat up, sleep driven from their eyes as they recognized gunfire on the roof of the train. Leanne tensed and slid closer to Anthony, who's arms quickly drew her to him. The bullets rained down for only a few seconds. As silence settled around everyone, an anguished cry came from Marc. Leanne painfully uncrunched herself from the tight ball she'd been in and crawled to Marc's side. Gerta was sprawled on the floor in front of them, her face drained of color. Her hair swept around her face. Blood slipped from her mouth. Her hands were wrapped around her stomach, and she was staring dazedly at the roof. Leanne gasped and felt the tears in her eyes.

"Gerta?" Leanne whispered, worried.

She didn't answer.

Nathan hurried over and placed two of his fingers on Gerta's neck. He waited for a few seconds, then pressed a little harder. Tears filled his eyes and he turned away. "She's gone."

Marc sobbed again. "*Non!*" He grabbed one of Gerta's unresisting hands. "Gerta! Gerta, answer me!" He bit his lip and sobbed.

WHEN THE SOLDIERS CAME

Leanne sighed. She expected tears to roll down her face, but they didn't. She'd cried so much in the last few days that she couldn't now. Anthony however turned away and crawled back to his spot, tears shining on his cheeks.

Albin and Dirk walked over. Dirk's face was hard. "Get away!"

Everyone else backed off, but Marc stayed beside her. Dirk raised an arm to strike Marc, but Albin caught his wrist. "*Naprawdę?* What are you going to do with the body? We'll be at a station before the sun sets; we can get rid of it there."

Dirk growled and turned away, his face melting into a scowl. Albin opened his mouth to say something but paused and thought better of it. Leanne watched the Nazi worriedly. His face was light, but pain filled. He kind of looked familiar but she couldn't place where. The soldier noted her ponderous expression and turned to her. "*Cześć.*"

She frowned. "What?"

He smiled, transforming his dark look to something bright.

"I said "Hi" It's Polish."

Leanne's eyes brightened, she always loved learning new languages. Polish is one she'd never thought of until she'd met Lovisa and Lidia.

"You speak Polish?" She knew she should be sad, but she couldn't think about losing Gerta right now. It was too painful. She slid to the other side of the boxcar before Nathan, Marc, and Anthony caught her excitement.

The soldier blinked in surprise. "*Ja.* And German."

"I'm Leanne." She sank against the wall, sticking her hand out.

The soldier hesitated. "Albin. And are you sure you're supposed to be talking to me? I am the enemy."

Leanne shrugged. The soldier did speak the truth. Everyone told her that she was supposed to hate the Nazis, but God had said love everyone. She'd rather do that than hate people.

"Maybe on Earth but not in Heaven. So, Polish and German?"

Albin smiled. "Yep. My father, Devid, is German. My mother, Julia, was Polish."

"Was?"

"She died when I was two. I was raised in Poland by my Grandmother."

"What about your father?"

"When he heard, he came and collected me. He brought me back to Germany to meet his new wife and my half brother. When I was ten I went back to Poland. After war broke out and Germany invaded Poland, my neighbors turned on me and would have killed me as a traitor because of my German blood, but my father was one of the officers posted in my village and saved me. He sent me to Germany and I became a soldier. Along with my brother, Kaleb."

"Kaleb's your brother?" Leanne couldn't keep the anger out of her voice.

Albin caught it. "*Przepraszam.* I find his actions horrible. You were his friends, he should have treated you all better."

The train shuddered and started moving. Leanne was silent for a moment. "You said your neighbors would have killed you because of your German blood. Why? You'd lived with them for a while."

Albin nodded sadly. "That wasn't enough apparently."

"So were the Germans glad to have you?"

"*Nie.* They too wanted to kill me, until they learned who my father was. I just don't belong anywhere."

Leanne went to answer but saw Anthony watching her. She gave a half smile and turned away from Albin.

Marc was silent for the rest of the day, his face was red and his eyes were rimmed constantly with tears. He hadn't spoken a word since they last saw Gerta's body. Nathan tried talking to him; tried getting him to eat whatever food they were given, but he didn't respond to anything.

Leanne laid awake for two nights straight listening to Marc talk to himself. She wanted to talk to him, but didn't think it would help. *'Father, spare us from this. We haven't even gotten to Dachau and already we're breaking. Please, Father, help us.'*

Anthony rolled over and clutched her hand. "Leanne, are you awake?"

She nodded. "*Oui.* Did you need something?"

"Why is God letting this happen? What did we do wrong? Where is He now? If he's already tested us, then why do these things keep happening?" His face was pinched in anger and sadness.

Leanne slid closer to him. "I don't think we did anything wrong. It's the Nazis and Hitler, they're making this happen."

Anthony frowned. "If God cares so much, then why? Why kill Esme? And Gerta? And Tristan? Why is so much evil happening in our world? He could stop it, we both know he could."

Leanne shook her head. "He could, yes. But he can't. All people came down to Earth and got agency, that was one of the main things in God's plan. He can't take that away just because evil seems like it's winning a battle. No, because there is good, there is and always will be, bad. We just need to trust Him. He can't run everyone's life to make sure no bad ever happens, but He will save us in the end."

The train shuddered and ran on in the night, its whistle squealing every hour. Anthony didn't answer and Leanne drifted off to sleep.

"Leanne! Leanne!"

Someone was calling her, but she didn't want to wake up. She tossed her head and rolled over, trying to get away from the voice. She was at home with Jameson and Maruis. It wasn't time for her to get up yet and Jaemson didn't have a reason to want her up right now. A hand touched her face. It was Jameson. She leaned into his hand, missing his touch. His eyes lit up and he smiled widely. Then he opened his mouth. "Leanne!" Leanne recoiled. It wasn't Jameson's voice. "Leanne!" the voice said again.

She sat up. "What?" she asked groggily, wondering where she was. Then she saw Marc and Nathan. Her stomach dropped and she wanted to cry. She wasn't home. She was still on the train. It had been a dream.

Anthony's grave face met hers. "We're in Germany."

Albin and Dirk walked over with cuffs in their hands.

"Stand up!" Dirk demanded, his voice edged on boredom.

WHEN THE SOLDIERS CAME

The four young adults complied, stifling moans as they stretched their cramped joints. Albin cuffed Leanne and Anthony as Dirk cuffed Nathan and Marc. Albin walked to the door of the train car.

"Do not speak unless personally addressed. Any noise will be met with swift punishment." He yanked the door open and disappeared in the blinding morning light.

Dirk used his gun to herd them to the entrance. Once there, they were dragged to the ground. Nazi soldiers by the hundreds were crowded around. Some were dismounting train stairs, others were boarding. Some were walking with girls, and others were romping with other soldiers. Leanne tried looking at the country she'd been told a lot about. The place was crowded. German citizens were walking down the streets, shopping and sightseeing as if there wasn't a war going on. The constant reminder were the soldiers, but the people walked by them, sometimes even starting up conversations as they passed. Leanne felt a rough hand shove her forward and stumbled up to a car. People gawked as they saw Anthony, Nathan, Marc, and Leanne's tattered clothes and dirty faces. They looked at these prisoners disgracefully.

The car door was yanked open and she was shoved in. She slid out of the way as the boys were thrown in after her. Just before Nathan got in, a German voice cried. "*Nien*. Not him. He's a doctor, he's going to the hospital."

Hands gripped Nathan's jacket and yanked him away from the car. His face was pale and worried. *'Au revoir.'* he mouthed as he was pulled away. Leanne looked down, allowing the tears to finally run off her cheeks. *'Father, protect him. And protect us.*

Keep us safe, Father, please.' Anthony bumped her lightly with his arm, but she didn't look up.

Two German soldiers got in the car, Albin was one of them. They started chatting about what was happening in the war in different locations. Leanne didn't know what to actually believe. They talked an awful lot about how Germany was winning. As the car started moving, Leanne looked sadly out the window, tears sliding down her face. Anthony's bound hands rested in her lap. Marc leaned back in his seat, his eyes closed. Leanne closed her eyes and leaned against Anthony's shoulder.

The stopping of the car made Leanne jerk upright. She blinked the sleep from her eyes and peered out the window. Her heart nearly stopped. In front of them was a wide gate. Thick brick walls ran from the gate out of sight. Through the bars of the gate Leanne could see a few buildings. What scared her the most was the inscription she read on the gate... *"Arbeit macht frei."* "Work sets you free."

She couldn't contain her tears. They had arrived. They were at *Dachau*.

Chapter 22

Leanne bet over and dug her shovel into the muddy ground. She ached everywhere. Her stomach pinched with hunger. She let her mind wander as she rhythmically dug a trench. *'They had arrived on June ninth. Spent two days being "Convicted and Charged" and then set to work. It was now July twenty fifth.'* She bit back a groan as she saw a Nazi soldier walking by. She looked around at all the people working with her. Nearly three thousand mud-caked, hardly clothed, starving men and women, all bending over in the rain, digging a trench to drain a marsh for more bunkers. She sighed sadly. *'Only three hours. Then I'll see Anthony and Marc.'* She dug the shovel deeper and tossed the mud over her shoulder. She felt weak and dizzy. Her stomach growled. She took a deep breath and tossed another shovelful of mud. A man beside her slipped in the pouring rain and struggled to get up.

A Nazi soldier, attracted by the other workers' shocked cries, hurried over and pulled a gun. "Get up!" he demanded. "*Jetzt!*"

Leanne watched in horror as the older man tried but was so overcome with fatigue that he sank back down again, shaking and shivering. The soldier yelled a few more times before coming to the conclusion that it was of no use and fired his gun. The shot rang loudly in the coming night, making everyone pause. Every prisoner turned to look at what happened before hurrying back to their work. Leanne could only stare as the man's body stilled in the mud. The soldier pointed at two other working men. "Take the body to the train!"

The two men, glad for the change of job, dropped their shovels quickly. One pulled himself out of the six foot trench and laid down on the side, his arms falling back into the trench. The other pulled the body from the mud and hoisted it up until the first man grabbed it. Then the second pulled himself out and helped haul the body away. Together, they lifted the dead man and shuffled up the steep incline that added to the depth of the trench, a soldier following them closely.

Feeling sick, Leanne turned away and got back to work.

An alarm blared loudly, signaling quitting time. The taller prisoners hauled themselves out of the trench, but the smaller ones struggled to reach the top. Leanne tossed her shovel first, hoping that it wouldn't slide back down into her face, and strove to get a good grip on the slippery mud. A man saw her and caught her hand. He wasn't strong, like other workers in the camp, but Leanne didn't weigh much and the man easily pulled her out.

"*Merci*," she whispered softly.

"*Værsågod*." the man responded.

Leanne blinked. The language was unfamiliar to her. He could have been saying "You're welcome" or "Shut up", but the kind smile on his face and the soft squeeze he gave her hand before walking off made her believe he'd said "You're welcome."

All the prisoners were forced into a line to march back to the bunkers. They passed a shed where they would place their tools for the night. By now, it was pitch black outside and Leanne made her way by the sound of footfalls and screaming Nazis. She stumbled along, making sure not to trip over her prison dress or slip in the mud. All the prisoners were herded into a tight line. A bowl was thrown into their hands, then a spoonful of dirty soup. They walked along to get a roll before hurrying to their bunks.

Leanne cradled the food in her hands. It wasn't much, and usually wasn't very edible, but at least it was something. She had to wait in what felt like a mile long line before even getting close to the bunkers. Taking a quick look around, she slid out of the women's line and into the men's. The two men she'd got between smiled a little, but fear was visible in their eyes. Leanne prayed that they'd stay silent and allow her into the men's bunker. As they passed the guard at the door, neither man said a thing and she breathed a sigh of relief as she slipped in unnoticed. By the time she got inside, her food was cold. Little insects were swimming around in it. She gagged as she looked at it, feeling sick. She waded through the thin boards and skimpy mattresses until she found Anthony's and Marc's. She settled on the bed and started eating the roll. Halfway through, she felt sick and placed it on the bed beside her. She pulled her knees to her chin, laid down on the skimpy mattress, and waited. Soon enough, the tall figure of Anthony made its way toward her. He had changed greatly, but was still handsome. He was thin, his eyes haunted and always looking for food. Fresh bruises and cuts on his face, arms, and hands mingled with old ones and scars, but the smile that lit his face when he caught her eye was the same as it had been four years ago. She sat up and made room for him, her heart feeling lighter than it had in days. He started eating, which made her gag again. Anthony laughed. "You know, they add a little flavor." He joked, flicking a bug from his food.

Leanne gagged. "Gross."

"Well, living in these fine conditions, I guess you can afford to be picky," he smiled at her, then grimaced as something crunched in his mouth.

Leanne turned away, retching.

Anthony smiled apologetically. "*Désolé.*" he offered.

"*Non*, you're fine." She turned back to him. "Where's Marc?" She looked at Anthony's food again. Her stomach flopped.

Anthony shrugged. "I don't know. I was on the wall. He was doing the fence ahead of me."

"Lucky." Leanne moaned enviously. "I had the trench." She motioned to the mud under her fingernails. She'd done her best to wipe it off her face, hair, arms, and dress, and she'd done pretty good, but she'd never been able to get the mud from her nails.

Anthony grinned. "How deep is it now?"

"Six feet, I couldn't get out by myself. Someone helped me."

"Kind of them." Anthony murmured through a mouthful of food.

Just then Marc walked up. He had changed from the fit young man of a few months ago, to a beat up and defeated version of himself. He half-smiled at them as he hauled himself onto the bed. Leanne sat between the two men so they could block her if any guard decided to patrol the bunks. "How was work?" Leanne asked, staring at the ceiling.

Marc swallowed. "Good." He spit something out of his mouth. "I think they get harder every time," he muttered, watching the bug hit the ground and scuttle off.

"Disgusting." Leanne shuddered. "How do you eat that?" She looked back down at her bowl and pulled out an inch long bug. She crushed it between her fingers and tossed it away.

Marc smiled. "They supply a surprise. You never know if it's a maggot or a grasshopper. Besides, they add vitamins."

"You're disgusting."

She flicked another one away. Something stung her arm and she slapped the large flea, itching the red bump it raised on her arm.

Anthony saw it and frowned. "The fleas get bolder, too. You'd think they owned this place," he scowled and swatted at one by his head.

Marc pushed his empty bowl to the base of the board. "I wouldn't mind giving it to them. I want to go home." He pulled his legs up and spun around. "Good night." Soon he was asleep.

Leanne leaned against Anthony. "How do we live like this?" she asked softly, her head laying on his shoulder.

Anthony wrapped his arm around her shoulder and pulled her closer. "It's not living. It's more like surviving. Even then, that runs out of meaning for some people."

Leanne nodded in agreement thinking of the man that had been killed this morning. He'd been too tired to even get up. She blinked back the tears in her eyes. *'Father, help us. Please. We can't go on like this.'*

"Do you ever think of home?" she whispered, changing the subject.

"Which home?" Anthony answered sleepily. He tightened his arm around her, pulling her to his chest. "The one I had with my uncle? The Lucroy's? The one I imagine having with you after the war?"

She nodded slowly. "Any of them." He'd said things like that a lot, but each time it made her a little happier.

He sighed. "*Oui.* All the time. But there's only one I like thinking of." He rested his cheek on her head and closed his eyes.

Leanne lay awake for a while listening to his strong heartbeat. *'Father, give us a way to find the home we both want. Please, Lord.'*

"Me too." she muttered before nudging him a little. "Anthony, I've got to go. The guards will be here soon."

He opened his eyes. "Good night. I'll see you tomorrow?"

Leanne shrugged. "I'll try." Then she slid off the bunk and melted into the darkness between the rows of beds.

Leanne stared in shock at the trench. Her heart sank to her toes as she glared at the two feet of water sloshing in the bottom. She teetered for a moment, her torn boots struggling to grip the wet incline. The rain had stopped, letting the sun come out with all its force. Already she was soaked in sweat, and knew that it would only get hotter. *'Father, why?'* she moaned silently.

The prisoner that had helped her out of the trench yesterday smiled as he walked up. "You ready?"

She grinned. "Best get started." She jumped into the trench, wrinkling her nose as her boots sunk into the water and mud. The water had soaked the ground, making it squishy. A bucket was thrown in after her and she quickly filled it up with water, giving a tug on the rope when it was full. As that bucket was pulled up, another was thrown on the other side.

Someone jumped in beside her. "This is awful." The man moved around a little, shuddering as the mud squelched under his feet. Leanne looked over as she recognized that voice, then laughed softly to herself as she saw Marc.

She glanced around to see if any guards were around before saying, "Nice of you to drop by."

Marc laughed quietly. "You've been doing this for a week and a half?"

"Yeah, it's pretty awful. Why are you here? How's the fence going?" She ducked as a bucket sailed over her head. A muttered apology in another language made her smile and nod in the direction it came from.

Marc grinned. "They thought I was too slow to keep on the fence. And I hate it. There's so much barbed wire and electrical things; it's so annoying. Glad I'm here."

Leanne grinned as she grabbed a bucket and filled it. "Well, by the end of the day, tell me what you think." She laughed quietly as she filled another bucket. Maybe today wouldn't be as bad. *'Merci, Father.'*

After half the day, a guard screamed at them to switch out. Marc jumped out with ease, and went to help Leanne when a guard kicked him and sent him sprawling. The guard turned to Leanne and ordered her out of the trench. She tried to obey, but the mud was too slippery and she was too short. She couldn't reach the top. The guard reached down and grabbed her arm, yanking her out of the trench, then dropped her at his feet. He sneered in disgust and struck Leanne across the face, whipping it to the side. He walked away, laughing darkly.

Marc crawled over to Leanne. "Are you okay?"

She nodded, pressing a hand to her bleeding mouth. "I've had worse."

Marc's face hardened. "Anthony will not be happy to hear this." He moved Leanne's hand and winced at the rapid swelling of her cheek and lip. "We need to leave."

Leanne stared at him. "Leave?" *'What was he talking about? They couldn't leave.'*

"*Oui.*" Marc replied cautiously. He lowered his voice. "Anthony and I have been talking about it for weeks. We're going to run away."

Chapter 23

Anthony caught Leanne's hand before she disappeared that night. "Leanne, get out of the camp and head to the hill beside the fence around midnight."

She frowned. "Tonight? We're leaving tonight?" Her voice rose in a controlled shrill. "We can't leave. We'll get caught and killed."

Anthony pulled her into a hug. "I'll protect you, like always. And God's here for us." He gave her a smile. "Aren't you always telling me He's there for us? I believe in Him. You believe in Him. So now we just have to trust in Him."

Leanne nodded shakily. "Okay. I'll see you tonight."

Anthony pressed his fist to his mouth as he leaned against the rough brick building at his back. Marc was on the ground beside him, his head between his knees. Anthony took a deep breath. "Marc," he whispered, wincing at the sound of his own voice. "Did anyone see us?"

Marc raised his head, blowing out a breath. "*Non.* They didn't," he gasped, clutching his chest.

Frantic and loud footsteps sounded around them. Anthony turned in panic, his eyes wide with fear. "Do you think they saw Leanne?"

The cry of soldiers and the barking of dogs echoed in the night air. Marc shook his head and tried to hide in the shadow. "Leanne's too smart. Only those that know her well would be able to find her, even in broad daylight. I think she's already at the hill, waiting for us."

Anthony took a hesitant step out of the shadows. "Follow me closely. I don't want us to get separated." Then, waiting a few seconds, he charged across the cloudy courtyard and into the shadow of another building. "Marc, you ready?" Anthony spun around to look at him. "Marc?" Marc was nowhere in sight. It was as if he'd vanished. "Marc!" he called in a whisper, praying silently that the soldiers wouldn't hear him. "Marc!"

Running footsteps and barking dogs made him draw back in fear. Then someone screamed in pain.

"Marc." Anthony whispered in horror as he took off running into the maze of buildings.

Leanne buried her face in the cool, scratchy grass as she struggled to quiet her frantic breathing. *'Where were they?'* She lifted her head slowly and searched the dark field. She was shivering, and the rain wasn't helping. It was running down her face and into her eyes, seeping into her thin dress, chilling her to the bone. *'Father, please help. Please!'* Footsteps nearby made her shrink back. Fear froze the blood in her veins.

"Leanne?" Anthony's hoarse voice whispered. "Leanne?"

WHEN THE SOLDIERS CAME

She sat up. "Here." The relief in her voice was very obvious. *'Merci, Father!'*

Anthony sank to the ground beside her. His breathing was uneven and sharp. He coughed and buried his face in his arms until he stopped. Leanne waited until his breathing evened out before looking him in the eye.

"Anthony, where's Marc?"

A pit formed in her heart as she feared the worst. By the look on Anthony's face, Leanne knew that something horrible had happened. He turned away but not before Leanne witnessed the pain in his eyes. "He is—We got separated. I was running in the shadows when I heard barking and shouts. Then a scream. Followed by hurried footsteps and a gunshot." He released a shuddered breath. "I snuck between the buildings until I found them. Soldiers were ringed in a circle, some holding dogs' collars. A man was lying on the ground in the middle of them. After a few seconds, I could tell it was Marc. He was still breathing, but I could tell it was slowing. I had to get away."

Leanne gasped. "*Non!* Anthony, why?"

"Don't." he warned, throwing an arm around her shoulders and pulling her into him. "We're not safe yet, you still need to be quiet." She buried her face in his shirt and forced herself to calm down. Sobs tore up her throat as she struggled to breathe. Anthony rubbed her back. "Come on, we've got to go."

She nodded sadly. "Okay." She hesitated a moment, whispering a small goodbye to Marc.

Anthony got to his feet and pulled her with him. "We've got to hurry."

Together, they ran through the darkness. The uneven field twisted beneath their feet. Searchlights flew around them, stopping every so often as the German in charge thought he saw movement. They ran for another few minutes before reaching the fence. The low humming assured them it was electrified. Anthony looked around. On the other side was a forest, but there was nothing that could get them over there. He took a deep breath and looked at Leanne. "Okay. I'll boost you over." He cupped his hands, dropped to a knee, and nodded to her.

She hesitated with her foot in his hands. "How are you getting over?" Since her hands were on his shoulders, she had to look down through the gap at him.

"I'll go to the gate. Get over to the woods and get safe. I'll meet you there." He started to straighten, getting ready to throw her over.

"*Non.*" She struggled to remove her foot, her face going pale. "*Non,* Anthony. We either both find a way over together, or we go to the gate together." She stepped down, but kept her hands on his shoulders.

"Leanne, *non.*" He got to his feet. "I promised I'd get you safe. You're going over right here." His voice was low and threatening, but also partially scared.

"Anthony, I'm not going to leave you. We need to get out of here together."

Anthony frowned. "Leanne—"

"Please?" She felt tears fill her eyes and looked away, unable to meet his hurt gaze.

Anthony bit his lip. "Fine. Let's go."

He grabbed her hand and pulled her away from the fence. They ran to the edge of the occupied part of the camp. Soldiers were patrolling the streets. The german shepherds barked every now and then, their noses quivering. Anthony's face became grave. "There is no way we'll both make it through there without getting caught. Could we please go back to the fence? I'll be able to sneak through the camp without getting seen. I did it once, I can do it again." He sounded so sure, that Leanne had to fight the urge to tell him to sneak through the camp.

Leanne forced the thought away, jerked him around, and glared. "God will give us an idea." They waited for a moment, then she perked up. "I know." She pulled on his arm. "Follow me." She led him to the trench. "This goes right to the wall. It will lead us there without the danger of being spotted. Come on." She jumped in.

Anthony rolled his eyes at the sky. "Oh, why?" He jumped in after her, wincing as the mud squelched loudly beneath his ragged boots.

Trying to be as quiet as possible, they walked along the deep trench, flinching and wincing as searchlights flash across the sky. Every now and then, they had to drop into the mud and hold still to avoid being seen by a soldier that was patrolling the trench. At the end of the trench, Anthony jumped out and pulled Leanne after him. The gate was on their left, two soldiers a few feet in front of it. Anthony raised a finger to his lips and pressed Leanne into the shadows. "Wait here," he whispered in her ear. "Watch what I do. then, if all is safe, I'll put my hand back in and wave to you." He pressed his back against the wall and slid slowly along it, then disappeared out the gate.

Leanne waited a few tense moments. As the seconds continued to crawl by with no change, her heart and lungs seemed to stop working. *'Father, what happened?'* she cried silently, tears filling her eyes. "Oh please be alright." she whispered breathlessly.

Just then, a pale hand reappeared around the wall and beckoned to her. She turned against the wall. The stone was rough and scraped the skin off her palms. It hurt, but she was careful not to make a sound. As she neared the gate, she felt iron bars in the wall and felt the rust rub off onto her hands. She gasped quietly, then froze, cursing herself for making noise. The soldier at the gate frowned, his eyes searching the darkness, but he was looking ahead of him not behind. Leanne was unable to move. She didn't realize how often she was holding her breath and her heart was beating so loud she was sure the soldier would hear it. After a few fear-heightened moments, the soldier relaxed, his posture slackened, and he stopped searching.

Leanne exhaled quietly and sucked in another quiet breath, her heart thudding painfully as she slid around the pillar then squeezed through the bars. Half way through she got stuck and had to pause before she steamed in panic. After a few more seconds, she slipped through and fell into Anthony's arms. He gasped as she leaned against him. She opened her mouth, but he placed a hand over it. "Not yet." He whispered in her ear. He took her hand and started off.

"Halt!"

Anthony spun around, his hand tightening around Leanne's. A soldier was standing in the center of the gate, his face shadowed, a gun pointed at them. "Vhere are you going?"

Anthony pushed Leanne behind him. "Who are you?" he demanded. He tried to make his voice sound strong and fearless, but he feared he'd failed. He was so worried that he and Leanne would get killed that that was all he could think about.

WHEN THE SOLDIERS CAME

Leanne stood shocked. Her hands shook badly. She wanted to cry but was too scared to even manage that.

"You forgot me already?" The soldier laughed and stepped forward into the moonlight.

"Kaleb." Anthony growled.

Kaleb's face darkened. "You're the reason Marc died. I didn't want him to, I thought he'd be okay. If only you hadn't tried to escape!" The despair in his voice shocked Leanne, again. "He could have gone free when Germany won the war! I would have seen to it!" he shouted.

"Shh." Anthony begged.

Leanne closed her eyes. *'Father help us! Please!'*

Kaleb leveled the gun. "Trying to escape is a crime punishable by death," he said calmly, "and killing an inmate is also punishable by death."

Anthony opened his mouth to argue, hoping to keep Kaleb distracted, but was cut off by the cocking of another gun. Kaleb froze, fear and wonder filling his eyes and reflecting on his face. A second soldier stepped from the shadows. The moonlight glared off his red hair and shone in his brown eyes. "*Cześć, Bracie.*" His face was filled with pain and tears were drying on his cheeks.

"Albin?" Kaleb growled.

"*Tak.*" Albin stepped to the right, making a small triangle. "Kaleb, why are you doing this?"

"For Germany," Kaleb responded curtly.

"But why?" Albin questioned again.

Anthony pulled a small pistol he'd stolen from his belt and aimed it at Albin, not sure whose team he was on. Albin caught the faint cocking of the gun and turned to them. "This is crazy.

We should all lower our weapons." He aimed his gun at the ground. Leanne watched in terror, worried that one of the soldiers would suddenly shoot Anthony. Anthony looked over his shoulder at her and gave her a worried look. She was too scared to acknowledge it. She placed a hand on his arm and tugged on it, hoping that if he'd lower the gun then the brothers would ignore them. Anthony was still stronger than her and was able to keep the gun straight.

Kaleb shook his head. "I would've done everything that Father asked me to, if it hadn't been for them!" His hands shook, the gun quivered. "I need to prove that I can do what he asked."

Anthony scoffed, realizinging what Kaleb was mad about. "I *saved* Lovisa! You were trying to doom her to a life of slavery!"

Leanne shook uncontrollably, but she stepped in front of Anthony, placing herself in the line of fire and forced her voice to become level. "Anthony, Kaleb, Albin, please. What is our leaving going to do to you? How will us going home hurt you?"

Kaleb swallowed but didn't answer, anger and confusion rippled across his face. Albin took a deep breath. "It won't. Just go."

"*Nien!*" Kaleb's face was dark and panicked. "Do not leave!" He leveled his gun. His eyes hardened.

Anthony pulled his gun and aimed it at Albin, then with his other hand tried to grab Leanne and drag her back behind him. Albin raised his gun and swiveled it back and forth between his brother and Anthony.

"Kaleb," Leanne stepped forward, making sure she got out of reach of Anthony. "Please, how will—"

WHEN THE SOLDIERS CAME

A gun fired, followed by two others. Anthony watched as the brothers fell to the ground. A soft thudding to his right made him look over just as Leanne dropped to the ground. He dropped his gun as he took a few steps toward her. Blood was quickly seeping through her dirty dress. He dropped to his knees beside her. "Leanne?"

She moaned. "We have to hurry. Someone had to have heard that." Pain twisted her mouth.

He picked her up and cradled her to his chest, then ran through the gate. He made his way toward the tree line, his steps slow but steady. At the edge of the forest, he looked back. He could see the brothers laying in the moonlight. Even now he didn't know who shot who. He believed he was the one that shot Albin, but wasn't positive. He turned and melted into the darkness. He moved at a quick pace, worried that someone would be after them, but was careful to keep Leanne steady. After half an hour Leanne moaned softly. "Anthony."

He dropped to the ground and placed her in front of him. "Leanne, are you okay?"

She shivered. "*Oui.* You're here."

He checked her and gasped as he saw a bullet hole in her stomach. "Leanne?"

Her breathing was shaky, but her gaze and words were steady. "It's fine. Anthony, look at me." He fearfully took his eyes off the wound and looked in her eyes as his shaking hands cupped her face. "I'll be okay." She raised her hand slowly and cupped his cheek. "Don't worry about me. I'll be okay."

Tears filled his eyes and he placed his hand over hers. "Leanne, don't leave me. Please!" Images of Tristan, Gerta, and

Marc flooded his mind, but he forced them away, focusing on Leanne in front of him.

Leanne smiled. "I'm going home. I'll see you there, okay?" her voice was hopeful yet sad.

"*Non*, Leanne. *Non!*" he growled, tightening his hand over hers, as if that would keep her there.

"Anthony, find them. Tell them for me." Desperation slipped into her voice. "Please! Jameson. Marius. Rose. Gael. Lidia. *S'il te plaît*. Tell them I'm home."

"Leanne, don't talk like that. Stay with me! Please, Leanne." He clutched her hand like a life line, as if he were the one dying instead of her. "Please." he sobbed.

She took a shuddering breath. "As long as I'm able," she whispered.

Carefully he slid his arms under her and pulled her onto his lap. Her hand stayed on his face. He held her gently, rocking back and forth, as tears rolled down both their faces.

Morning began to come. The sky turned a hazy gray. Anthony shook his head to chase sleep away and looked at Leanne. She wasn't moving, her face still and calm. "Leanne?" Fear clutched Anthony's heart as she remained silent. "Leanne?" He shook her gently, willing her to wake up.

"Anthony?" Her voice was weak and shaky, her eyes lit up as she saw him and a pain twisted smile curved her lips.

He sighed in relief, but quickly became worried, "Do you love me?" he asked, trying to keep her talking.

WHEN THE SOLDIERS CAME

"More than anything in the world, that will never change. Do you love me?" Tears made her eyes shimmer.

He blinked back tears of his own. "Of course I do. You are the only one that will ever have my heart. I promise." He squeezed her hand, biting his lip.

She looked up at him. He was distressed to see pain behind her eyes. "You never answered me last night," she said, her voice barely above a whisper. "Will you tell them I'm home?" She returned her hand to his cheek.

He swallowed painfully. "*Bien sûr.*" He brushed a piece of her hair behind her ear, wiping tears away with it.

"Trust God." Leanne whispered. "Trust Him. I..." she gasped, tears rolled down her face, falling into her hair. A look of panic settled in her eyes as she struggled to finish her sentence. "I...I love—" She tensed, her words stopping suddenly. Her head slid off his arm, her hand fell from his cheek, her eyes became fixed on his, and her breath blew warmly across his face.

He caught her hand before it hit the ground. "Leanne?"

Her face remained still. In her eyes, the orange, pink, and red of the brightening sky were reflected, making it look like they were filled with the defiant fire they always had been, but looking closer he could see they were empty.

"Leanne, answer me! Please!" He shook her gently, tears falling down his face. "Leanne!" He broke down sobbing. "Come back!" he moaned, gasping. "I can't do this without you," he cried, then buried his face in his hands and sobbed.

The warm sun fell on the back of Anthony's neck, arousing him. His head pounded. He didn't know when he fell asleep, but now that he was awake, he felt like he was living a nightmare. He straightened and fearfully looked in front of him. Leanne was in the same position. A calm, almost peaceful look on her face, her eyes blank, and her hair billowing around her head.

He took a shaky breath. "I love you, too." He brushed a hand down her face and for the first time in his life pressed his lips against hers. Fresh tears rolled down his cheeks and landed softly on her face. "I'll miss you, my love." He slid her off his lap and arranged her carefully on the old fallen leaves and newly blooming flowers.

He gently closed her eyes. "You gave me something to fight for. You believed in a free country and you were willing to lay down your life for it. I'll tell you I love you every day and I know you'll hear me. I'll struggle every day to live without you. *Au revoir.* Be safe in God's keeping." He kissed her again. "I love you," he whispered against her lips, then pulled himself to his feet. He cast one last glance at her then looked at the sky. "Keep her safe 'til I get there." He turned and disappeared into the trees.

Epilogue

April 10, 1946

Anthony walked unsteadily through the English streets. England was very different from the calm France that he was used to. People were calling out, trying to attract attention. Children were running down the street, dodging men, women, and animals. Car horns honked loudly as they struggled to get to where they were going. Anthony felt a sudden wave of homesickness.

He missed Reims; the easy life where no one was in a hurry.

'How does anyone live like this day to day?'

A well dressed man caught Anthony's eye and hurried over to him. "Hello." The English greeting sounded strange. "Can I help you?"

"Yes," Anthony smiled gratefully. "I'm lost. I'm trying to get to this address?" He pulled out a small slip of paper with English words on it.

The man read it and nodded. "You're almost there, you just need to go down a few more blocks and turn right. You'll see it." He smiled kindly.

"*Merci.*" Anthony grinned in return.

"French, huh? Welcome to England."

Anthony nodded then tucked his hands into his pockets and started down the street. The spring wind blew gently and he pulled up his collar, shivering. As he kept moving, his steps slowed. His heart beat excitedly but fear wasn't far behind it. He turned the corner and glanced at the addresses. The house he wanted was only a few yards away. It was quaint with a small porch and crisp green yard. The owner was kneeling in the grass, planting flowers. His back turned.

Anthony stepped closer, his hands shaking. *'This had to be right. Father, please let it be right.'* He cleared his throat. "*Bonjour?*"

The man straightened at the sound of a French greeting, his head cocked, but he didn't turn. "*Bonjour,*" he answered cautiously. Fear and uncertainty tinting his voice.

Anthony's heart leapt at the familiar voice. "Gael?" He felt breathless as if he'd just run miles. Gael turned. His face had darkened and the start of a beard covered his chin. His eyes widened in shock and filled with tears.

"Anthony?" He took a step forward and Anthony saw the slight limp in his step. "Anthony, is that you?"

Anthony nodded slowly, tears filling his eyes. "*Oui.* Oh, Gael!" He ran forward and threw his arms around his old friend.

Gael slapped him on the back. "You're so tall! I can't believe you're alive. We thought all of you were dead. How did you make it out? Where are the others?"

Anthony swallowed painfully and decided to ignore the questions. "Is Lidia here?"

Gael nodded quickly. "*Oui.*" He turned back to the house. "Lidia!

"*Oui?*" a voice called from inside.

"Come out here for a moment! We have a visitor."

The door opened and Lidia stepped out. She was wearing a light blue dress and her hair was pulled back away from her eyes. A little girl held her hand. The girl had Gael's hazel hair and Lidia's green eyes. Her elfish-like face was beautiful; complete with a small dimple on her cheek. Lidia closed the door behind them and shaded her eyes. "Gael, what did—" She stopped mid sentence. Her eyes widened with disbelief. "Is this...?"

"*Bonjour,* Lidia." Anthony offered, biting his lip.

Lidia gave a cry, dropped the girl's hand, and threw herself down the stairs, tears filling her eyes. "Anthony!" Lidia threw her arms around his neck. "You're here! You're alive!" she sobbed.

Anthony squeezed her gently. "I missed you!" They broke apart. He turned to Gael who had retrieved the little girl. "Who's this?"

Lidia met his kind eyes with a sad smile. "Esmé." she answered softly.

Anthony caught his breath. "Esmé?" he repeated. "For...?"

Gael nodded. "*Oui.*" He peered over Anthony's shoulder, as if someone was behind him. "Where are the others?" he asked again.

Anthony's heart thudded painfully. "They're dead," he spoke reverently, barely above a whisper. "All of them, except Lovisa; I don't know where she is now."

Lidia gasped in horror. "*Non.*" Pain creased her face.

Gael shook his head in disbelief. "How did it happen?"

"Could we talk inside?" Anthony asked softly.

"Of course."

They turned and walked inside. Anthony took Esmé onto his lap and played with her as he told the story. After Anthony finished, Gael got to his feet. "How long are you able to stay?"

"If it's alright with you, I'd like to stay until I can find Leanne's brother and the two friends she had missed so much." Anthony said.

Lidia nodded. "Of course it is!"

Lidia hugged him again. "Stay as long as you need."

Anthony walked up Gael and Lidia's walkway and sighed. He'd finally got a link to Rose. Someone had approached him that morning and introduced herself as Angelica Bonnet Vannier. She had heard that he was looking for a Rose Bonnet and told him that Rose had gone to Reims a few months ago with her new husband. Angelica informed him that she was Rose's sister and asked why he needed her. He'd given her a small portion of the story and Angelica had instantly pressed some English coins into his hands and wished him luck.

Anthony pulled the door open and was instantly hugged around the leg by Esmé. He smiled and pulled the little girl into his arms. She grinned and hugged his neck. Lidia walked over, a smile lighting her face. "*Bonjour.* Did you find anything?"

He nodded, placed Esmé back on the floor, and rubbed a hand through her hair. "*Oui.* I got a lead. I was told Rose is in Reims."

Lidia gasped. "Anthony, you know that Reims is still trying to rebuild after what happened. It won't be safe there."

WHEN THE SOLDIERS CAME

Anthony sighed. "I know. But Rose is my best shot at finding Jameson and Marius."

Lidia nodded. "When are you leaving?" she asked, hoping he would prolong his time with them a little longer.

"As soon as possible." He looked Lidia in the eye. "When does Gael get home?"

"Around five. Could you stay for one more meal?"

Anthony nodded. Without saying so, both of them knew that once Anthony went back to Reims, he'd never leave it again.

Anthony hugged Lidia and Esmé tightly. "I'll write you," he promised Lidia.

She laughed through her tears. "You better. We lost you once, I don't want to go through that again."

Anthony smiled at her as he turned to Gael. Gael wrapped his arms around him. "Be safe, Anthony. I don't know how people feel in Reims. A lot of people joined the Germans. They still may be supportive even though the Nazis are no longer in France."

Anthony nodded. "Don't worry. I know."

The ship behind them rang its bell and the captain called *'All Aboard.'* Anthony hugged the small family. "Lidia if you get Lovisa's address would you send it to me? I want to know how she's doing."

He'd learned that Lovisa had made it to England, but she'd been so scared with the bombs and gunfire that the king had decided that she'd be safest in America. She was living there now.

Lidia promised over and over that she'd send it as Anthony glanced over his shoulder at the boat. Passengers were walking up the gangplank, handing their tickets over. Anthony turned back to his friends. "*Au revoir.* God bless you and keep you safe."

Lidia smiled and waved then broke down in tears and buried her face in Gael's chest. He wrapped an arm around her shoulders, cuddling her to him. Anthony watched them as he moved backward. His heart longed to stay with them, but he knew that he had to fulfill his promise to Leanne. Thinking of her made his heart ache. '*I love you.*' he thought for the tenth time that day. He turned at the gangplank and walked up. Numbly, he handed his ticket to one of the sailors and moved toward the back of the ship. He watched as England became a smudge on the horizon, then made his way to the front, willing France to come into view.

Anthony took a deep breath as he stepped off the train. Reims' station was half deserted. There were a few people on the platform that were getting ready to board. He looked around and realized he was the only one to get off here. He stared at his home. It hadn't been a good home. His months here were spent in fear, but this is where he met Tristan. And Esmé. Nathan. Marc. Gerta. Lidia. Gael. Lovisa. And…Leanne. Tears filled his eyes. He moved out of the station, trying to run away from the hurt.

WHEN THE SOLDIERS CAME

Reims was slowly rebuilding itself. Bullet holes and bomb craters sprinkled the roads and sidewalks. People shivered as they walked, their faces drawn in fear and worry; but there was a hopefulness in their steps, a whisper of joy and happiness in the wind. The repair of buildings was underway with rubble being cleared off the streets and slowly taken out of the city. One day, in the future, Reims would be back to what it used to be and Anthony would make sure he helped it along.

He moved slowly through the streets, ignoring the fearful and suspicious looks thrown his direction. He followed the signs until he found the Bonnet's old address. He rang the bell. It pealed loudly but no one came to the door. He tried again. The door flew open and he was face to face with a thin woman bouncing a chubby baby. "Can I help you?"

"*Oui*. I'm looking for a Rose Bonnet. She lived here before the war and I was told I could find her here."

The woman smiled sadly. "She's not here. I don't think she's been back in this house since the war. I did hear that Rose was somewhere in Reims. I think you could check with the Martin boy. His shop is down the street and off to the left, third to the end. I don't know if he's alone or not, but I'd say that's your best bet."

"*Merci.*"

"Hope that helps." She disappeared back into the house.

Anthony followed the woman's instructions and was half-shocked, half- conflicted when he stopped in front of the old clock shop that he'd come to with Leanne two years ago. He swallowed nervously. His hands were shaking. He forced himself to move and push open the shop door. A bell rang happily but was quickly drowned out by the ticking of hundreds of clocks. A man was seated at the counter. He looked up and smiled. Anthony knew that he'd been in the war. His eyes were haunted and scars covered his face. He nodded kindly to his customer. Anthony unbuckled his watch and laid it on the counter.

"*Bonjour,*" the man grinned. "You're not one of my regulars. Did you move here or are you just passing through?"

"Actually," Anthony said, watching as the clockmaker disassembled his watch with amazing speed, "I'm looking for someone. Someone that has been said to live here?"

The clockmaker put the watch together as quickly as he took it apart. "I am Jameson Martin. My wife is Rose Bonnet Martin. The only other person living here is Marius Decrocles. But who is it you are searching for?"

Anthony felt his heart grow heavy. *'This was Leanne's brother!'* Looking at him he could see the same determination in Jameson's eyes as he'd loved about Leanne. "I'm searching for you, in fact." he said huskily.

Jameson started with a slight smile on his lips. "Who are you?" His hand slipped under the counter and Anthony heard the faint cocking of a gun.

He stared calmly at the man. "My name is Anthony Tremblay. I was Leanne's boyfriend."

Jameson gave a strangled cry and dropped both gun and watch. The watch broke into a thousand little pieces. "Leanne?"

Anthony nodded as sadness filled his eyes. His heart beat painfully before seeming to stop as he tried to figure out exactly what to say next. Quick footsteps sounded from the living room and a beautiful woman stood in the doorway. She wore a wine-red skirt and white blouse. An apron was tied around her waist. Her swollen stomach announced that she was close to having a baby. Her blonde hair was pulled back revealing diamond blue eyes. Flour covered her face, hands and apron. "Jameson?" She glanced at her husband, then at Anthony. "Who's this?"

Jameson got to his feet and captured Anthony's hand. "Rose, this is a friend of Leanne's." Rose's hands flew to her mouth. "Leanne? Where is she?" Her blue eyes filled with desperation.

More footsteps. A huge man appeared and held the door open. His face was hard. His blue eyes, too, were haunted. His cheeks and chin were blanketed in a thick brown beard. Brown hair fell to his shoulders. Anthony noticed that one hand was missing two fingers. He glanced at all three of them. "Rose, Jameson, what's wrong?" His voice was deep and pained.

Anthony shifted uncomfortably under the man's gaze. Jameson glanced at the man. "Marius, this is Anthony Tremblay. He knew Leanne."

The intimidating face disappeared, replaced by a worried and fearful one. "Leanne? Where is she? Is she alright?"

Anthony held up his hands. "Could we go somewhere private?"

Jameson's eyes softened. He caught the despair in Anthony's tone. "Sure." He hurried and closed the shop door then motioned for Anthony to follow Rose and Marius into the living room.

Anthony gratefully took a seat on the small sofa and looked at the man he'd been searching for for almost a year now. He slipped his hand into his pocket and pulled out a small photograph. It was creased and blurred along the fold lines, but he could still easily see the nine year old Leanne grinning at him. He'd found it tucked into Leanne's pocket the day she'd died. He didn't know how she'd kept it, but had taken it, determined to return it to her brother. Quietly, waiting for Rose to come back from the kitchen, Anthony compared the fourteen year old boy in the photo to the twenty-five-year old man seated across from him. Both looked prepared for anything and the slight lifting of their determined chin. Notably, the fourteen-year-old was happy and excited for life. The man sitting across from him was slumped, with worried eyes, and a sad curve to his mouth.

Anthony turned to Marius and compared him to the nineteen year old version in the photograph. Again, the younger version had a confident air to his stance and gaze and a bright vision for his future. This older version was slightly defeated with a look that said plainly he didn't know what to do with the rest of his life. Rose came back holding a teapot and four small white teacups. "Cider?" Her voice was gentle, but Anthony caught a strain and knew that she was struggling not to cry.

He nodded and graciously accepted the cup. Jameson took a cup, but placed it on the sofa table without drinking it. He fixed his gaze on Anthony in a pleading glance. "Monsieur Anthony, where is my sister?"

Anthony took a deep breath. *'Leanne, I kept my promise.'* Fighting back hot tears, he held out the photo. "She's gone home."

Also by Kesli Gleason

The Kingdom of Cavrain
When The Soldiers Came

About the Author

I'm a fifteen year old girl that is interested in a lot of random things that most teenagers aren't.

I love reading, I've read every book I can get my hands on. My favorite genre is medieval fiction

I love animals, dogs are my favorite. I own two of them, a Border Collie named Squirt and a Shepneese named Splash.

I love hanging out with my siblings and my friends.

I hate math but love English and Language Arts.

I love everything small, like figurines and stuff like that.

I enjoy legos and 3D puzzles, I like building things that aren't that hard but do require you to think.

I love the mountains and the forest. I could spend every weekend camping and not complain once.

I enjoy looking at the stars, I love how they sparkle and shine all at different times.

I love being outside in the summer, but winter is my favorite season, I love playing in the snow.

I enjoy singing in my school choir and performing in the concerts.

I'm not a very social person, but am always willing and open to making new friends.

Milton Keynes UK
Ingram Content Group UK Ltd.
UKHW021416220524
443105UK00038B/775